FURY'S LOVE

LOST LADIES - BOOK ONE

TESS MATTHEWS

Published by Blushing Books
An Imprint of
ABCD Graphics and Design, Inc.
A Virginia Corporation
977 Seminole Trail #233
Charlottesville, VA 22901

Tess Matthews
Fury's Love

EBook ISBN: 978-1-64563-501-7
Print ISBN: 978-1-64563-502-4
Audio ISBN: 978-1-64563-503-1
v1

CHAPTER 1

"*D*arcy Pendergrass, you should not ask such things!"

"Come on, Belle," Darcy pleaded with the petite brunette sitting beside her in the surrey." We are supposed to be best friends, and best friends tell each other everything. I would tell you if a boy kissed me."

"Girls, what are you two chattering about?" Mr. Pendergrass asked from the front seat of the surrey.

"Why, Richard, the girls have been to a dance. I'm sure they have plenty to talk about that is none of our business."

"What our daughter does is *our* business."

"Richard, you know so little about girls."

"Oh, all right, you ladies share your secrets," Richard Pendergrass moaned.

"Thank you, Ma." Darcy leaned forward and kissed her mother's cheek then slid back in her seat.

"Well?" Darcy turned back to Belle.

Belle giggled, enjoying the look of desperation on her friend's face.

"All right," Belle leaned closer to her friend's ear," yes, he kissed me."

"I knew it. I knew it." Darcy drummed her feet against the carriage floor. "Tell me everything!"

"Well," Belle took a deep breath," first, he is a *man*, not a boy. And," she grasped Darcy's arm," he's a ranger."

Darcy's jaw dropped." You mean a Texas Ranger?"

Belle's head bobbed.

"Wow! A grown man. Oh, Belle, how did you get so lucky? Not only did you get your first kiss but with a grown man—a Texas Ranger." Darcy exhaled a dreamy sigh. "I should be jealous. But how could he resist you, especially with you wearing the blue dress your ma made. It practically sparkles. The only one after me was Joe Carter."

"Why, Darcy Pendergrass," Belle scolded, "Joe is a nice guy, and he likes you a lot. I saw him following you around like a lovesick pup."

Darcy shrugged. "He's still a boy, not a man like your ranger."

"Darcy, you know Joe is not a boy. He's twenty-one, and that's not a boy."

"He seems like one to me. Maybe I don't see him as a grown man since I've known him most of my life. But enough about Joe. I want details. What's it like to be kissed? How did it happen? I need details, Belle." The blonde ringlets of Darcy's hair bounced as she fidgeted with excitement.

"All right. We finished our dance, and he went to get us some punch. But I was so hot, I couldn't wait for the punch, so I went outside to cool off. I sat on the bench right outside the church hall, and then I heard this deep voice—

"What did he say?" Darcy jiggled in her seat.

"There you are, young lady," Belle lowered her voice to imitate a masculine tone.

"He called you a *lady*?" Darcy squealed.

"Yes." Belle giggled.

"Imagine," Darcy sighed, "being called a lady, like in one of those romantic books about a knight and his lady."

"Oh, Darcy, you are such a romantic."

"You are too, Belle Alston," Darcy chided. "Now go on; tell me the rest."

"Well, I turned and looked up, and he was standing next to the bench with a glass of punch in each hand."

Belle's mind drifted back to the dance, the memory of the evening playing in her mind.

"There you are young lady. What are you doing here all alone? I left for a moment to get us drinks and when I came back, you were gone."

"Thank you," Belle answered as she held out her hand for the drink.

"Oh." He handed her the drink and motioned for her to scoot down on the bench. He sat down next to her.

The warmth of his body near her, mixed with the scent of leather, soap and pure masculinity, made her tremble.

Even though he was sitting, Belle needed to tilt her head to meet his gaze. She realized he must be over six feet tall, almost a foot taller than her five-foot-five self.

"I'm sorry. I didn't mean to be rude. I thought I might faint from the heat, it's so warm in there."

"You're not going to faint for real, are you?"

"No, no," she giggled at his alarm," I'm fine."

"I'm glad you are fine, but you know you really shouldn't come out here alone. You should at least have let someone know you were out here," the young man lightly scolded.

"I turned eighteen last week, I'll have you know. I'm old enough to care for myself," Belle huffed.

"Feisty little thing, aren't you?"

Belle laughed at being called feisty; it was the last word she would use to describe herself.

"I'm sorry. I have a bit of a temper."

"Not to worry. Anyway, I didn't come out here to argue with you." He smiled, and Belle felt a warmth growing inside herself.

She studied his face.

Wisps of dark hair rested on his forehead. His green eyes sparkled against his tanned skin. They were kind eyes, but she imagined a hidden flame ignited from within if a dangerous situation arose or his temper flared. Beyond his warm smile was his strong jawline, covered with a shade of dark stubble that would make other men look unkempt, but it made him all the more attractive.

He is the handsomest man I have ever seen.

"Why, thank you. I can't recall anyone ever calling me handsome."

Belle's face turned crimson. "Oh my gosh, I said that out loud, didn't I?"

He smiled and nodded.

"I'm sorry." She clamped her hand over her mouth.

"Why are you doing that?" He chuckled as he removed her hand from her face. "I think it's charming that you say what you think."

"I do it when I'm nervous." Belle shuffled in her seat. "It's embarrassing. I mean, I just met you and I don't even know your name, then I go and say something like that. I'm mortified. She looked at her lap.

The light touch of his fingertips gently raised her face, and she was captured in his mossy, green eyes.

"I have to admit, meeting you makes me a bit nervous too."

"It does?"

"Yes, so don't feel mortified, and the name's Travis—Ranger Travis Parker. And just who might you be?"

"Belle," she said, her voice quivering.

"Belle," he repeated, "how appropriate. 'Belle', I believe that means beautiful in French, and you, Belle, are uniquely beautiful. I don't think I have ever seen eyes like yours. They are not quite blue, are they? They're almost violet."

"Huh?" Belle blushed and tried to swallow but found her mouth was dry. "I don't know, I suppose. I mean, that's what I'm told, about my eyes. Oh, and umm... my name, I'm named Belle because of this birth-

mark." Belle showed him the birthmark on her arm. "See, it's shaped like a bell. Oh, Belle, stop talking," she admonished herself. "I'm sorry I'm rambling."

"No, you're not, sweetheart."

His endearment shot like a flaming arrow, igniting something inside her.

"Tell me about yourself, Belle."

"Well, um, my father is Judge Alston. He was a lawman before he became a judge and—

"Belle, honey."

"Yes?"

"No disrespect to your father, but I want to know about you."

"Um, well, there is nothing to tell." She shrugged. "I'm Belle Alston. I'm eighteen. I've lived in Faulkner all my life and probably will live here till I die."

"Come on, Belle, what do you like to do?"

Belle replied, "I don't know. Well, I like animals and books. I can't think of anything else. I'm boring Belle, that's all."

"Aw, darling, you are anything but boring. You are beautiful and charming and witty, and," he smiled, "I believe you have a bit of a temper."

Belle blushed. How can he tell so much about me; he doesn't know me.

"I can tell you how; I'm a Texas Ranger, and it's part of the job."

Belle's eyes widened, "Oh no, I did it again. I said that out loud too, didn't I?"

Travis nodded with a chuckle.

"That's it," Belle held her hand up, "I am going to stop talking. You can tell me about you for a while. I'm going to keep my treacherous, damn mouth shut!"

"Belle!"

She flinched at the sternness of his tone. His soft eyes flashed with a hint of disapproval.

"What?" Her voice weakened.

"Don't curse. You are far too pretty and sweet for such words to cross your precious lips."

"Oh," she muttered, "I'm sorry. I mean, I don't usually curse, you know. I'm a bit flustered."

"You're forgiven." He smiled and tapped her nose. "Now, let's get to more pleasant conversation."

"I don't know what to talk about. I already told you about me. What about you? You're a ranger? I bet it's exciting, chasing bad men."

"I doubt I know everything about you, Belle, but I will someday, I'm sure. And chasing 'bad men' is not all excitement. Most of the time, you're too cold or too hot and hungry, but the worst part is the loneliness." His voice dipped as Belle witnessed a sadness cross his face. "And, not to mention, it's dangerous, but I do get to help people and protect them from harm. I tend to be the protective type, so it suits me, at least for now."

"I think it would be so exciting."

Travis laughed at her innocence.

The conversation paused and the silence made Belle uncomfortable. She gazed up at the clear night sky.

"I love looking at the stars."

"So do I, and it's a perfect night for stargazing."

"Do you know much about stars?"

"Well, I know that's the big dipper." Travis pointed at the group of stars.

"Oh, yes, I see it. My father taught me the constellations when I was younger. Oh, look, Travis," her finger jutted toward the sky, "it's a falling star. Travis?"

"What is it, honey? You look worried."

"I know it's silly, but I heard seeing a falling start means something bad will happen."

"I don't think so." He smiled at her. "I think they are lucky."

"How are they lucky?"

"I feel like I'm lucky tonight."

"You do?"

Travis leaned his face closer to hers, and she fought the urge to scoot away.

"Yes, I found you tonight."

Belle felt the soft touch of his rough hands as he cupped her face. Her heart hammered in her chest as he drew closer. She closed her eyes and felt the tender, warm caress of his lips on hers.

"Belle? Belle, honey, open your eyes."

"W-what?" She floated in a dream of bliss.

"Open your eyes, darlin'."

Belle fluttered her eyes open, to see Travis smiling at her.

Oh, I'm such an idiot. He's going to think I'm such a little girl, mooning over her first kiss. Or maybe he will think I'm a loose woman, letting him kiss me; after all, we just met.

"First kiss. I'm honored." Travis gently traced his thumb across her jaw, stopping to tuck a stray lock of her chestnut hair behind her ear. "And you could never be a loose woman."

"I did it again, didn't I? I said that out loud," she murmured, but this time she felt no embarrassment as she gazed into his warm eyes.

"Please," Belle whispered, "do that again."

"Gladly," Travis said as he leaned toward her.

The church hall door flung open. The twanging sounds of banjos, mixed with the whines of a fiddle and the nasal voice of the dance caller, spilled out into the night, ruining Belle's romantic moment.

"Belle!" The booming voice of Mr. Pendergrass made Belle jump and Travis retreat to his side of the bench.

"Yes, sir, Mr. Pendergrass, I'm out here."

She gave Travis an apologetic glance as she stood.

"Oh, Belle, here you are." Mr. Pendergrass stood with his wife and daughter in tow. "It's time to go home, Belle. Come along."

The trio walked past Belle and Travis. Darcy smiled at Belle.

With a weak smile and gentle wave, Belle said goodbye to Travis and turned to walk away.

Travis jumped to his feet and reached out, grabbing her arm. "Please, Belle, may I see you again?"

"Yes, please do," she replied, beaming. "My father is Judge Alston, and we live outside of town. Ask anyone. They will tell you how to get to the Alston place."

"Good, honey." He placed a quick kiss on her forehead and released her arm. "You can expect me soon, Miss Alston."

~

"BELLE, BELLE," Darcy's voice broke through Belle's reminiscing." Well, how was it, the kiss? Oh, Belle?"

"Y-yes…the kiss…it was…" She sighed and let her shoulders drop. "…wonderful."

"Oh, oh, Mr. Pendergrass." Belle suddenly realized they were near her home. "Please drop me at the path to our house. I can walk the rest of the way."

"I don't think I should, Belle. I need to see you safely to your home."

Belle did not want an abrupt end to her night. She craved time alone to think about Travis and to moon over her first kiss.

"I'll be safe, Mr. Pendergrass. It's not that far, and besides, Mama's been sick. You know that's why they couldn't take me to the dance, and, oh, I am so grateful you took me, but, Mr. Pendergrass, we could wake Mama with the sound of the carriage."

"Well," he croaked," I suppose you are right, but you hurry along home."

"Oh, thank you so much, Mr. Pendergrass."

Darcy grabbed Belle's arm as she stepped off the carriage. "I want more details next time I see you, Belle Alston."

"I promise," Belle said.

Darcy released her grip and Belle waved and turned up the well-worn path to her home.

~

BELLE TWIRLED her way down the path to her home as her parents lay dying in the parlor.

The best night of my life. Travis and my first kiss. I will remember tonight for the rest of my life.

As she continued to dance, her blue satin dress shimmered in the twilight, giving her an angelic appearance. The joy of the night and her bright future filled her heart, then she heard a horse whinny. *Strange?*

Belle's dance came to a stumbling stop. *A horse? I'm too far from the barn to hear the horses. Papa's never careless with the team. It couldn't be one of them*

Careful steps led her to the sound. There, off the main path, she spied the dark outline of two horses. *Who do they belong too?* Belle cringed. *Oh, come on, Belle; they are probably someone's lost horses. I need to go tell Papa.*

Her eyes darted left, then right, as she crept to her house. The cringe in her stomach tightened as her home came into view. *Something's wrong.*

Her throat thickened. The lamp Mama lit in the foyer burned its usual warm glow, but upstairs, an eerie light shone. Not a light from someone's nightstand, but from a lamp someone held. Belle's heart thudded as the lamp moved from room to room, casting odd shadows and, at times, the outline of a person.

The night air, crisp and clean just moments ago, became hot and thin. Belle struggled to take a breath. *I must go in. I must find Mama and Papa.* Belle found her way to the back porch. She removed her shoes and opened the door, careful not to allow a creak. The kitchen was dark, except for a shaft of light from the foyer. Belle heard the creaking groan of footsteps above her.

She froze. Were they her parent's footsteps she heard or someone else's? Then she heard a pained whimper.

With gentle footsteps, she made her way to the parlor where she believed the sound originated. A sense of foreboding washed over her as her chest cinched tighter with every step. An odd copper scent drifted in the air; Belle refused to accept the smell of blood.

The parlor also benefited from the foyer light. Her eyes struggled to accustom themselves to the dim lighting. Shapes formed then outlines of objects, tables and chairs, but something lay on the floor; she could not make it out. The feeble sound of gasping breaths coaxed her to what lay near her feet, but icy trepidation fought to pull her back.

"Belle," she heard a weak whisper of her name.

"Papa?"

The voice confirmed her fear.

Her body shuddered as she drew close.

"Papa!" Her heart wanted to scream his name, but she spoke in a terrified whisper. She crouched by her father.

"Belle, run." Her father's voice trembled.

"Papa, you're hurt, Where's Mama?"

She scanned the dark room. There, a little way from, her lay another form, and she knew it was her mother. She dragged herself to the lifeless body.

"No, Belle," she heard her father's weak protest.

"Wake up." Belle gently shook her mother's body. "Please, Mama, wake up." She touched the side of her mother's face, only to draw back when a sticky substance covered her hand.

"Belle," her father's voice reached her, "she's gone, and I will be soon. Don't look at her. Remember her life, Belle, not her death." Belle's father struggled to talk, his breathing growing shallower as the seconds ticked by.

She crawled back to him and cradled his head in her lap.

"Belle, run...live."

"Papa, I can't leave you and Mama."

Belle heard the clunking of heavy boots making their way down the stairs.

"Belle." Judge Alston racked his body to gain a gasp of air." Go now, Belle...remember us as we were," he wheezed, "don't let this moment define your life...live, Belle, be happy."

Belle wiped a tear from his eye and leaned her head down against his. "Don't leave me," she whispered.

Judge Alston's hand shook as he raised it to cup his daughter's face. "Run." His hand dropped with a thud.

"I'm not leaving you or Mama. I'll save you, Papa." Denial flooded her heart as she refused the reality in front of her. She got to her feet and made her way through the kitchen. She edged her way through the foyer, hugging the wall with her back.

One of the intruders whistled a tune as she slid into the stairwell closet. Belle shrank into the back of the closet, her back pressed against the wall. She slid down, crouching in the solitude of a dark corner.

Her frenzied mind hindered her ability to focus and think. Rubbing her temples with her fingertips, she attempted to clear her mind, but to no avail. She drew her legs up to her chest and wrapped her arms around her knees, hugging herself. Desperate to do something but helpless, she remained in the darkness and trembled.

What do I do? What if they find me?

Small bands of light leaked through the louvers of the closet door, casting eerie shadows. Belle's eyes darted in the dim light searching, searching...

A weapon...a weapon. I need a weapon! Mama's sewing basket. Yes...scissors in there...I could...I could stab one of them. If I had to.

She rose on wobbling legs and rummaged the shelves, searching for her mother's sewing basket

Bam!

Belle's body jolted at the sound of the gunshot, and fear drove her back to her hiding place.

Bam! Bam!

The murmur of voices reached her ears. Her limbs wobbled and shook as she crawled to the door. She needed to hear them.

"What ya go and do that for? They's dead already."

"Just making sure."

"Come on; let's finish and get outta here."

A shudder of grief racked her small body and agony seared her heart. As hot, bitter tears washed her face, she clasped both hands over her mouth to stifle a scream. With rapid, shallow gasps, she breathed in the rank air and felt sick.

Hideous laughter broke into the darkness.

Belle shoved her small body under the lowest shelf and curled her legs up to her chest like a baby in its mother's womb. But unlike a babe in the womb, there was no sense of safety, only terror.

A spider crawled on her hand. Belle swallowed hard as it proceeded to crawl up her forearm. Sweat gathered on her brow as she saw the red violin and realized it was a black widow. Not able to move, she watched as the spider crawled off her arm and onto the floor. It then walked past her face and into a hole in the wall. Taking a deep breath, Belle rolled out from under the shelf. She sat in her dark corner and listened as her parents' murderers destroyed her home.

Between the sounds of furniture being overturned and precious objects being smashed, she heard the melodious whistling of one of the intruders. She thought the foreboding tune would drive her mad as she heard it over and over. But the maddening sound was driven from her mind when she heard footsteps approaching her hiding place. Fear should have kept her crouching in the darkness, but she spied a broken slat on the bottom of the louvered door. Desperate to see if she could spot anything that would identify the murderers, Belle pushed through her fear and crawled to the door.

She rubbed her eyes in a feeble attempt to sharpen her vision, and she could see red boots in front of the door. Belle's heart pounded in her throat and sweat ran down the curves of her face.

Dear Lord, she silently prayed, *please let him pass by.*

"I wonder what they keep in here?"

Belle's breathing slowed as she heard the voice of the man who had just shot her parents. Her eyes centered on the doorknob as it began to turn. The sound of her heartbeat hammered in her ears, and the lump in her throat became a burning desert. Belle's eyes widened, watching the knob turn. Left. Right. Left. Right. The door jiggled, and a cold numbness washed over her body, sinking to her core. Her breathing became mere puffs of air as she waited for the one turn leading to her discovery. She trembled at the thought of what they would do to her if she were found.

"Damn door is stuck."

He yanked on the door.

After a few more attempts, Belle knew the door would open.

"Hey, lookie here!" the whistling man shouted out to his partner.

The man with the red boots released the doorknob.

Belle crumbled to the floor.

"What?" he shouted.

"Come here and take a look. I think we hit the jackpot."

Belle heard footsteps walking away from the door, but she received no sense of relief.

She had no idea what they'd found. Maybe it was the money her father hid in his desk or her mother's jewelry; she didn't care. She could hear them talking in the foyer.

"Let's get out of here; we done what we wanted and got this to boot."

"All right, but there is one last thing I want to do. I want to burn down this fine house. I don't want nuttin of that judge's life left standing. Let's start it in the old judge's study. There's plenty of paper and books in there. I'll toss this lamp to start it going; should burn in no time."

Belle heard the commotion from her father's office, her father's precious books thudding as they hit the floor, furniture upended and the smashing of glass, followed by a pause then laughter.

"Let's get the hell out of here; this place will be an inferno in a few minutes."

The sound of a few quick footsteps and Belle knew they were gone.

She sat paralyzed by fear, unable to move, even when she smelled the smoke. *Fire! They set the house on fire!* For a moment, Belle accepted her fate, willing to sit in the closet until the smoke overtook her.

Knowing her parents were dead stole her desire to live without them. Her eyelids drooped closed. She waited. But there in the darkness as she awaited death to overcome her, a thought came to her. *What if they are still alive? What are you thinking? They were shot multiple times, but what if?* The thought nagged at her, and her eyes popped open. *I must go to them.*

A light stream of smoke leaked into the closet. Springing to her feet, she tried with all her strength to open the door, but it wouldn't budge. Stuck, maybe from the heat, she didn't know but she did know she must get out. Fear tried to take her over once more, but something inside of her changed and she did not give in to the fear. Belle plopped down on the rough wood floor and began kicking the door. Over and over, she kicked, pounding the door with all the strength she could muster, burning the bottom of her feet and sending jagged shockwaves of pain up her legs, but still, it wouldn't budge.

"Come on, Belle," she ordered herself, "you can't give up. You can't let Mama and Papa down."

She sucked in a deep breath then harnessed all her fear and anger into one decisive last blow. *Crack,* wood splinters flew, and the door flung open.

A light haze of smoke drifted in the foyer. Belle began to cough. She tore a piece of her dress and tied it around her face, using it to cover her nose and mouth. The fire began to crawl from the study to the foyer. Belle could feel the heat on her skin, and a part of her wanted to quit, but determination pushed her forward as she crawled on her hands and knees to find her parents.

Come on, Belle, come on, she repeated to herself, *you can do this; you have to do this for Mama and Papa, keep moving.*

She reached the parlor. Even though she could feel the heat growing behind her, Belle continued to crawl. The smoke grew thick and clouded her vision. She bumped into something—her mother.

"Mama! Mama!" she cried but heard no response. Belle placed her head gently on her mother's chest and cried from the root of her heart.

"Papa!" Her eyes searched though the smoke. Then she spotted a dark figure. She crawled over to find the dead body of her father.

Her petite body shuddered as grief wrenched at her soul again. Tenderly, she kissed her father's face.

Uncertain if her own will to live spurred her on or her father's last wish that she live. Whichever it was did not matter; Belle was going to get out.

The smoke thickened as the heat grew unbearable. Belle needed to get her bearings. She tried to gauge where the fire spread. As far as she could figure, the flames crossed the foyer and now were licking their way to the parlor. Precious time ticked away, demanding she find a way out. Her burning eyes darted around, trying to discern an escape. She found herself disoriented, lost in the thickening smoke. Belle could not fathom which way to go, and even with her face covered, she could feel the smoke burning the back of her throat, trying to choke the life out of her.

"I'm sorry, Papa, I know you want me to live, but I don't know the way to go. I am lost, Papa."

A childlike instinct for security spurred her to reach for her father's hand. Her fingers began to wrap around his but were hindered by an object still clutched in his grasp. She slid her hand down the smooth metal. It took a moment for her to identify the fireplace poker. Did he try to use it as a weapon? Running her hand down the length of the poker, she reached the end and a sense of hope washed over her as she realized it rested on the edge of the fireplace.

Hope jumped in her heart. She found a guide to help her find her way in the smoke. *If this is the fireplace, then Papa's chair is only a few feet away.* She grabbed the poker and stabbed the air, and after a few attempts, she hit something solid.

Reaching out, she touched the soft leather of her father's chair, a landmark to the route of her escape. She crawled from landmark to landmark. The farther Belle moved from the fire, the thinner the smoke became, making her path to the door clear. When she reached the kitchen, she stood and stumbled her way to the door and flung it open. Clean air hit her face. Belle removed the protective cloth and drew in a breath but dropped to her knees in a coughing fit. The coughing subsided and she pulled herself to her feet. She stumbled along on flimsy legs until she reached the old oak tree on the hill behind the house. She crumpled to her knees at the sight of her blazing home. Belle buried her face in her hands and wept. When she could weep no more, she raised her head, and gazing down at the palms of her hands, she saw traces of her parents' blood mingled with the dampness of her own tears. She turned her eyes up at the flames consuming her home and her parents.

The searing pain of grief ripped through her, burying deep within her being all the qualities that defined Belle. A coldness grew inside of her as the flames reflected in her eyes. At that moment, Belle died with her parents, and only Fury remained.

CHAPTER 2

*H*ank Black Hawk woke with a feeling of dread. He credited his Indian blood for his sense of premonition. *Ain't nothin' gonna happen; you're just feeling old today.*

He studied his reflection in the mirror as he buttoned his shirt. The majority of his shoulder length hair shone coal black, invaded by only a few streaks of grey. He joked, claiming the grey to be premature, inherited from his white mother. Although, her hair was a glorious shade of pearl, while his was gunmetal grey. Hank tried to ignore the concern he recognized in his own dark eyes, but from the center of his being, he sensed a calamity approaching.

"Good morning," he said to his wife Little Dove when he came into the kitchen.

"Good morning, old man," she teased," sit down. Your breakfast is almost ready."

"All right, old woman," he retaliated and kissed her cheek, knowing full well Little Dove's age never overshadowed her beauty. Not a hint of grey could be seen in her silky black hair which hung loose, draping to her small waist. Her soft sable eyes were what first drew Hank to her. Like her husband, she was labeled a "half-breed". Not fully accepted in the Indian or white man's world, they became each other's world.

He pulled out a chair but stopped short of sitting when he heard a weak rapping at the door.

"Who could that be this early in the morning?" asked his wife

"I don't know. You stay back," he ordered as he reached for the rifle hanging over the fireplace.

He raised his rifle so he could see the sights and then slowly reached and swung the door open.

Black Hawk dropped his rifle at the sight of Belle leaning on the door frame. "Belle!" he reached out and caught her before she fell to the floor.

Her hair, which only last night had decorated her head like a crown, now hung in a disheveled mess. Scratches and soot covered her beautiful face. Her dirty, tattered dress, scorched by the fire that had consumed her home and smeared with her parents' blood, no longer resembled the beautiful gown sown by her mother.

"Belle!" he shouted, seeing her on the verge of fainting. "What happened? Where are your parents?"

"Dead. They killed both of them," her weak voice whispered. "They killed them and burned the house."

Hank's heart panicked, his thinking muddled refusing to believe what he heard.

"Hank, lay her on the bed in the boy's old room," said Little Dove, her voice bringing him back to reality.

Hank lifted Belle, cradling her in his arms as he carried her to the bedroom and laid her on the bed. Little Dove began examining her for injuries.

"I've gotta go and see what happened." Hank's strong voice trembled.

"Hank, get the doctor and the sheriff."

Little Dove's words broke through the haze in Belle's mind.

"No, please…no doctor, no sheriff."

"Why do you not want the doctor or the sheriff?" Little Dove queried.

"No, no, no…please!" Belle thrashed in the bed.

"Calm down, honey," Hank tried to comfort her."

Little Dove rose to her feet.

"Hank, we must get help."

"Yes," said Hank, "but first, I'm going to see what happened, and then I'll go to the sheriff. I won't tell him Belle is here. I want to talk to her first. Do you believe you can treat her injures?"

Little Dove came from a family of medicine women and possessed a great knowledge of healing. "Yes, I do not see any serious injuries, but I don't know how much smoke she breathed. I will give her herbs to strengthen and cleanse her lungs, but, Hank, I may be able to heal her body, but I cannot heal her mind."

"I know," he answered. "I need to go and check the Alston home. Take care of her."

Hank picked up his rifle and headed to his best friend's home.

Hank had served as John Alston's deputy when John was the sheriff. John ignored the protest from some of the citizens concerning hiring an Indian and stood by his choice. Hank served the people of Faulkner with bravery, often risking his life for the townspeople, gaining their respect and loyalty. An unfortunate injury kept him from becoming sheriff when John became a lawyer. Hank caught a bullet in the leg while he was trying to apprehend a bank robber.

The injury left him with a limp and the inability to sit a horse for long periods of time, but today he ignored the searing pain and blazed his way through the woods. He smelled smoke before he spotted the small, black clouds rising from the direction of the Alston home.

Anguish racked his body, plunging to his soul, when he saw the smoldering remains of his friend's home. Hank drowned his feelings; he needed to check for survivors.

Everything in him wanted to rush to the house and look for

his friends, but his years as a lawman taught him prudence. The murderers may have returned, so he waited and watched.

When he felt certain that no one else was present, he crept closer to the house.

The heat from the smoldering remains grew in intensity as he approached. His heart pummeled his chest. Hank was not afraid of many things, but the thought of losing someone he cared for frightened him more than anything nature could throw at him, be it a grizzly bear or a man.

He entered the burnt home and took slow steps as he watched for falling timbers. His boots offered little protection from the scorching heat rising beneath them, and air tainted by smoke burned the back of his throat. He placed his bandana over his mouth and nose, ignored the pain from his leg, and continued his search.

"John! Martha!" He knew he called their names in vain, but hope struggled to remain in his heart.

A few more steps and the toe of his boot nudged something. Dread flowed down his body as he gulped.

He grabbed hold of his lame leg and struggled to bend down to the floor. Reaching out his hand, he touched a body. Grief wanted to overtake him, but he could not allow it. He rose and walked a few more steps and found the second body. The bodies were his closest friends, his family. He released an anguished cry.

LITTLE DOVE FOCUSED on tending to the girl instead of her concern for her husband and what he may find. She removed Belle's tattered dress, washed her wounds, and applied an herbal balm. Rest is what the girl needed so Little Dove coaxed Belle into drinking a tea to help her sleep.

She closed the door to the room where Belle lay and busied

herself by washing the dishes used to prepare her remedies. Little Dove turned when she heard the creak of the cabin door.

Hank stood in the threshold; his proud, upright posture now caved at the shoulders. His noble features were fixed with sadness, and the life in his eyes were empty with grief. Words were unnecessary; his face conveyed his news.

Little Dove rushed to him. They embraced and wept bitter tears in the comfort of each other's arms.

After that, Little Dove and Hank took turns sitting with Belle. She thrashed about, babbling her horror in her sleep and crying out for her parents.

BELLE'S EYES FLICKERED OPEN. The clouds of sleep dissipated as the reality of her situation sharpened in her mind. She bolted upright in her bed. "Mama! Papa!"

Little Dove, exhausted from the chaos, woke with a start when she heard Belle scream. She jumped from her chair and rushed to Belle's side. "Shh, shh, shh," she said as she put her arms around the girl to comfort her.

The warmth of Little Dove's embrace caused her heart to want to cry out, but Belle would not allow it.

"What's going on?" Hank shouted as he ran into the room.

"Hank," Little Dove spoke in a calming voice, "it's all right. Belle woke up."

"Oh," he answered as he eased to Belle's bedside.

He crouched, as best he could, next to the bed. Little Dove sat on the bed next to Belle, keeping one arm around the girl's shoulders.

"Belle, honey," Hank kept his tone soft, "do you remember what happened?"

Belle's body stiffened. "Yes," she replied with a cold emptiness in her voice.

"Hank," Little Dove interrupted, "maybe we should discuss this after Belle has something to eat."

Hank nodded, but Belle gave no response. Her gaze remained lifeless.

"Belle, I'll go get you one of my dresses to wear."

"No!" Belle snapped. "I do not want to wear a dress."

"But, Belle," Hank implored, "I'm sorry, honey, but your clothes are ruined."

"Don't call me Belle. You raised four sons; don't you have some of their clothes here?"

Little Dove and Hank exchanged a perplexed look. "Yes," said Little Dove, "there are some of the boys' old clothes in the dresser. You are welcome to wear whatever you find."

"Belle, I want you to know—

"Do not call me Belle!" she shouted.

Hank inhaled. "Why?"

"Belle is dead; she died with her parents."

"Then who are you, and what do we call you?"

"Belle is dead. I am Fury; you will call me Fury."

Hank looked at his wife. "All right, Fury, you get dressed and come get some breakfast."

Fury nodded.

Hank hesitated and then added, "We need to talk about this."

"Not now, Hank," Little Dove pleaded. "Come help me with breakfast."

Hank rubbed the back of his neck. "All right," he muttered, then he followed his wife out the door.

THEY ATE BREAKFAST IN SILENCE. Fury toyed with her food as Hank and his wife exchanged nervous glances.

Fury rose from the table and walked to the door.

"Where are you going?" asked Hank.

"I need to go think."

"Bel—Fury, we need to discuss what happened and go see the sheriff. He will want to talk to you."

"Go, talk to the sheriff. Do what you think you must, but I'm not talking to anyone, and do not tell him I am here."

"Why?" asked Hank.

"The sheriff will want to talk to Belle, and Belle is dead; only Fury remains. And I, Fury, have a mission, and I will not be deterred from completing it."

"What mission?" asked Hank, fearing he already knew the answer.

"To find and kill the men who murdered my parents."

Fury walked out the door.

Hank rose to go after her, but Little Dove stopped him. "Let her go, Hank. She needs to be alone for a while."

"Fine," he replied," but I need to talk to the law, see if they know anything."

"Belle—I mean Fury—told you to do what you need to do, but not say she is here."

"I will honor her wishes and keep her whereabouts secret, for now."

CHAPTER 3

*T*ravis dug his spurs into Chief's sides, hoping to make up for lost time. He was not in town when word came about the Alston home. Town gossip said bodies were found. He prayed it was only a rumor, but dread swept through him at the thought of losing the young woman he'd held in his arms last night.

Belle, please be alive.

Rainclouds crowded out the sun. Travis cursed as a few spattering drops became a drenching rain. The sky cleared by the time he arrived at the Alston home, but he knew the rain would wash away the chance of tracking anyone.

Travis flung himself from his horse. Even after the rain, the smell of smoke lingered in the air. As he walked up to the house, Travis could hear the hot embers sizzling from the rain. He surveyed the charred skeleton of the Alston home, of Belle's home, and a deep sadness yanked his heart as he considered the chance anyone survived the blaze.

"Travis!"

He turned to see Ranger Tom Greene walking up to him.

"Fill me in."

"It's bad, son."

"I know it's bad, Tom, now tell me what happened," Travis snapped at his boss.

"Travis, I know the Alston girl is the girl you told me about, the girl from the dance. Maybe you should let the sheriff's posse and a few of the other rangers here handle this."

"Is she dead?" Travis strained to control the quiver in his voice.

"No, son, I don't think so. We found two bodies. They were identified by Hank Black Hawk as Judge John Alston and his wife Martha."

"And what about Belle, their daughter?"

Tom shook his head. "We know she left the dance with the Pendergrass family. We have yet to question them."

"I'll do it," Travis replied. "I'll look for Belle; the posse doesn't need me."

"Travis," Tom sighed, "I don't think that's a good idea. I think you are too close to this case."

"Look, Tom, I know you are trying to protect me, but I can keep my personal feelings separate from my job."

"Can you, Travis? I know you, son, I raised you since you were sixteen. I know you don't let people in, and how quickly you developed feelings for the Alston girl has me worried, and, damn it, I have an obligation to the job, to her. I need a man who is thinking clearly to look for this girl."

Travis clenched his fists. A part of him knew Tom was right, but the other part didn't give a damn.

"All right, Travis, I'll let you question some of the people who can give you background on Belle, then we'll go from there. Start with her grandmother; she lives in town. Then question the Pendergrass family and anyone else they may suggest."

"Thank you, Tom."

"Don't thank me; I'm risking this girl's life on your skill, not on your emotions. Put those emotions away, son. I'm depending on you, but more importantly, Belle is depending on you."

IT WAS late afternoon when Hank came back home. He found Little Dove in the kitchen, but there was no Fury.

"Did you talk to the sheriff?"

"Where is Bel—Fury? I will never get used to that name," said Hank

"She went to sit out by the pond after the rain. I took her some lunch, but she refused to eat. Hank, please tell me what the sheriff said."

"I met him at the Alston house, what's left of it. He has no new information. The sheriff formed a posse, but with the rain, there will be few tracks to follow. I identified the bodies. He promised to have them removed for a proper burial. The sheriff asked if I knew where Belle is, and I lied. I wanted to join the search for the killers, but he said my leg might make that impossible."

Hank hit his leg with frustration. "Damn leg!"

"Hank, it's all right. You will have your hands full caring for the girl. Are you going to tell the sheriff she is here?"

"I don't know yet. I want to talk to her first."

"She should still be by the pond. See if you can get her to come inside."

"I will."

Hank made his way to the pond and found Fury sitting on a rock by the water.

"Papa's favorite fishing spot," Fury said, keeping her eyes on the water.

"Yes, I remember when you were younger, John and I would bring you and my boys here to fish. We had some great times."

"Yes, we did, and Mama would make us a picnic lunch."

"Best fried chicken ever, but don't tell Little Dove," Hank said with a painful grin.

"Hank," Fury asked," did you go to the sheriff?"

"Yes, I did. They are forming a posse to look for—

"For the men who murdered my parents," Fury added.

"Yes."

"And what did you tell them about m-me…Belle."

"I haven't told anyone you're here, but they are searching for you too."

"Good."

"How is it good? There are a lot of folks who care about you, like your grandmother. Surely, they have a right to know you are all right."

Fury thought about the people she knew, her friends, but most of all, she thought of her grandmother.

"Grandma has always been special to me, but right now it's best she doesn't know where I am."

"Why? She loves you, and you two can help each other through this."

"No, she can't know where I am—not yet—maybe never. I have a duty, a mission I must complete."

"What duty? What mission?"

Fury's dead gray eyes penetrated Hank's sight. "I told you, I must find and kill the men who murdered my parents."

"No!" Hank shouted. "Fury, you can't; the lawmen will find them."

"No, they won't," she answered in a matter of fact tone. "Oh, they will hunt for them for a while, but they will give up. They have nothing to go on."

"And you do?"

Fury did not answer.

"How do you plan on doing this; you're a little girl. You're no match for these murderers."

"I know, but you are going to help me. You are going to teach me all I need to know."

"I don't think so."

"Hank, I don't mean to be rude, but if you weren't lame, what would you do?"

Hank drilled his fingers through his hair.

"Damn it, Belle, it ain't that easy to say."

"You mean you would let the posse find them, and my name is Fury."

Hank shook his head. "You know I loved your father like a brother. I would go after them. But there is a difference between you and me."

"What? Because I'm a girl?"

"Yes, that's part of it," Hank railed," but you ain't just any girl, either. You're my best friend's daughter. I need to watch out for you now that he is gone. And you are also too young and inexperienced."

"Don't you want my parents' death to be avenged?"

"Of course, I want justice for your parents. But not vengeance."

"Well, if you won't help me because of my father, know this. If I am taken from here, wherever I end up, I will run away and go after them on my own. So, you can teach me what to do or leave me to myself."

Hank shook his head. *She would make as good a lawyer as her father.*

He rubbed the back of his neck. "Let me think on it, and I will tell you my decision in the morning."

"All right," Fury muttered.

"Let's go back to the cabin. I don't want to worry Little Dove."

CHAPTER 4

*M*rs. Alston, may I get you some lunch?" asked Milly Nelson, the housekeeper.

"No thank you, Milly," replied the older woman." I am not hungry."

"I know you are grieving, ma'am, but you need to keep up your strength. And, ma'am, if you don't mind me saying, who is gonna take care of your granddaughter when they bring her home?"

"My Belle," Kate Alston whispered to herself. Her thoughts were broken by a rapping on the door.

"Do you want me to send them away?" Milly asked.

"Yes, please do; I do not want to see anyone."

Milly opened the door to find a handsome man with dark hair and kind, green eyes standing on the front porch. He towered over Milly, and the sight of his toned muscles made her wish she were a younger woman.

"Sorry," Milly said before Travis could speak, "Mrs. Alston isn't seeing anyone today."

Travis caught the door as it began to close. "Wait. Wait, ma'am. I'm a Texas Ranger; my name is Travis Parker, I am investigating the Alston murders and the disappearance of their daughter. May I please come in and talk to Mrs. Alston?"

He pointed to his badge, and Milly nodded.

She ushered Travis into the foyer. "Wait here, please."

Milly entered the parlor to see Mrs. Alston sitting in her favorite overstuffed chair, staring blindly out the window.

"Mrs. Alston, I'm sorry, it's a Texas Ranger by the name of Travis Parker. He would like to...ask about...what happened to—

"My family?"

"Yes, ma'am."

Mrs. Alston took a deep breath. "Show him in, Milly."

TRAVIS ENTERED THE PARLOR, carrying his hat in his hand. His heart clenched when his eyes met the lone figure sitting across the room. Except for her black dress, most people would not know she was grieving. Travis studied her, a habit born from being a lawman. Mrs. Alston was not a large woman nor was she frail, her silver hair gathered into a tight bun. Her eyes were similar in color to Belle's but not as violet. He observed the stiff way she held her body, the proud way she held her head high, but he also noticed the glimmer of tears in her eyes and how she clutched her hands together to keep them from trembling. Even in her grief, she maintained an image of controlled elegance. Travis knew he needed to remain professional. He would keep his own emotions in check and not tell Mrs. Alston he knew Belle.

"Please sit down, Ranger Parker," Mrs. Alston said as she pointed to the floral sofa across from where she sat.

"Thank you, ma'am."

Travis dusted the back of his jeans with his hands, hoping not to get the fine furniture dirty.

"I am sorry for your loss, Mrs. Alston, thank you for meeting with me today. I will try to be as brief as possible."

"Thank you; now how can I help you?"

"I am here to ask you questions about your granddaughter. Sometimes background information helps us find missing persons."

"What kind of information?"

"Well, to start with, tell me about your granddaughter, what kind of girl she is, what are her likes and dislikes, who are her friends, anything you think might help us get a better picture of who she is."

Mrs. Alston sat quietly for a moment that seemed an eternity to Travis. She reached for a stack of papers on the table next to her and handed one to Travis. Travis stared at the picture of the young girl. Her grandmother, desperate to find her, had printed the handbills with Belle's picture and a caption, *Have You Seen This Girl?*

Grief girded Travis' chest as he gazed at the image of Belle. "She is a special young girl, isn't she?" His voice tightened.

"Yes, very special."

"Tell me about her."

"How do I describe Belle? Her name is Belle. Belle is the kindest, gentlest person you could ever meet. I have never heard her say a harsh word about anyone, always is concerned with the wellbeing of others. Anytime someone was sick, Belle would make them soup and homemade bread and take it to their home. She is a good daughter, never gave her parents trouble. Well, she does have a bit of a temper. But Belle is a good girl."

Travis scribbled on a pad of paper. *All right, Travis, ask the routine questions, even though you know the answer you still have to ask.*

"Mrs. Alston, could you give me a detailed description of Belle —how tall is she? What color is her hair—anything like that?"

"Belle is not a tall girl, but not short, either. I guess you would say average height. She has a small frame; some might say delicate but not sickly. She is ethereal in her movements and soft in her touch. Her hair is long, chestnut brown, with streaks of reddish gold when she spends too much time in the sun. Her eyes are violet-blue."

Travis wrote on his pad. *Average height. Small build. Brown hair and violet-blue eyes. Ethereal. (whatever the heck that means—look that one up)*

"Does she have any identifying marks, like a scar or birthmark?"

"Yes, she does, a bell-shaped birthmark on her right forearm; it is how she got her name."

Travis smiled and added the birthmark's description to his list.

"And don't forget her eyes."

"Her eyes?" Travis asked.

"Why, yes, they are quite remarkable, don't you think?" Mrs. Alston pointed to a portrait that hung over her fireplace.

Travis looked up at the painting. A younger, maybe from two or three years ago, Belle stood in the painting. She wore a white dress with a violet sash. He thought she looked like an angel.

Travis, how in the world did you miss that painting? Some ranger you are. You didn't even notice a portrait of Belle. Travis shook his head. *And her grandmother is right. Who could miss those eyes?*

"Ranger, Ranger Parker?"

Travis roused from his daydream. "Oh, I'm sorry, Mrs. Alston. How about friends? Is there anyone she would go to if she were in trouble?"

"Well, there is Darcy Pendergrass; her father manages the Faulkner bank. They live outside of town, not too far from my son's home. Belle has other friends, but they would be the ones she would go to for help. But that is doubtful, Ranger Parker. Mr. Pendergrass would go straight to the sheriff if Belle showed up at his home."

"Even if Belle did not go to them, her friends may still be some help. Thank you, Mrs. Alston."

Travis stood up and turned to leave.

"I will see you to the door, Ranger."

"Thank you, Mrs. Alston."

Travis reached for the doorknob and turned the knob.

"Wait! I just thought of another person she might go to."

"Who?" asked Travis, his hand resting on the doorknob.

"Hank Black Hawk. He and my son were the best of friends. Hank and his family live in a cabin on a piece of land my son gave him. Belle could have gone to him for protection, especially since he would be the closest person for her to go to. Give me your pad, and I will draw you a map."

Travis took his pad out of his vest pocket and handed it to Mrs. Alston. She sketched a map to Hank's cabin and handed the map to Travis.

"Oh, Ranger, be careful when you approach Hank's cabin. Let him know right away that you mean no harm, so he does not shoot you."

"Thanks for the advice."

As Travis opened the door, Mrs. Alston reached out and grabbed his arm. "Please find my granddaughter."

He gazed at the picture of the girl clutched in his hand. "I will."

Travis surprised himself with his answer. He never told a family member he would find their lost loved one; he would only say he would try, but this time everything was different, this time, *he* needed to believe he would find Belle.

EVERYONE IN BLACK HAWK'S cabin went to bed early, but no one slept.

"I don't know what to do," said Hank as he lay in bed next to Little Dove.

"Hank, if you don't teach her what she wants to know and send her back to live with her grandmother, do you think she will try to run away and go after the murderers?"

"Yes, I'm sure of it."

"And do you think she would succeed in running away?"

"Yes."

"So, if you do nothing, she will go after those men and be killed."

"I know. I will have to teach her."

Hank watched the sunrise as he drank a cup of coffee. He contemplated his decision and felt its weight. He could be sending his best friend's daughter to her death. Knowing the fear dancing in his gut would work against him, he gripped his emotions and put them away.

Hank drank his last gulp of coffee and said a silent prayer for wisdom and guidance.

He heard Little Dove clanging cookware as she prepared to cook breakfast. Hank took a deep breath and went inside.

"Good morning," he muttered to his wife.

"Good morning, Hank. Pour yourself another cup of coffee and sit down; breakfast will be ready in a few minutes."

Hank did as his wife asked.

"Can I help?" Fury asked as she walked into the kitchen.

"No, thank you," Little Dove answered, "breakfast is almost done. You can get a cup of coffee and sit with Hank."

Hank's eyes followed Fury. He watched as she fought to control her shaking hands as she poured her coffee. She took a sip then sat down next to him.

After breakfast, Hank left the house, leaving the women to clean up.

The ladies were stacking the dishes in the cupboard when he returned.

"Little Dove, if you don't mind, I need to talk to Fury."

"Sure. Fury go ahead with Hank; I can finish up."

"Let's go for a walk," Hank said to Fury.

She nodded then followed him out the door. They walked in silence until they reached the back of the barn. Fury saw bottles lined up atop a fence rail.

"So, you have decided to help me."

"Yes, God help me, I have. Show me how well you shoot."

Hank handed Fury a gun.

She aimed and shot at the bottles, hitting most of them.

"You are a good shot."

"I know," Fury replied with a slight tone of smugness in her voice. "Papa made sure I learned how to shoot."

"Don't be so sure of yourself. I said you were a good shot, but to go after murderers on the run, you need to be a great shot."

Fury swallowed her pride; she knew he was right.

"You've practiced enough for today."

"But we've only been out here an hour."

"I know, but you need rest. You're still on the mend."

"I'm all right, Hank."

"Fury, let me give you some advice. If you want to stay sharp, you need to take care of yourself. Being exhausted will get you killed."

Fury sighed," All right, you win."

"Good, but before we go in the cabin, I want to show you a couple of things."

"What?"

"Follow me."

Fury followed Hank to a fence that ran along his pasture. He propped his arms on the top rail.

"Look there," Hank said to Fury as he pointed to a painted horse running in the field.

"Nice horse."

"It's yours."

"Mine? Hank, I can't take your horse."

"You can, and you will. You asked me to help you, and getting you a good horse is part of the deal. Watch her run."

Fury watched as the horse galloped in the tall grass.

"Mighty fast, isn't she?"

Fury's eyes were glued to the horse. She was amazed that an animal that fast could move with grace and agility.

"What you want to call her?"

"Huh?" Fury's attention focused on the horse. "She is swift."

"All right, Swift it is?"

"Wait. What?"

"Her name—Swift."

"I didn't mean that to be her name, but she is the fastest horse I've ever seen, so, yeah, I'll call her Swift."

"Well if you can tear your eyes away, I have something else to show you in the barn."

"You don't need to give me anything else," Fury said. "The horse is more than enough."

"Remember what I said. If I'm training you, you take what I give you, no questions asked. Anyway, what's in the barn is already yours. Come on."

Fury nodded and treaded her way to the barn with Hank.

"All right, Hank, what do you want to show me?" Fury asked as they walked into the barn.

"This way." Hank led her to a stall.

"See there." He pointed to a black and white dog being tormented by a scrawny brown pup. The mother dog lay patiently while the pup attacked her ears.

"Oh, him," Fury's voice dropped.

"What do you mean, '*oh, him*'? Your parents gave him to you for your birthday."

"I know, but that was before. What am I going to do with a dog when I'm tracking murderers?"

"Don't be so quick to judge; a dog, a good dog, can help you."

"What do you mean?"

"Well, for one thing, he would be a watch dog. He will hear things long before you do. He also can be trained to protect you. He can sniff out people. There are a lot of things a dog can be trained to do."

"You think *that dog* can help me?" Fury nodded her head toward the pup, who was now hopelessly chasing his tail.

"Yes, I do. His mama is the smartest dog I've ever owned."

"Sally is a smart dog, but that doesn't mean he will be, and I don't have the time to train him."

"Give him a chance. You've worked with me and your father, training hunting dogs. As I recollect, not only did you train them to hunt, you taught them to do tricks."

"I don't think dog tricks are going to help me hunt killers."

"I'm not saying that. I'm saying you are a natural when it comes to training animals. Work with him for a while, and if you don't think it's worth it, then leave him with me."

"All right," Fury sighed as she watched the pup bark at his own shadow, "but he doesn't seem very bright."

"Come on; he's a pup. You gotta give him a chance. What are you gonna call him?"

"I named him when I was here with Papa. His name is Max."

"Good, you stay here with Max for a while and get acquainted. I'm going in to clean our guns."

Fury watched as Hank disappeared into the cabin, then she turned her attention back to the runt of a pup. "What am I supposed to do with you?"

Max looked at her and whined.

"Hey, don't take it personally."

The pup sat back on his haunches and cried.

"Oh, come on," Fury said as she entered the stall.

"It's not like I don't like you," she said as she picked up the pup. "I just don't think it's a good idea to take you with me."

Fury chuckled when the pup began to lick her chin. "All right,

Max, I'll spend a little time with you, but that doesn't mean I'm taking you with me."

From Mrs. Alston's description of Hank Black Hawk, Travis expected a dilapidated shack not a quaint cabin nestled in the serene countryside. He envisioned broken windows and holes in the roof, not flowers and a porch swing, not smoke billowing from the chimney, not a home. Travis hoped the man would be as inviting as his homestead.

Travis needed answers, his visit with the Pendergrass family the prior evening proved fruitless. Darcy sobbed the entire time and her parents were filled with self-recrimination. Travis hoped his visit with Black Hawk would make up for the precious time he lost, time he needed to find Belle.

Travis remembered what Mrs. Alston said about Black Hawk, he was cautious as he approached the door. He knocked on the door.

He heard the rasping sound of a chair scraping against the floor. The door opened and Travis was greeted by a rifle.

"Whoa!" Travis shouted, as he raised his arms, "Put your rifle down, mister. I'm a Texas Ranger I need to ask you some questions concerning Belle Alston."

Hank slowly lowered his gun.

"What you want to know about Belle?"

"May I please come in?"

"No! Ask your questions."

Travis let out a frustrated sigh.

"I am investigating Belle's disappearance and I understand you were close to the family. Did Belle come here after the murder of her parents?"

"Belle is not in my home." Hank hoped saying Belle was not in his home would save him from a lie. He valued honesty.

"Do you have any idea where she might have gone?"

"Sorry, can't help you with that either. Look, son, John Alston was my best friend and I considered his family, my family, if I knew where Belle was, *right now*, I would tell you."

Again, he took his honesty to the limit, technically Hank did not know where Belle was 'right now'.

"I have nothing else to say," Hank added.

"If you think of anything please inform the sheriff and he will pass on the information to me. Thank you for your help Mr. Black Hawk."

He extended his hand to shake Hank's but was met by a closing door.

Travis did not know that the girl he searched for was just a few feet away in the barn.

AFTER SIX MONTHS, the search for the Alston murderers and for their daughter faded away. Only two people held on to the hope that Belle lived—Kate Alston and Ranger Travis Parker. Although the official search for Belle had ended, Travis continued to look for her. No matter what assignment, Belle remained ever present in his mind.

Over the months, Fury trained with Hank. They began every day early and ended every day late. Under Hank's tutelage, Fury improved her shooting and riding skills. He also taught her to track and fight. In the evenings, they sat by the fireplace as Hank shared his knowledge as a deputy with her. When she was not with Hank, she could be found training Swift and Max. But training with the animals was not always work; sometimes she would play games with them. They loved playing a kind of horse and dog hide and seek. Fury cupped her hands like blinders over the horse's eyes and commanded Swift to find Max. Usually, the horse found him in no time. Fury wondered if he wanted to be found. The pup proved to be as smart as his mother, and Fury was pleased at how quickly he learned.

The walk back to the cabin was silent, and Fury knew something was on Hank's mind.

"Hank, what's going on? Did I do something wrong today? Is there something you want me to work on?"

"No, you've learned everything I wanted to teach you, Fury." Hank's voice hitched. "You are ready to leave if you still want to go."

"Yes, I do."

Hank nodded. He hung his head as they plodded along in silence. They were almost to the cabin when Hank stopped and turned to face her. "Fury, what will you do to support yourself?"

"I been meaning to tell you that." Fury shifted her weight. "I'm going to be a bounty hunter."

"What?" Hank yelled. "Do you know how dangerous that is?"

"Yes, I do, Hank, but hear me out. I want to find my parents' murderers, and I need information. Who better to get information from but other criminals?"

"You think some criminal is just gonna spill his guts to you?"

"No, I know it won't be easy, but you taught me well. I know I can do it because I have to do it."

"What about the fact you are a girl; that will bring you a world of trouble, especially if you are hunting criminals," Hank growled.

"I've thought of that. I'm gonna pass myself off as a man."

Hank almost laughed. "A man! You could barely pass yourself off as a boy."

"I believe if I dress in loose fitting clothes and a jacket, no one will know I'm female. And I will have to cut my hair off."

"Cut your hair off?" Sometimes Hank could not believe how much she'd changed. Belle would have never cut her hair, but as she said, she was not Belle; she was Fury.

"It has to be done, Hank. Also, Hank, there is something else I want you to do for me."

"Let's hear it."

"I want you to spread rumors about me, about Fury."

"What?"

"Hear me out, Hank. You start telling the right people about a new bounty hunter named Fury. You could give me a reputation the criminals will take seriously. Warn them. Tell them there's a new bounty hunter, only goes by the name Fury. You heard people say don't let his age or size fool you. Hank, you could tell them things like that, and it might make things easier for me."

Hank was silent. He thought about what Fury said and knew she was right.

"All right," he answered," but you need to stay here a bit longer, to give time for the rumors to get around. And, Fury, remember, I didn't help you so you could get revenge. I helped you so you could get justice."

Fury nodded. "Thank you, Hank."

Hank told his tall tales of the bounty hunter named Fury at saloons and general stores. He went anywhere he knew people gathered to gossip. The name Fury soon became a name to be respected.

"Don't judge Fury by his size," he heard people say. "He is the best shot around and can fight like a grizzly bear." It didn't take long for the stories of Fury to spread and become embellished with each retelling.

When Fury believed enough time passed for the rumors to take hold, she announced she was leaving. Hank and Little Dove gave nervous goodbyes, and Fury thanked them, promising to do her best to keep in touch—a promise she knew she would break.

CHAPTER 5

"*B*oy, it's hot." Travis wiped the sweat from his brow.

"What's wrong? Ya getting soft in yer old age?" Dave chuckled.

"I've tracked every kinda criminal there is, hot days, cold nights, and stormy weather. Used to never bother me, but today I'm hot. I'm getting tired of this job."

"You, Travis Parker, tired of being a ranger? Huh, I don't believe it. Ya used to say ya wanted to join up since ya was a young'n."

"I don't know why you don't give it up, Dave. You got a wife and a baby on the way. That's a life I dream of, but that's a dream, not real life. Dreams and real life ain't the same thing. Women don't marry lawmen."

"Hey, remember, I'm married."

"That's cause Mary is a rare woman, and you're a lucky man. Don't matter anyhow, haven't ever met a gal I would want to court." Travis shifted in his saddle. "Cept'n one," he muttered.

"What?" Dave pulled the horse reins. "You met a girl?"

A warmth spread across his face. *Great, he heard me.*

"It ain't nothing. Come on; let's go." Travis kicked his horse's flanks.

"No. I ain't movin' from this spot until ya tell me about this gal."

"Come on now, Dave, we gotta get to Greenville, to fetch the prisoner then escort him to Clairton so he can stand trial."

"Then ya better start talking."

Travis sighed. "All right, all right, I'll tell you," he said as he dug in his pocket, retrieving a folded-up paper. He took a deep breath and handed it to Dave.

"What's this?"

"Just read it."

"Missing, Belle Alston," Dave read aloud, "5'5", brown hair, violet-blue eyes, birthmark right arm, bell shaped. If you have any information—"

Travis snatched the paper from Dave's hand and returned it to his pocket. "Go on now; have your laugh."

"Travis, who is she?"

Travis sucked in some air. "Belle Alston. Her parents were murdered, and her home burned to the ground, but we couldn't find Belle. I was assigned to search for her. That was three years ago."

"And you fell in love with a picture?"

"No, you idiot. I met her at a dance. Her parents were murdered the same night."

"And you fell in love with her?"

"You can laugh at me if you want, but I did, or at least I was startin' to. I've never given up looking for her."

"I ain't laughing. Same thing happened to me when I met Mary. The first time I saw Mary, she was workin' in her pa's store. I came in the store and went up to the counter, didn't see anyone there, so I yelled out. Well, up pops Mary from behind the counter, scared the shit out of me. She was the purdiest girl

I'd ever seen. Knew right then and there, I would marry her, and I did. So, I ain't laughin', Travis."

Travis saw a look of concern cross Dave's face. "I tell ya what, partner," Dave said. "We are almost to the road to Serenity. Why don't you go there and take a break, get a good meal, and sleep in a real bed. I'll go on to Greenville and get the prisoner and meet up with you in Serenity, then I'll hand over the prisoner and you can take him the rest of the way to Clairton, and I can go home to Mary and maybe the baby if'n he decides to come."

Travis was silent. He mulled over Dave's idea. "You can handle Dale McGraw alone?"

"Hell, McGraw is a banker, arrested for stealing from his own bank. If I can't handle him, I need to turn in my badge."

"Yeah, I reckon a middle-aged embezzler wouldn't put up much of a fight."

"Come on, Travis, you can use a break, and I want to go home to Mary."

"All right, all right, I'll go if it means you might see your baby born, but I wouldn't call the town of Serenity a break."

Dave laughed aloud." No, I guess not."

A few minutes later, Travis and Dave reached the road to Serenity.

"Here's where I leave you," Dave said." See ya tomorrow."

Travis sighed." Yeah, see ya tomorrow."

I SHOULD REACH Serenity before nightfall. Tired from travel, Fury hoped she had enough money left from her last bounty to get a room in the hotel and sleep in a real bed. Even with the training she received from Black Hawk, the years she'd spent as a bounty hunter had not been easy. There were long days of travel and nights of sleeping on the ground. Rain or shine, cold or hot, the weather did not offer any reprieve, the job had to get done.

Bringing criminals to justice offered her survival and a way to search for those who murdered her parents. She had a few close calls and knew one day she would probably be killed, but she hoped she would find her parents' murderers before she met that fate.

Fury tried her best not to think of her parents and her life with them, because those thoughts made her feel and she found feelings and emotions a detriment to her survival. Perhaps fatigue kept her from keeping her memories buried. She thought of her papa's laugh and her mama's sweet smile. Tears attempted to form in her eyes, but she forced them back. A sad smile swept her face as she remembered how easily Belle would cry. Sweet Belle, soft and feminine, replaced by hard, cold Fury. Not a trace of Belle's femininity remained. Fury walked like a man and spoke in a low voice if she spoke at all. She wore men's clothes—jeans, shirt, and a jacket, to cover her womanly form. Today, the jacket was troublesome. It was a hot day, and she didn't dare remove it, so she settled on rolling up her sleeves, hoping that would bring relief.

Fury kept her hat low, to hide her feminine face. She didn't bathe often, using her offensive smell to keep others away, and added an extra layer of dirt to her face so her lack of facial hair would be obscured. To add a final touch to her masculinity, Fury smoked a slender cigar and taught herself to like the taste of whiskey. She smiled when she remembered how sick both habits made her in the beginning, but now, they were a part of Fury.

The town of Serenity glowed from the light of the setting sun as Fury arrived at its outskirts. She stopped for a moment as she heard the wild sounds coming from the town. Serenity did not live up to its name. It had become a town where people of dubious reputations often gathered due to the lack of effective law enforcement. Fury was no stranger to Serenity; she found the Golden Nugget saloon a place with a wealth of information if you knew the right people to ask, and besides, she had grown to enjoy the whiskey they served.

She tied her horse to the hitching post outside the saloon, and a dirty brown dog followed her into town and lay next to her horse. Even though the saloon served as a good place to gather information, at times it could be dangerous.

Fury checked the tilt of her hat, making sure it covered her face. She took a deep breath and pushed through the saloon doors. She knew she would get a reaction; she always did, but her reputation as a bounty hunter had grown past the rumors that Black Hawk had spread. At first, a reputation gave her an advantage, but now she was a target for want-to-be gunslingers hoping to make a name for themselves. Fury approached the bar with her usual confident swagger. She wanted to be left alone to drink her whiskey and look for a particular type, the kind of person who could have the information she needed and would willingly part with it when plied with enough whiskey. Fury had become an expert at singling out informants.

"Whiskey," Fury said as she slapped down money on the bar.

"I'm sorry, young fella," the bartender replied," we don't serve kids. Come back in a couple of years."

Fury lifted her gaze to meet the bartender's eyes.

"Oh, it's you." The bartender quickly retrieved a shot glass and placed it on the bar in front of Fury. He filled it with whiskey.

"Hey, bartender!" bellowed a large man sitting at a poker table. "You gonna serve a kid?"

Fury drew her expected share of unwanted stares, murmurs, and snickers, but experience had taught her that the reaction soon dissipated as everyone returned to playing cards and drinking. But on occasion, Fury drew trouble and she felt this would be one of those occasions.

The blustering drunk, in a mood to cause trouble, thought it would be great fun to antagonize the boy at the bar. Fury had dealt with similar situations a few times; men wanting to feel manly by bullying someone they perceived as weak.

It will blow over, as long as the bartender doesn't tell him who I am.

"Hey, kid!" the drunk barked again. "Does your mama know you is here?"

He laughed as chuckles waved across the room. The reactions of others egged the drunk on.

"I bet if she knew you was here, she would come in and grab you by the ear. Then she would take you to the woodshed when you got home." He howled with laughter.

"For heaven's sake, Morley, shut up! Don't you know this is Fury? You fool."

Fury glared at the bartender. *I don't know who is the bigger idiot.*

She hoped her reputation might frighten the man, but it made him more determined.

Morley slapped his knee and laughed. "This...this is the dangerous and deadly Fury? He don't look that deadly to me; in fact, I would say he is downright scrawny. Why, I don't think them thin little arms could even hold a gun."

Fury turned to face the blowhard when she heard someone speak from the end of the bar.

"Mister, move along, you have had your fun. Leave the boy alone."

Nothing infuriated Fury more than someone thinking she needed to be rescued. If she ever allowed anyone to intervene for her, she would appear weak and her days of bounty hunting could be over. The last thing she needed or wanted was a knight in shining armor.

Fury turned and glared at the man who spoke. *Travis!* Fury had learned how to keep her emotions in check, but seeing Travis, she struggled to keep her composure. She would not, could not, let a rush of emotions take over.

"Butt out, mister!"

"Well, folks, he kin talk. And I do agree with the boy, mister, you need to butt out."

"It's ranger, not mister. Texas Ranger Travis Parker, to be exact, and if you don't do as I say, I will arrest you for disorderly conduct and threatening a minor."

"Minor!" Fury was livid. "Who are you calling a minor?"

"You. I'm calling you a minor. Now be quiet, kid, and let the grown-ups talk."

"Shut the f—"

"Don't say it, kid." Travis was losing his temper with this ungrateful boy. "All right, kid," Travis held up his hands, "have it your way. I'll be here by the bar if you need me."

"Fat chance," she sniped at the ranger.

Fury returned to her drink sitting on the bar.

"Hey, kid!" Morely bellowed once more." I ain't done with you yet. Turn back around and face me, or is the great Fury scared?"

Fury took a gulp of her drink; she liked how whiskey burned the back of her throat. She turned toward the man.

"Well, Mr. Fury, the great bounty hunter, could take on ten men at a time, I heared. Why don't you just take on one man, me, and let's see what you can do. Here," he said, pointing at his chin, "take a free shot."

Fury rested her back against the bar, both arms extended across the top of the bar propping her up.

"Morely. It is Morely, isn't it?" Fury asked.

"Yep!" the big man gloated.

"I will oblige you, but first I need to ask you something."

"Sure," sneered the oaf.

The entire room went silent. Even Travis leaned forward to hear Fury's question.

"Well, while I have been talking to you, I've noticed something curious about you. I have noticed, as I am sure everyone here knows, that you are quite a large man."

"That I am," Morely answered with pride.

"Yes, you are," Fury added, "but I also noticed that you have very small feet for a man of your size."

Morely looked down at his feet. "So?"

"I would like you to clear up a question I have. Is it true what people say about men with little feet?"

There was a moment of silence, then the room broke out in a cacophony of laughter. Even Travis joined in. It took Morely a bit longer to realize that Fury had insulted his manhood. His face burned crimson red as his temper reached its limit.

Fury studied him, waiting for his reaction. Then she saw it. Morely leaned forward and charged straight for Fury. But Fury was quick. She stepped toward the charging drunk then moved to her right and stuck out her foot. Morely tripped over her foot, and with his forward momentum, ran his head straight into the side of the bar. He was out cold.

The room roared with applause, but Fury was not happy. Because of this altercation, she would not be able to question anyone tonight. She turned and walked out of the saloon.

"Damn idiot," she grumbled as she untied her horse from the hitching post.

"Hey, kid!" Travis called out.

Fury turned to see the interfering ranger had followed her out of the saloon. *Steady.* She tried to calm the butterflies in her stomach. She looked at him but did not respond.

"Kid, I loved how you handled that drunk. I haven't laughed that hard in a long time."

Travis, why him? I need to get rid of him. Sadness plopped down in her heart. She needed to get rid of Travis, the man who, for a short time, she had felt she might have a future with, the man she thought she could love. But those were Belle's dreams; they could never be her dreams, or could they?

"The name is Fury."

"Sorry. Fury, do you need any help or a place to stay?"

Fury tossed him a confused look. "Why in the hell would I need your help? No thanks, I have my own money."

"Didn't your mother teach you to watch your language? I was trying to help you, you ungrateful brat."

Fury mounted her horse and gazed down at Travis. "No, my mother didn't teach me to watch my language, and I don't need help."

Fury nudged Swift's flanks with her boots and rode toward the livery stable.

TRAVIS SHOOK HIS HEAD. Never had he met such a stubborn, rude kid. Then he chuckled, remembering he used to be just like the kid, stubborn, proud, not needing anyone's help. Travis lost both his parents by the time he turned fourteen. Alone in the world, he probably would have ended up in jail, but fate had been good to him when a ranger took him in and gave him a home. Maybe that's why he went after Fury, to return the favor and help another lost, lonely young boy.

CHAPTER 6

"*Y*ou're just in time; I was about to close up and go home," Fury heard Miles Keaton shout out as she came into his livery.

"Hi, Miles."

"Fury, is that you?"

"Yes." Fury dismounted and handed the reins of her horse to her friend.

Miles Keaton was one of Fury's few friends. She'd tracked down his wife's murderer, and Miles would do anything for Fury.

"Whatcha doing in town?" Miles asked.

"Lookin' for someone, of course. Miles, you got any information on Dan Davenport, also known as Cutter Dan? He is 6-foot-tall, about two hundred plus pounds of muscle, dark hair, and dark eyes."

"Cutter Dan. I've heared of him. Not a nice fella. Evil."

"Yes, he is evil for sure. He hunts, murders, and mutilates young women, then he cuts his initials C.D. on their forehead." Fury was silent then, waiting for Miles to respond.

"You know, Fury, it's funny how people are with their animals."

51

"What?" Fury replied, believing the man had not listened, but she knew that sometimes Miles took time to get to the point.

"Fury, you ever talk to your horse?"

"Sometimes."

"A lot of folks do. Before they leave their horse, they will stand there and tell the animal all kinda things. Folks who leave their horses here forget I am even around, so I hear a lot."

"And?" added Fury, losing her patience.

"A week or so back, a big fella come in with his horse. He kinda fits your description. If I'd known he might be Cutter Dan, I woulda hightailed it to the law."

"Go on."

"He left his horse with me, and I put him in the stall over yonder. Thirty minutes later, he comes back, telling me he forgot to get his saddlebags. I pointed him toward his horse's stall, and I go back to working. Well, when he gets to the stall, sure enough, he starts talking to his horse. He forgets I'm there. Most people do, and he tells his horse it won't be much longer, and they will be in Mexico. But first, they have to lay low and wait for the law to get tired of looking for him. This fella tells his horse they've got a long ride ahead of them, to Langston. It's a few days south of here; anyway, he says he knows there is an abandoned cabin outside of town where they can hole up. Then he tells his horse there are grassy meadows where the horse kin graze and cool water to drink from a river. There is no sweeter tasting water than the water in Spiny River."

Miles paused and smiled at Fury.

"Funny how some horrible people kin care about an animal."

"You be careful," he said with a smile and turned to walk Fury's horse to the stall.

"Miles, don't tell anyone else your story," Fury said.

Miles raised his hand as he walked away, his way of signaling Fury that he heard what she said.

Max passed by Fury as she left to go to the hotel. Fury figured the dog wanted to bed down in the livery with her horse.

Her hollow stomach growled. When she hunted a bounty, she lived on limited provisions and learned to ignore her hunger. But being in a town with some money in her pocket meant treating herself to a real meal. The thought of a home-cooked meal, especially one cooked by Nora Bailey, the owner of Bailey's restaurant, enticed her. Even the thought of Nora's juicy fried chicken and melt-in-your-mouth chocolate cake made Fury's mouth water.

"Hey, kid."

Fury sighed when she recognized the man in front of her. She was annoyed at herself that she'd broken one of Hank's most important survival rules—always be aware of your surroundings.

"I'm not a kid," she answered as she attempted to walk around the large ranger standing in front of her.

The top of Fury's head barely reached the middle of his chest. Fury hated to look up at someone; after all, how can you be intimidating when someone is towering over you? She reluctantly tilted her gaze slightly up, ready to give the ranger her best intimidating stare, but something happened—a bit of Belle slipped by Fury's wall as she considered his jade eyes enhanced by his tanned skin. She remembered his brown sugar-colored hair and the strong angular lines of his face. He was the kind of man Belle dreamed about when she imagined her future husband.

A warm smile broke across his face. "Kid, you all right?"

"Um, yeah, what?"

"I asked if you are all right. You looked a bit lost for a moment."

"I ain't lost," she said as Fury pushed Belle back and regained control. "What ya want from me, mister?"

"I want to help you. Do you have a place to stay? Have you eaten?"

"I thought you were a ranger, not my fairy godmother," Fury said with a shadow of humor in her otherwise flat voice.

Travis grinned at the insult. "No, I'm not your fairy godmother. I want to help you like someone helped me once. You see, when I was around your age, I was orphaned. I drifted from town to town and got in some trouble. A Texas Ranger took me in, and he changed my life. I would probably be in jail or dead if someone hadn't reached out and helped me."

Fury folded her arms across her chest.

"Uh huh, and you want to change my life. Well, no thanks, go find another charity case."

Fury stepped around him, but as she passed, Travis grabbed her arm. "But, kid—"

Travis noticed something on the kid's arm. Even in the fading evening light, it was plain to see the bell-shaped birthmark.

Fury felt him tighten his grip as he pulled her arm closer to get a better look. She tried to retrieve her arm from his iron grip, but he held on.

"Belle?" Travis half whispered. He glared at Fury's eyes, a faded violet, not the piercing shade they once shone. Maybe the harshness of her life had robbed them of their uniqueness. Travis searched them, hoping for recognition but received only silence.

His hold weakened, and Fury succeeded in yanking her arm from his grip. She jerked her sleeve down to cover her birthmark.

"Have you gone loco? Why in the hell are you calling me a bell?"

Travis shook off his stunned trance. "Because it's your name. You are Belle, the girl who went missing a few years ago, the girl with the bell-shaped birthmark."

"Listen, Ranger, I don't know what you've been drinking, but my name ain't Belle and I sure as hell ain't no girl. Leave me alone, mister, or I may have to shoot you."

Travis chuckled at her warning and watched as Fury stomped away from where he stood. He knew he'd found his Belle.

~

FURY DRUMMED her fingers on the red gingham tablecloth, contemplating what to do about the troublesome lawman.

"Here you go," Mrs. Bailey said in a cheery tone as she plopped a bowl of stew and a stack of fresh baked bread in front of Fury.

Fury nodded her approval, and Mrs. Bailey left to tend to her other customers.

How could I be so stupid, so careless? She picked at her food. *That meddling ranger knows who I am. What am I going to do?*

Fury scooped up a spoonful of stew and guided it to her mouth. *I could shoot him. Naw, Fury, you can't shoot Travis. Besides, he's a ranger. There would be too many questions. I don't recall him being so damn irritating. I gotta step up my plans and avoid that infuriating ranger.*

The aroma of the stew overpowered Fury's worries concerning the ranger. She ate like a starved animal, enjoying every juicy warm morsel. The meal warmed her insides and comforted her worries until an unwelcome visitor sat down across from her.

"I don't recall invitin' anyone to eat with me," Fury said, not lifting her gaze from her meal.

"You didn't; I invited myself."

"Well, you can just uninvite yourself, mister."

"Not until we talk."

"You sure like to take risks with your life, mister."

"Who's threatening my life?" Travis chuckled.

Fury raised her gaze and glared at him. "If I have to tell you, then you are a bigger fool than I thought."

"Listen here," Travis leaned in, "I've had just about enough of your threats. I'm here to help you."

"I told you I ain't no charity case."

"I was planning to leave you be," Travis said as he leaned in closer, "that is until I found out you are Belle."

The hair on the back of Fury's neck prickled as she felt the heat of anger rising on her face. "Shut the hell up; you are begging for a bullet. I told you I ain't this Belle, and I certainly ain't no girl!"

"Well, if I am wrong, you won't object to showing me your arm again." Travis grasped her arm.

Fury yanked it from his hold. "I'm warning you, mister; I have killed men for less."

"Look," Travis said, keeping his voice down, "I don't intend to bring you any harm, but I am sure you are Belle, and I'm not gonna leave you alone until you admit it. Let's go somewhere and talk."

"I ain't going anywhere with you." Fury stood, scraping the legs of her chair on the wooden floor. "Stay the hell away from me."

Fury reached in her pocket and removed some money. She slammed the money on the table and walked out, leaving Travis sitting with only the remainder of her stew to keep him company.

When she got to her room, Fury slammed the door and threw her saddle bag on the bed. "That insufferable clod of a man is going to get me killed. I need to get out of here and away from him as fast as I can."

She plopped down on the bed and rubbed her temples. Anger boiled inside her; she needed to breathe, to settle down. Fury never let anger or any other emotion take over. She needed to regain control. A small dust cloud came off her jacket as she removed it and draped it on a chair with her tattered hat. Fury began to unbutton her shirt but was stopped by an unwelcome pounding on her door.

"Great, what now?" She rebuttoned her shirt and put her

jacket and hat back on. Keeping her hand on her gun, Fury approached the door.

"What you want?" she asked.

There was no response from the other side of the door. The pounding resumed.

"You can wear out your hand for all I care, I ain't answering that door until I know who it is."

"It's me, Travis."

Fury rolled her eyes. "Now I'm sure I ain't opening that door. Go away, Ranger." Her ears perked, listening for the sound of his footsteps leaving, but no sound came. "Suit yourself; you can sleep there if ya want, but I better not find you there in the morning."

Silence. Then the clanging sound of keys, and Fury's door swung open.

Fury drew her gun on Travis who stood in the doorway holding a bowl of stew.

"I suggest you put that gun away. You didn't finish your stew." He held the bowl out toward Fury.

"How in the hell did you get the keys to the room?"

"Oh, me and the desk clerk came to an understanding." Travis smiled. "Now, where do you want me to put your stew?"

"You know where you can put that stew; you can put it up your—"

"I wouldn't finish that statement if I were you; put your gun down and eat."

His brazen behavior stunned her.

"You gotta be some kind of peculiar crazy, mister."

"I told you to put your gun down." Travis took a few steps toward her.

Her mind contradicted itself. Part of her wanted to shoot him, but part held back. As a bounty hunter, she didn't allow indecision, but here she was wanting to shoot the man in front of her but unable to do so.

Travis reached out and grasped her gun from her hand as if the weapon were a toy in the hands of a naughty child. "I'm gonna hold on to this for a while." He placed the bowl on a small nightstand. "Eat, and we can talk in the morning."

Fury froze; she remained standing with her mouth hung open, trying to understand her inability to react.

Travis strode over to the door." I will see you in the morning." He began to turn the knob then stopped. "Oh, I suppose I should leave this with you." He held up her gun and then placed it on the floor next to the door. "Goodnight."

Fury picked up the bowl of stew and hurled it at the closing door.

The door crept back open, and Travis peered in. "Smashing a bowl against the door?" Travis smiled and shook his head. "That's what I would expect an angry woman to do, not a notorious gunman." Travis tipped his hat and closed the door.

Fury shook her head. *What in the hell just happened?* She ran over and picked up her gun then locked the door.

His key.

Fury spied a wooden chair sitting next to the door. She scooted the chair in front of the door and propped it under the doorknob. *I gotta get out of here and away from him, quick. Damn it, Fury, why are you letting this man get to you? You should shoot him and be done with it.*

Fury hurled her hat at the chair, flinging her coat after it. She walked over to the bed and flopped down. She struggled to get her boots off then threw them in a corner and lay back on the bed. The bed was every bit the soft luxury she wanted to give herself tonight, but the worrisome ranger occupied her aware-ness, stealing this bit of pampering from her. The moment Travis discovered her birthmark played in her mind.

Stupid, stupid, stupid, Fury? Why didn't I remember to roll my sleeves back down when I got to town? Hank warned me; it's the little things that will get you. I really messed things up this time... Damn that eagle-eyed Travis. Those damn, mossy eyes, yes, they were green, and his hair, what I could see of it, was kinda wavy brown, and his smile, what a warm smile. And I think he has dimples—w-what in the hell is wrong with you? Fury slapped the palm of her hand over her face. *Why in the hell are you mooning over a man who could get you killed?* Her hand slid down to her chest." *Where did all this come from? Holy smoke, it's like Belle mooning over a boy. Well, Belle, I corked you and your emotions up a long time ago. I must be tired for them to slip by so easily.* Fury yawned, her body sinking into the plush comfort of the bed.

"Just put all those thoughts away," she mumbled. *Gotta stay focused, gotta stay away from Travis, yes, stay away from Travis.* Fury's eyes drifted closed. *Stay away from that smile, away from those dimples. Gotta stay away.*

IN ADDITION to the key to Fury's room, the desk clerk, with a bit of persuasion from Travis, arranged for him to stay in the room adjacent to Fury's.

Travis removed his boots and shirt. His years as a ranger made him prefer to keep his pants on and his gun lying next to his head, ready for any unwelcome visitor.

He stretched his long body across the soft bed. Usually, the luxury of a bed would cause sleep to come quickly, but not tonight. Tonight, his mind raced as fast as his heart pumped in his chest. He propped up on the pillow, cradling his head against his arm, and listened to his thoughts.

I found her. After all these years, I found Belle. It's hard to believe that dirty, ill-mannered and foul-mouthed bounty hunter is the sweet, angelic Belle. But wait, what if I'm wrong? What if I see what I want to see? Am I fooling myself?

Travis scratched his head. His smile drooped as he questioned himself.

Wait, wait a minute, the birthmark was definitely bell-shaped, but is that enough proof? I have good instincts about people, after all, I am a ranger, it's practically a requirement to be a good lawman, everything in me tells me Fury is Belle.

Travis lay quiet for a moment; then the smile returned to his face.

Travis, you idiot, you forgot those eyes. Yes, Fury's eyes are tired, but they are the same shade as Belle's eyes. They may not be as piercing as they once were, but it is the same blue-violet color. Two people cannot have that same color eyes along with a bell-shaped birthmark. Fury is Belle, and she is in the next room.

Travis reached back, resting the palm of his hand on the wall behind his bed. He found comfort in knowing Belle's bed and his shared this common wall.

I know it's you, Belle, and I'm taking you home.

CHAPTER 7

*F*ury put on her boots, ignoring the pale shades of orange-gold light filtering through the window. A few years ago, the beauty of the morning light would have won her attention but not now, and especially not with Travis on her mind. She did not sleep well. Nightmares of Travis exposing her as Belle competed with pleasant dreams of the handsome man with his sea green eyes.

Fury sat reflecting on the images of her dreams still fresh in her mind. She rubbed her forehead. The thought of his interference with her mission wrestled those troublesome, pleasant images down, fueling a rage in her.

Damn him! I gotta get out of this town quickly, before his big mouth ruins everything. Don't lose your head, Fury. Remember, Hank said the quickest way to get killed is not to keep your wits about you. I need a plan. I'll get all my gear, then I can make one more try to get someone at the saloon to talk, and if that doesn't work, I'll just have to go on with the information old Miles gave me. It's too dangerous to stay here any longer.

The aroma of bacon and coffee drifted up to her room from the restaurant across the street. The enticing smells filled her nose and caused her mouth to water in anticipation. *Oh, I just gotta get one more home-cooked meal in me before it's back to jerky, beans, and hard tack.*

Fury sprang to her feet, put on her dirty coat and dusty, tattered hat, and went down the stairs on her way to the last good meal she would have for a while.

"Excuse me?" the desk clerk called to Fury as she passed by. "Excuse me please, Mr. Fury."

"What?' Fury's voice croaked as she stopped and glared at the clerk.

"Will you be staying another night with us?"

Fury thought for a moment. She wanted to leave today if she could but didn't want the clerk to know for fear of him telling his acquaintance, the ranger.

"Yeah," Fury answered and walked out the door, following the enticing smell of bacon and freshly brewed coffee leading her to Bailey's Restaurant.

TRAVIS FILLED the basin then set the pitcher down on the table. The shock of the cold water as it hit his face washed away any remnant of sleep. He rubbed the rough towel over his face and across the back of his neck then left the towel hanging from the rim of the basin. He grabbed his shirt from the chair where he'd tossed it last night.

Hope Belle—Fury, I mean Fury—gotta remember to call her Fury or I could bring a heap of trouble for that girl. Dang boy, no, young man, gotta remember she is a young man. Hell, I can't wait until I get her back home. Trying to keep this straight in my head is gonna drive me crazy. Get her home, how am I gonna get her home?

Travis fastened the last button on his shirt and then looked at himself in the mirror. He rubbed his hand across his stubbled face. *Maybe I can find time to get a shave?*

He stepped back and studied his reflection.

"You're looking pretty rough there, son." Travis smelled his underarm. "Dang, and you stink too."

He chuckled at himself. "It ain't like you're courting her, Travis. She already hates you, and she is gonna hate you more when you try to drag her home."

He raked his hand through his thick brown hair. *Gotta think this through. I gotta meet Dave today and take his prisoner to Clairton.* Travis scratched his head. *I'm gotta convince Dave to take the prisoner so I can take Belle home. Belle...damn, I mean Fury. I gotta go find her. I don't need her gettin' away from me.*

Travis put his hat on and left his room to find Fury.

"Fury," he said as he pounded the door. "Fury, come on; it's Travis, open the door. Fury?" *Better check and see if she is in there,* he thought as he removed the key from his pocket.

He edged the door open halfway, expecting to be shot at. "Fury, you in here?"

Travis surveyed the room, but there was no Fury. To his relief, her saddlebags lay on the chair, evidence that she was still in town.

He shuffled down the stairs and up to the front desk. "Henry," he called to the desk clerk.

"Yes, Ranger, how can I help you?"

"The kid, Fury, do you know where he is?"

"Left here about thirty minutes ago."

"Damn, you got any idea where he went?"

"He didn't say, but I would try Bailey's if I was you. The smell of her breakfast cooking is mighty alluring this morning."

"Thanks Henry."

The wooden boards of the sidewalk squeaked as Travis shifted his weight. He stopped for a moment to scan his surroundings, making sure he didn't miss Belle if she had already left the restaurant.

Something had changed.

Everything appeared normal as Travis watched the town waking up. Dust clouds still drifted in the air as riders and wagons passed by. The storekeepers were opening their shops like they had a hundred times before. A few drunks waited for the saloon to open, and townspeople scurried about their daily tasks. The town didn't appear different and yet Travis sensed a change. Realization hit him like a bolt of lightning—he was different, not the town. Finding Belle had fueled the change in him.

Yesterday, he'd pondered his empty life and unattainable dream of a wife and a home, but now he'd found Belle. Did someone hear his thoughts, or was it a coincidence, finding the one woman he dreamed of marrying. Was he crazy to want to marry a woman he knew only from the recollection of one evening and a picture he kept in his pocket? And what about Fury? There were no similarities between her and Belle, yet her spunky tenacity intrigued him.

For years, memories of Belle had haunted his mind. As time flowed by, she became a dream, living in his imagination, but yesterday, he woke from his dream, and now she was a reality. A walking, talking, cursing, fighting, tough, reality, now eating breakfast a little way from where he stood.

Travis drew a deep breath of the sweet morning air then walked to Bailey's restaurant.

FURY TOOK her last sip of coffee and sat back in her chair. She had relished every morsel of her breakfast, thankful the pesky lawman did not plop himself at her table as he did last evening.

She gave in to a yawn and stretched her arms. Her relaxed countenance left her when she gazed out the window and spotted the meddling lawman coming her way.

"Back door?" Fury questioned the cook.

The cook pointed. "That way."

"Don't tell anyone you saw me here," she said in her most intimidating tone.

"I won't, Mr. Fury, I won't," the poor man's voice cracked.

"Good."

Fury made her way out the back door. She circled behind a few buildings then turned down the alley leading to the general store.

~

"MORNIN'," Travis said as he entered the restaurant.

"Let me find you a table," the nervous cook said.

"No need. I'm Ranger Travis Parker. I'm looking for a young man, goes by Fury. Have you seen him?"

"You mean Fury the bounty hunter?"

"Yes."

"Look, Mister Lawman, Fury is a dangerous person to tangle with. If he ain't done anything major, it's best to let him be."

"I ain't gonna arrest him. Fury has information I need for a case I worked a few years back; all I want is to talk to him."

"Sorry, but he ain't here."

Travis didn't buy his answer for a minute but thanked him anyway. He figured Fury scared him enough, so he didn't want to add to his misery.

~

I CAN'T BELIEVE I'm doing this. I'm Fury, people are afraid of me, and here I am sneaking around the back of buildings and going down an alley to avoid one man, one irritating ass of a man. I should have shot him already.

Fury rounded the corner of the alley and stepped on the sidewalk. She was in a hurry and ran smack into a large man.

"Get out of the way," Fury demanded.

"Didn't your ma teach you any manners?"

Fury's eye's darted up to confront the man before her. "I shoulda known it would be you. Get the hell away from me, Ranger."

Travis smiled. "We need to talk."

"No, leave me alone. You are trying my patience, Ranger, and my trigger finger is beginning to itch." Fury circled around him, making her way to the general store.

"Oh, we will talk," Travis said.

Fury stopped in front of the store and glared at Travis

"I'm giving you a chance to pick a place, but I'm about out of patience." Travis walked up to where Fury stood on the steps in front of the store. They were eye to eye. "Listen, Fury, I'm trying my best to keep your secret, but if you don't agree to meet with me, I may have to expose you."

Fury leaned toward Travis and locked her eyes on his. "There ain't nuttin' to expose, and if you cause me trouble, it will be the last thing you will ever do. Do I make myself clear?" Fury snarled, puffing up her chest.

"You know," Travis said as he looked at the angry little bounty hunter, "I'm about tired of all your threats, and I'm gonna give you one hour to meet with me. I will be at the hotel. If you don't show, then I will come looking for you."

"You can wait till Hell freezes over."

Travis smiled, tipped his hat, and turned to walk back to the hotel.

"Hey, Ranger!" Fury shouted.

Travis stopped and turned to face her.

"You'd better get your will written while you are waitin" for Hell to freeze over."

Travis chuckled. "You'd better get some warm clothes while you are in the store. I think a freeze is coming…oh, and by the way, while you're in the store, you ought to buy some soap. I've smelled skunks that smell better than you."

"Some of your family, I assume," Fury retaliated.

Travis laughed out loud. "You got an hour, kid."

Fury's hand brushed the top of her gun. *Damn, why can't I shoot that jackass?*

The warm greeting jingle of the bell over the door did not match Fury's foul mood. She slammed the door shut. The smell of coffee, pickles, and tobacco greeted her.

"Be with ya in a minute," said the old storekeeper as he finished an older woman's order.

"You can sit with them and wait, young fella." The storekeeper pointed to a group of chairs next to an old potbellied stove. Most general stores hosted a common gathering area primarily used by men. Some men passed the time there while their wives shopped, but most came to socialize. On any given day, one could stop by and engage in conversation concerning weather or farming as well as heated political debates. There would also be a fair amount of tall tales also known as lies. Two of the chairs were occupied by older men playing checkers while a third man watched.

"No thanks, I'll wait," Fury grumbled.

She sauntered over to the post office occupying the far corner of the store. There, on a worn bulletin board, hung the wanted posters. Fury scanned the various faces searching for one. She paused when she reached the third wanted poster on the second row. There before her, hung the image of the man she hoped to find. His broad face with small, close-set eyes, cold stone evil as the man they belonged to, his thick lips framed by his stubbled beard, clearly the picture of a man you did not want to tangle with.

Wanted for murder. Dan 'Cutter Dan' Davenport. Reward of one thousand dollars dead or alive.

Fury was not certain anyone other than Miles knew that a

man fitting the description of Cutter Dan had passed through Serenity a few days ago. If only she had more time, she would go to the saloon and attempt to gather more information, but with that interfering ranger on her heels, she didn't know how she could manage it. The last thing she wanted was for anyone to find out she was searching for Davenport and warn him, or worse, try to take him and collect on the bounty. How could she be discrete with Travis trailing her everywhere? Fury knew she had to do something about the ranger, but what?

She yanked the poster from the board, folded it, and shoved it in her pocket.

"All righty then, young fella, what can I help you with?" the storekeeper called out to Fury.

"You got a piece of paper so I can write a list and then you can deliver it to the hotel?"

"Sure thing, but I'm gonna need your name."

"Fury."

"Fury?" The storekeeper's voice shook. "The bounty hunter?"

"Yeah. Deliver it to the hotel."

"Right, right," the nervous storekeeper said, "have it right over to you, Mr. Fury."

"Good," Fury answered and left to return to the hotel.

TRAVIS PACED the floor of his hotel room.

She'd better show. The last thing I want to do is drag that girl out of town, I don't want to expose her by letting her secret out, but I needed to give her some extra motivation to meet with me. Hopefully, she will meet up with me and not shoot me. What time is it?

Travis pulled out his pocket watch. It was not the kind of watch one would expect a lawman to carry. Tom Greene, the ranger who had taken him in when he was a young man, had given it to him when Travis was sworn in as a ranger.

Good, I've got a couple of hours before Dave gets to the jail. Dang it, Fury, you have fifteen minutes, then I'll have to hunt you down.

Travis smiled when he heard a rapping on the door. "Fury," he said as he turned the doorknob, "I'm so glad you—

His smile faded when he saw a boy with a note in his hand standing in front of him. "Whatcha want, son?"

"A man at the jail told me to bring ya this here note. Are you Ranger Parker?"

"Yes, that's me." Travis took the note from the boy's grimy hand. "Here," Travis said as he handed the boy a coin.

"Thanks, mister."

"Uh huh," Travis muttered as he closed the door. He unfolded the note.

Hey, Travis,

Made good time, got here early with the prisoner. I'm at the jail. Come and take this scum off my hands so I can be on my way.

Dave

"Damn, of all the times for Dave to be early, it had to be today."

Travis grabbed his hat, left his room, and sprinted down the stairs. "Henry," he shouted at the desk clerk on his way out," Fury is supposed to meet with me but I gotta go out, gotta meet someone at the jail about a prisoner. Tell Fury to wait in my room. Tell him I might be a while, maybe an hour, but to wait."

"All right," the nervous clerk answered.

Fury shuffled her way to the hotel. She was not in any hurry to meet up with Travis but did not know how to avoid him since she needed to get back to her room.

Damn, he is a sly one, wanting to meet up at the hotel knowing I would have to go back there. I guess it's time to deal with him once and for all.

Fury patted her gun.

The hotel lobby was deserted. Fury glanced at the long oak desk where the clerk usually stood, but no one was there.

"Good," Fury mumbled as she crossed the faded carpet on her way to the stairs.

"Oh, Mr. Fury." She heard a familiar voice call out to her.

Fury stopped at the foot of the staircase and turned; her eyes glared at the desk clerk as he closed the door to a storage closet.

"Whatcha want?" Fury demanded.

"I-I'm sorry, Mr. Fury, s-sir, it's just the ranger wants—

"What the hell does he want?"

"Well, he said, you was supposed to meet up with him and, uhm, F-Fury, sir, well, he needed to get down to the jail. Sum'n about a prisoner, but anyhow, s-sir, he's gonna be late, said for you to wait for him in his room. Oh, and he said he might be a while, maybe an hour."

"Uh huh…so that's what he said…wait for him in his room."

"Y-yes, sir, that's what he said."

"Good," Fury said with a smile, something she rarely did. She turned and walked up the stairs. *Fury, sometimes luck smiles on you. This is the break you need. He expects me to be here waitin' on him. Ha.*

She closed the door to her room. *My delivery from the store should be here soon, then I'm getting out of this town and away from one Ranger Travis Parker for good.*

Fury heard another rapping at the door. *Great.*

Fury opened the door to see the desk clerk with a package in his hand.

"Sorry to bother you, sir, but Mr. Adams from the general store dropped this off for you."

"Good," Fury said as she grabbed the package.

"Y-you thinking about leaving soon, M-Mr. Fury, sir?"

"No," Fury replied.

"All right, bye, Mr. Fury."

"Wait."

"Yes, sir," the desk clerk said with a tinge of fear in his voice.

"You said the ranger wanted to meet with me."

"Yes, sir."

"Well," Fury said, "I have business to attend to; he can find me at the saloon."

The clerk nodded. "Sure, Mr. Fury."

Fury leaned against the closed door of her room. *Good, another way to slow down that man. Yes, Mister Ranger Travis Parker, Fury will be long gone before you notice he's missing.*

Fury was quite pleased with herself. She packed her supplies in her saddlebags and threw them out the window to the alley below. *Gotta hurry before someone steals my bags.*

Fury raced down the stairs, slowing her pace as she crossed the lobby. She made sure the clerk noticed her leaving.

"Have a good day," the desk clerk chimed.

Fury grunted her response and walked out the door. She walked at a normal pace not to draw attention. Turning the corner into the alley, she found her bags. *Now to the livery and out of this town and back to bounty hunting, with no Ranger Travis following me.*

A strange mix of emotions stirred within her at her mention of the ranger's name. Part of her would be happy never to see that man again, but another part felt a twinge of sadness.

"COME ON, Dave, I really need this favor."

Travis stood with his hat in his hand pleading with Dave.

Dave leaned back in the only chair in the dank jail. Sheriff Tate occupied the other chair.

Dave sipped his coffee. "Look, Travis, I traveled most of

yesterday with the prisoner. You're supposed to take the last leg of the trip to Clairton so he can stand trial. You promised to take him so I can get home to my wife before the baby is born."

"Yes, I know," Travis argued," but that was before I got a lead on an old case of mine, a murder case. Come on, Dave, it's only an hour to Clairton and back, and besides, your wife has already had five kids. I think she knows what to do if she goes into labor."

"Sorry, friend, but you know, a deal is a deal, and like you said, it's only an hour of your time. I'm sure your lead will be here when you get back."

"I'm not sure if this lead will keep."

"Can't help you there."

"You sure you won't reconsider?"

"I'm sure."

"All right, Sheriff," Travis grunted as he turned his attention to the grey-haired man behind the desk," let me get my prisoner and we will be on our way."

CHAPTER 8

*F*ury relished her freedom. She received a sense of security and control in her regular routine, even though it involved hunting wanted men. But with this bounty, she embarked on the most dangerous bounty hunt of her life. The man she hunted, Cutter Dan, was arguably one of the most violent men in a sea of criminals.

Fury did not dwell on the caliber of assailant she hunted. Sure, her path crossed with various criminals but none like Cutter. She pushed back her doubts. After all, she needed the money from his bounty, one thousand dollars. A few weeks ago, she had found an informant, a man known as the gambler, who claimed to know the whereabouts of her parents' killers. He demanded a steep price for his information. Fury knew the information could be bogus, but she needed to follow this clue on the remote chance it led to the men who had killed her parents.

"Slow down, girl," Fury said to her horse as she tugged on the reins." I think we are far enough from that lawman, we can relax some. Besides," she smiled, "Max looks tired." She rode up onto a grassy area with a few clusters of trees scattered about. "We can stop here and rest a bit."

Fury dismounted. "All right, horse, graze away. It's a good thing you aren't the type of horse who would run off." She rubbed the animal on the nose.

"Now," she said to the dog," let's see what I might have for you."

Fury reached into her saddlebag to find some jerky. Instead, her hand landed on something else in her bag. "What in the world is this?"

She pulled her hand out and found her fingers wrapped around the bar of soap she'd bought at the store. "Oh, damn soap. You tell me," she said to the dog, "why did I let Travis get to me so much that I bought soap?" Fury tossed the offensive item.

"Here it is," she said as she retrieved jerky from her bag. "Want it, boy?"

The mutt's ears perked up as he licked his nose in anticipation. "You know you gotta earn it."

The dog cocked its head as if he were asking a question.

"Sit," Fury commanded, and the dog sat. "Good boy." She tossed him a piece of jerky. "Now lie down."

The dog dropped down on the lush, thick grass.

"You're a good dog. Now, the one you are learning. Up."

The dog sat back on his haunches then raised his front legs.

"Ready?" Fury held up her hand and shaped her fingers into a fake gun. She pointed at the dog. "Bang! Your dead!"

The dog fell to the ground, rolled over and played dead.

"Good job, up. You sure are a quick study. We can work on the harder ones later."

Fury paused and turned her head. "What's that noise?" She focused on the babbling sound. "Water. Come on, boy, sounds like we're near water, and I want to fill my canteen."

Fury walked a few feet then spotted something on the ground. She bent over and picked it up. "It's the soap, boy; I guess I didn't throw it far enough."

Fury juggled the soap in her hand then thrust it into her pocket. "Come on; let's get some water."

DAMN, she had better be here. Travis flung open the door to the hotel lobby. He was tired, hungry, and frustrated. The trip to Clairton and back had taken longer than he thought.

"Hi there, Ranger. I was beginning to think you weren't coming back today," the desk clerk said.

"I was beginning to think the same thing. Where's Fury?" Travis said with a snarl.

"Fury ain't here. Been gone a while. I'd stay over an hour."

"What do you mean? Did he leave?"

"No, last I saw of him, he was headed out to the saloon. He told me to tell you he would be there."

"Why would Fury go to the saloon?"

"Oh, he's a young man, Ranger, and young men like whiskey and women. Why, I suppose one of the fine saloon girls could be entertaining him and that's why he is still gone."

"Not likely," Travis grumbled to himself then headed out the door to the saloon.

He slung the saloon doors open and scanned the room, but no Fury.

"Hey, bartender, have you seen Fury today?"

"Fury? No, he ain't been in here today, and I hope he stays away, always brings trouble, that one."

"Are you sure Fury ain't been here?"

"Yes, but ask around if you don't believe me. Hey, Lil," the bartender called out to an older saloon girl.

"Ya seen Fury in here today?"

"Fury, that little bounty hunter? Nope, besides, he never visits any of the girls. He just drinks and talks sometimes to men in the bar, but I ain't seen him today."

"Thanks just the same. I'm gonna ask some of your customers."

"Suit yourself."

Travis questioned the few men scattered about the bar, but no one recollected Fury being in the saloon.

Sum'in ain't adding up. Travis pushed back his hat and scratched his head. Then he stopped and righted his hat. *No, no, no, she couldn't have...oh yes, she could.*

Travis ran to the hotel and up the stairs, taking them two at a time.

He could hear the voice of the clerk trailing him up the stairs. "What's wrong, Ranger, what's wrong?"

Travis was focused on Fury and did not pay any attention to the clerk. He rifled through his pocket until he found the key and jammed it into the lock. The door flung open. Travis' eyes darted around the room. No clothes, no saddlebags, and no Fury. The only evidence Fury had left was money on the dresser for her hotel bill and an open window.

"Damn it," Travis said as he looked out the window.

"I don't understand, Ranger."

"I'm pretty sure Fury flung his saddlebags out the window then went downstairs and told you he was going to the saloon, but what he was doing was escaping and the saloon was a way to delay me. Damn it all, I fell for it."

Travis rammed his hand into his pocket and pulled out some cash. "Here," he said as he slammed the money into the clerk's hand. "That's for the room."

Travis headed for the general store. He needed to get supplies before he rode off after Fury. He cursed, yet another delay.

The friendly bell rang announcing his arrival.

"How can I help you, Ranger?"

"I gotta make a quick trip out of town. I need to get some jerky, beans, and bacon if you got it."

"Sorry, Ranger, I'm out of bacon and beans. All I have is jerky."

"Then jerky it is."

"All right, Ranger, give me a minute and I'll get that for you."

Travis spied a bin of apples. "And throw in some of these apples."

"All right."

Travis paced in front of the counter but stopped when he spotted the wanted posters by the post office window. He noticed an empty space; one of the wanted posters was missing.

"Hey, Fury, the bounty hunter, was he in here earlier?"

"Yes, he was. Said he needed some supplies and such."

"Did he by any chance take one of these posters?" Travis pointed to the vacant spot.

"Well, he must have. I keep that organized, and there was a poster hanging right there."

"Of who? Do you know who it was?"

The storekeeper stroked his beard. "Well I don't recollect. I see so many of them, I can't remember them all. Any you men know what wanted poster was hanging here?" he asked the men gathered by the wood stove.

All the men shook their head except one. An old man with a toothless smile and a twinkle in his eye said, "I do."

With a couple of long strides, Travis stood next to the man. "Please, it's very important. I must know who was on that poster."

"It was that lunatic, Cutter Dan."

"Cutter Dan," Travis repeated, his voice dripping with dread.

"That little idiot is going after Cutter Dan," he muttered. "Thank you, sir," Travis bolted out the door. He knew exactly where to go next, the livery. He wracked his brain as he walked to the livery, trying to remember Cutter Dan's last whereabouts.

"Hey!" Travis shouted as he entered the livery. "Hey, anybody here?"

"Hold on, mister, I'm a comin'," answered a faint voice from the back of the livery.

Travis paced, waiting for the man.

"Whatcha need, mister?"

"I need my horse, Chief, but before you go a looking for him, I need to ask you something. I know Fury kept his horse here, along with that mutt, and I know he's gone. I need to know if you know where he went?"

"Yeah," old Miles rubbed the stubble on his chin, "but why should I tell you anything about Fury?"

"I'm Ranger Travis Parker, and it is very important I find Fury before he does something foolish that could cost him his life."

Miles chuckled. "Mr. Ranger, you must not know Fury. If'n he is after someone, then they're the one who ought to worry. Haven't ya ever heard of Fury?"

"Yes, yes, I have," Travis said, trying to be patient. "What you don't understand is Fury is after a very dangerous criminal."

"Ya, ya, I knowed it; that's what Fury does."

Travis removed his hat, raked his fingers through his wavy brown hair, then put his hat back on his head. "Mister—"

"Miles."

"Mister Miles—"

"No, just plain Miles."

Travis's lips tightened. "Miles, you gotta believe me. There is something about Fury you don't know, and that something could get him killed."

Miles chuckled again. "I guess I'm about the only one around here who knows anything about Fury. If'n ya was to ask him, he would tell you I'm one of his few friends. Ya see, Ranger, Fury tracked down the man who killed my wife. There ain't nuttin' I won't do for Fury, and that includes telling anyone where he is or what he is doing. Now which horse is your'n?"

"Miles," Travis pleaded, "I promise you, you don't know this about Fury. Please, sir, if you care about her, you gotta talk to me."

"Her?" Miles laughed. "You're a bit confused there, Ranger."

"No, I'm not." Travis knew he'd slipped.

"I don't think Fury would like bein' called *her*."

"Miles, you care about Fury, don't you?"

"I done told ya I did."

"I imagine you would keep a secret, to keep Fury safe."

"Yep, have and will. What you gettin' at?"

Travis looked down at his feet and rubbed the back of his neck. He returned his gaze to Miles. "Miles, I've something important to tell you about Fury, and if you spread this information to anyone, Fury could be killed."

The grin on Mile's face dropped. "What is it then? I won't talk."

"Fury isn't who you think he is. I should say, who *she* is."

Miles' eyes widened. "You tellin' me Fury is a girl?"

"Yes, let's sit down," Travis said as he pointed to a couple of haybales, "and I will tell you Fury's story."

It didn't take long for Travis to hit the main points, even with Miles interrupting with, "Ya don't say," every now and then.

"Miles, do you understand why I need your help?"

Miles stood up and walked a few feet away from Travis. "I don't know, Ranger, ya make a convincing argument, but I ain't sure."

Travis pulled the handbill with Belle's picture from his pocket. "Look, Miles, this is Belle. This is who Fury really is. Does she look anything like Fury to you?"

Miles studied the picture. "Well, maybe, around the eyes, but it's hard to tell. Kin you read me the words, maybe something will help me figure this out."

Travis grasped the paper from Miles' hands.

MISSING, *have you seen this girl?*

Belle Alston, eighteen years old, five feet five inches tall, brown hair, blue-violet eyes.

Distinguishing mark—bell shaped birthmark on right forearm.

. . .

TRAVIS SAW the light of belief spark in Miles' eyes when he looked up at him.

"The description fits, the height and hair and eyes, but what's got me is the birthmark. I seen it once when Fury took off her coat to tend to her horse."

"You believe me now?"

"Yeah, yeah, guessin' I do."

"So, you will help me?"

"I will. I will," Miles softly said." Ya know, I'm thinkin' part of me knew, but I owed so much to Fury, I didn't pay any mind to the signs."

"Signs?"

"Well, I've known Fury a while, figured he was maybe eighteen or so, but so small, I figure he might do some growing but never did. And then there was the way Fury dresses, always with a jacket, even when it was hot as hell. Suppose he were covering his...I mean her figure. And there were a few times, her voice didn't sound so deep."

"Miles, I need to hurry; tell me what you know."

"When Fury got here, she asked me about Cutter Dan. Oh shit, I forgot she is after that bastard!"

"Yes, yes," answered an impatient Travis, "that's why I'm in a hurry."

"I told her a man fitting that description was here and I overheard him talking to his horse, like some folks do. He said they was heading for Langston and then Mexico."

"Langston?"

Miles nodded. "Yes, it's a few days ride south of here, but you better hurry. Fury left here a few hours ago, and knowing how fast her horse is, I'm betting she got a pretty good lead on you."

"You don't know my horse, Chief. I need you to get him for me."

"Sure, and you get Fury, or Belle, safely home."

"I intend to."

Miles brought the horse to him. "Chief, boy, we gotta make up for some lost time." Travis kicked the sides his horse, spurring the animal to go faster.

Belle, how could you think about going after Cutter Dan, especially by yourself?, Even the lawmen hunting him go out in a group. I read the report on the poor girl in Clanton he murdered. I'll never forget beaten, murdered, those letters cut into her forehead, his 'CD'. That ain't happening to you.

"Come on, Chief, faster!"

CHAPTER 9

*T*ravis varied Chief's pace between a gallop and a trot, occasionally letting him walk. The last thing he needed was for his horse to fail him.

"Holy Smoke!" Travis said when Chief reared up. "Shh, shh, Chief, calm down." Travis petted the side of the horse's head. "What the hell was that?" The ranger scanned the area. His eyes locked onto the culprit.

"Well, look at you," Travis said to the mutt standing in the road next to him. He dismounted. "Easy, boy," he said as he extended his hand toward the mutt's nose.

The dog took the bait and sniffed Travis's hand.

"Good boy, see, you don't want to bite a friend." Travis risked patting the dog's head. The dog responded with a wag of his tail and a lick on his hand. "Where's your traveling companion?"

Travis' body straightened up when he heard a scream. "What the hell!"

The mutt ran, with Travis close behind. Tall blades of grass were trampled as the pair ran, and the land began to slope. Travis half slid down the path, right into a group of bushes. He drew his gun, his ears perked, listening for any sound. What he heard was splashing. He spread the limbs of a bush, then he sat back and relaxed. He couldn't help but chuckle at the sight.

"No denying it now, Fury, you certainly ain't a boy."

FURY SQUEALED when her body hit the cold water. She dunked herself a few times to get accustomed to the temperature. The cool, crisp water helped her relax. She managed to keep the slippery soap in her hand when she jumped in the water. She lathered the soap on her body.

She sniffed the bar of soap, curious if it had a scent. *No, nothing like the soap I used to use. I remember the smell—lavender, yes, lavender—I miss soaking in a hot bath, breathing in lavender. Stop it! Stop reminiscing over something you can't have; you are Fury now, not Belle.*

Fury continued her bathing ritual, unaware that someone lurked behind the bushes. After she finished bathing, she swam a little then headed back to where she'd left her clothes and gun.

She was not paying attention when she walked out of the pond, then she realized her clothes were gone, along with her gun. Fury ran back into the water. Was someone watching her?

Stupid, how could I be so stupid? That's what happens when I remember Belle; I don't keep my mind focused on what is important, and now my gun is gone.

"Hey!" Fury shouted. "You out there, you'd better leave. My partner will be here soon, and he's mighty handy with a gun."

Fury's eyes skimmed the shore. The bushes where her missing clothes were laid moved. An unwelcome figure emerged from behind the bushes.

"What the f—

"Now, Belle, you know ladies shouldn't use that kinda of language," Travis teased with a broad smile on his face.

"I told you I ain't Belle and I definitely ain't no lady. Now give me my clothes, you son of a bitch, and my gun."

"Belle." Travis chuckled. "I know for sure you're a girl."

Realization hit her, causing her face to burn from embarrassment to anger.

"Y-you were watching me—you saw me?"

"Calm down. I came down when I heard a scream, and yes, I saw you—all of you—but I did what a gentleman would do and looked away."

"Well, you didn't look away until you saw everything, did ya? And you stole my clothes and gun."

Fury spied Max sitting next to Travis. "Get him, boy," she commanded, but the dog cocked his head.

"You ain't talking to this dog, are you? Well, me and him are friends. He ain't gonna help you now."

"Traitor," Fury muttered. The dog hung his head as if he understood her.

"Your clothes ain't gone; I got them right here." Travis held up his arm with her clothes draped over it. "As for your gun, I think I'm gonna hang on to it for a while."

"You don't expect me to come out with you standing there, do you?"

"Well, I am a man, "a mischievous glint sparkled in his eyes, "so, the thought did cross my mind, but I consider myself a man of good morals. I will toss your clothes over the bushes and turn my back so you can git dressed."

"No, you will leave while I dress," Fury demanded.

"I don't think so. You can either stay in there all night or trust me and come out now."

"Damn, I regret not shooting you when I had a chance."

Travis grinned then turned around.

Fury crept out of the water, keeping her eyes stuck on Travis. "All right, I'm done."

Travis turned to face her. His smile faded.

"What's wrong?"

"Guess I prefer you the other way."

"You ass." Fury leapt at him, ready to fight.

Travis wrapped an arm around her waist, picked her up, and threw her in the pond.

"Cool off, Belle, and while you're in there," he tossed her the soap, "you might as well wash your clothes. Taking a bath doesn't take the stink out of them."

Fury began to ford the water back to the shore.

"Oh no, I mean for you to wash those clothes," He wagged his finger at her. "If you come out now, I will throw you back in."

"I swear, when I get out of here," Fury growled, "I'm gonna—

"Yeah, yeah, you're gonna shoot me, I know, I know. Hurry up. We got some talking to do."

TRAVIS CHUCKLED as he watched Fury try to scrub her clothes while still wearing them.

"Well, genius," Fury said with a scowl as she trod to the shore, "what the hell am I supposed to do now? My clothes are soaked, thanks to you, and I don't have anything else to wear. Am I supposed to stand here dripping wet until I dry?"

Travis sat on a rock. "You could take them off again and hang them on the bushes to dry," he said with a devious smile.

"Yeah, and you could go to Hell."

"Now, now, Belle, I told you not to cuss. Follow me up to our camp, and I will give you a blanket to wrap in while your clothes dry by the fire."

"Fire, what fire? I didn't make a fire." Fury stood before him, with water running off her clothes, pooling at her feet.

"I know you didn't make a fire, but I'm going to, so we can camp here for the night."

"Like hell I will. There is still a few more hours of sunlight, and I intend on going on until dusk."

"Hmm, no, I don't think so, Belle. We are staying here tonight, and in the morning, we will start on our way back to Faulkner."

"Stop calling me Belle. I told you I ain't damn Belle, and I sure as hell ain't going anywhere with you!"

Travis stood up and took a step toward the soaked girl. Fury fought the urge to step back.

"Listen here, Belle, I'm about to lose my patience with you. I will call you Belle because that is your name. I will, however, call you Fury if we are in a situation that would threaten you if someone knew your identity. I know your plan was to go to Langston and find Cutter Dan. Well, young lady, you can get that notion right out of your head. You are going home, even if I have to hog tie you to your horse."

Fury's eye's narrowed as her breathing became short and shallow. She tightened her fist. "Now you listen to me, you bastard, you ain't got no claim on me, and I go where I want and do what I want—

Travis grabbed Fury's forearm while she was in mid rant. He spun her and delivered six sharp, stinging swats to her backside, then he spun her back around to face him. He grabbed hold of her shoulders and leaned down to meet her wide eyes.

"Now, young lady, I have had enough. No more cussing and no more arguing. You best git yourself up to where the horses are before I sit back down on this rock and finish giving you the spanking you earned."

Fury's mouth gaped open and her eyes widened, her face locked in disbelief.

"Git!" Travis shouted as he pointed up the path.

Fury grumbled as she trudged up the slope to where the horses were grazing.

Travis could not help but smirk every time she reached back and rubbed her sore behind.

No CLOTHES, no gun, how in the hell did I let this happen? I didn't; it was that no good ass of a man. He'd better hope he's a light sleeper. No one treats me like that and gets away with it!

Fury sat by the fire, wrapped in a blanket and sending dagger eyes to the man tending the horses.

Just look at yourself, the great Fury, naked and under the thumb of a man you should'a shot when you met him. What on earth is wrong with me? Have I forgotten who I am? Oh, no, Mr. Ranger, you are going to be sorry you ever tangled with Fury.

She sipped her coffee and contemplated his demise. She continued to scowl at Travis, then someone else attracted her attention. She spied Max sitting near the horses.

Traitor, she mouthed the words to the shaggy mutt. The animal cocked his head as if he heard her, then Fury grinned. *All right, boy, ya wanna make it up to me?* A devilish smile bloomed on Fury's face. She signed a command to the mutt, excitement bubbling in her stomach as the dog reacted.

"Come on, boy," Fury coaxed, "come on; don't let me down."

The dog stood up and closed the gap between himself and Travis. Without hesitation, Max lifted his leg.

"What the hell!" Travis shouted and jumped away from the dog. He danced around, shaking his leg as if it would remove the offensive wetness. "Damn dog!"

Max ran with his tail between his legs, as Travis continued to shake his foot and cuss.

Fury slapped her hand across her mouth. She thought she would burst, trying to hold back the laughter. When she could contain it no longer, her hand dropped, and her laugh bellowed out much louder than she intended.

Travis stopped and stared at her.

Part of Fury knew she should remain cool and indifferent, but she lost all self-control.

The angry ranger advanced to where she sat, limping as if his leg were injured not wet.

Fury held on tight to her blanket as she pointed at Travis' wet boot and belly laughed.

"So, you think this is funny?"

Fury sucked in air, struggling to speak. "Wait," she held up her hand, "wait." But she was doomed, and the laughter burst out of her once more. "It seems we are both wet, but I prefer my way more than yours. Oh, by the way, there's a bar of soap somewhere by the pond. You should take a bath. I'm sure you got another blanket to wrap up in." Fury's laughter died down to a chuckle as her glance met the smoldering grey-green of Travis' eyes.

He glared at her with his hands on his hips. "Somehow I think you were behind this attack by your dog."

"Look, Ranger, he ain't my dog; he just travels with me. Besides, how in the hell could I have done anything? If you forgot, I'm sitting here wrapped in a blanket without a stitch of clothes on. You really think I'm gonna traipse around, risking this thing falling off then, somehow, magically make a dog pee on you. I think he's a good judge of character, even if it took him a while to decide how he really feels about you."

Travis grumbled to himself as he stomped over to his saddle-bags in hopes of finding something to clean his boot.

Fury heard a rustle of bushes.

"It's all right, boy," she said in a low tone.

The dog peeked through the bushes.

"Good job." She smiled at the dog and heard the thumping of his wagging tail. "I'll get you a treat later."

"What you lookin' at, Belle?"

She snapped to attention when she heard Travis. "I ain't looking at nuttin', but I sure smell something." Fury sniffed the air. "Hmm, smells kinda...like...well, smells kinda like a mix between a pain in the ass ranger and dog pee. Oh, I think its wafting in from your direction, Ranger Parker."

"Ha ha ha," Travis said. "Well, at least *you* don't stink anymore and," he touched Belle's clothes lying on a rock near the fire, "I believe your clothes are dry."

"Good, you go away, so I can get dressed." Fury rose to get her clothes.

"Now, Belle, honey, you know that ain't happening. I'll turn around."

"No. I'll go behind those bushes."

"Belle, don't argue with me, or I won't turn around." Travis folded his arms across his chest.

"Fine!" Fury seethed. If there was one thing she hated, it was giving in.

"Hurry up, Belle. I guess there is one thing about women that doesn't change, no matter how they dress. They still take an eternity to get ready."

"You can turn around now, Ranger Asshole." Fury's anger fumed out of every pore.

"This is your last warning," Travis said as he watched Fury struggle to get her boots on.

"What are you warning me about, Ranger. I don't scare easily."

Travis covered the space between them in a few strides of his long legs. He stood in front of her, his hands posed on his hips.

Fury kept her eyes down, ignoring the giant of a man.

"Look at me, girl," Travis ordered.

"I'd rather look at a horse's a—"

"Don't say it." Travis pulled her to her feet, put his hands under her armpits, and picked her up to his eye level.

"Let's get one thing straight, Belle, you will obey me, or I will tan you good. And that goes for no cussing. I gave you your last warning; you'd better remember that."

"Put me down, put me down!" Fury kicked her feet in the air, nearly hitting Travis' knees.

"Oh," Travis chuckled at her desperate fight, "no tantrums, either."

Fury stopped kicking and gave Travis a murderous glare.

"I am Fury. I *do not* have tantrums."

"Oh yeah," Travis said, "and what do you call all this kicking about?"

Fury wiggled and twisted, trying to get loose of his iron grip.

"Ask me nicely, Belle, and I will let you down." Travis laughed.

"You can go to H—" Fury stopped herself, remembering his warning as she swallowed her pride.

"Put me down, Ranger," she asked in a calm voice.

"Say please, Belle."

Oh, I'm definitely gonna put a bullet in him.

"Please," she asked through clenched teeth, almost choking on the word.

Travis smiled and gently set her on her feet. "Now, you see, that wasn't too hard, was it?"

Fury's body quaked with anger. A litany of curse words fought to escape her lips, but she held her tongue.

"Sit, Belle, we have some serious talking to do."

"I'll sit," Fury answered, "but I ain't talking to a jackass."

"You'd better be glad I think that's funny. You don't need to talk, but you are gonna listen if you know what is good for you," Travis grumbled

"You'd better think about what is good *for you,* Ranger. Just as soon as we get to a town, I'm gonna have you arrested for kidnapping."

"Ain't it like a woman to say she ain't gonna talk but does anyway."

Fury scowled at him, hoping for the day she could wipe that smug look off his face.

"No, you won't, young lady. I have every right, as a ranger, to bring you in. You see, you are the only witness to a double murder, and I worked the case, so I have every intention to bring you in."

Memories of her parents' murders materialized in Fury's

mind. She fought hard to keep them buried, but Travis' mention of their deaths jiggled the lock of the door she had hidden them behind. Suddenly, she felt sick and the world began to spin.

A strong grip wrapped around her slim waist. "Belle, honey, I'm sorry."

Her head spun as she tried to focus her eyes.

"Belle?"

Her vision cleared, to see Travis' worried face staring at her.

"Let me go," she demanded.

"Not until I'm sure you ain't gonna faint. Your face went white as cotton. I'm sorry, honey, I shouldn't have been so callus about your folks."

Fury shook herself from his grip. "What are you talking about? I'm hungry is all. Now let me be."

Travis grumbled. "You've got to be the most stubborn, ornery woman I've ever met, Belle Alston. You sure ain't like the Belle I met three years ago. You sit still while I make us some supper, then we will talk."

Fury grimaced. *I have no intention of ever being like her again.* She sat in silence as Travis cooked beans. She was fighting a quiet battle inside herself, one she thought she'd won long ago, but with this damn ranger calling her Belle and stirring her painful memories, the battle between Belle and Fury reignited. Being quiet helped her push Belle and her emotions back behind the door she kept locked tightly inside herself.

"Belle? Belle? Are you all right, honey?' Travis asked, concern painting his words.

Fury snapped herself out of her thoughts. "Don't call me Belle. It's Fury, and don't ever call me honey!"

"Well, I see you are back to your sweet, normal self," Travis joked.

"Oh, shut up."

"Hmm, no manners." Travis shook his head. "We'll have to work on that some."

"*We* ain't working on nuttin', you empty-headed baboon."

"Here," Travis said as he shoved a plate into her hands, "eat."

Fury looked down at the plate of beans. She was hungry and her mouth watered at the smell of the food before her.

I'd rather throw these beans in his face, but it ain't right to waste food and I'll need all my strength to get away. Fury grumbled and shoved a spoonful of beans into her mouth, surrendering to her protesting stomach.

TRAVIS SAT down across from her, the fire blazing between them. The setting sun and the light of the fire played on Fury's face, reflecting the beauty he remembered when they first met.

He contemplated the small, tough girl sitting across from him. *She is so small, fragile, some folks might think a delicate little thing like her would be weak, but they don't know her like I do. No, there ain't nothing about Belle Alston that's weak. She may look delicate on the outside, but inside, there is steel in this girl.*

Travis tossed another log on the fire. *Damn it, Travis, you really put your foot in it when you brought up her folks. I could kick myself. Under that steel in her, there is still the scared little girl who lost her parents, and I hurt her. But she's sure got guts, this one, to take on the life of a bounty hunter and think she could go up against someone like Cutter Dan. She may be scared, but she don't show it, and she certainly is brave. A little idiot but a brave little idiot. Yet, I admire Fury's bravery, her determination; there is a fire in her. If I could just coax out, the sweet, demure, loving little lady she buried within herself, if she allowed her softer side out and mingled Belle with Fury, she would be one hell of a woman.*

"Belle, honey?"

Fury stared at her plate.

"Belle? All right then, have it your way." Travis sighed. "Fury?"

"What?" Fury answered, not taking her eyes off her plate of beans.

"We need to talk."

"You mean, you need to talk, and I'm supposed to listen."

Travis chuckled. "You're just asking for it, ain't you? Look at me, little girl."

Fury sighed and rolled her eyes up. "Whata you want now, Ranger?"

"I want to talk about taking you home."

"Talk all you want; I ain't going back."

"So, you are finally admitting you are Belle Alston."

Fury grimaced. "I ain't admitting nuttin', and I ain't going anywhere with you. I've a job to do, and the longer you keep me from it, the more likely someone's gonna die."

"Belle—"

"Fury!" she snapped.

"Belle!" he insisted, "you ain't getting away from me, and you sure is hell ain't going after Cutter Dan."

Fury leapt to her feet. "How'd you find out about Cutter Dan anyway? Who told you my business?"

"Never you mind about that, young lady; now sit down," Travis ordered.

Fury plopped back down on the log.

"I don't know how you found out, but you got no say in what I do to earn a living."

"First thing, Belle, you ain't running away from me, and you know what to expect if you do. Tell me, why in the world do you think a little girl like you could bring in a butcher like Cutter Dan?"

"Don't be so sure of yourself, Ranger. I've brought in murderers before, ain't no different bringing in Cutter."

"Yes, it is, and you know so. I wager the other murderers you brought in were nothing like Dan. Why don't you tell me about some of the men you brought to justice?"

"Why should I tell you anything? You've heard of Fury; I'm a bounty hunter. I bring in criminals and get paid for it."

"Oh, yes, I've heard the stories of the famous bounty hunter Fury, but now I'm trying to separate the real stories from the bullshit stories you or someone spread to give you your badass reputation."

Travis watched as Fury's face turned scarlet red with anger, her chest heaving as she huffed. "I don't need anyone spreading lies about me to help me with my job. I am Fury, and what you hear is true, so you better watch yourself. I'm biding my time before I shoot—"

"That's enough of that, young lady. No more talk of shooting me, and if you pull a gun on me, I will paddle your backside. You got me?"

"I hate you."

Travis smiled. "Sure, you do."

"Some ranger you are, letting a man like Cutter Dan get away."

"I ain't letting anyone get away. I'm taking you home and keeping you out of harm's way."

"I don't need you to keep me safe."

"You don't? Well, tell me then, what do you know about Cutter Dan?"

"I know he is a murderer who likes to kill women."

"That's putting it lightly. You know...huh...well, let me tell you what I know. One of his victims lived long enough to talk. That's how we know his identity, for all the good it's done. Cutter Dan, just so you know, is insane. He kills for no reason other than he likes it. I witnessed what this man does to a woman, and it ain't pretty. He takes young women—the lucky ones, he kills right away, the others, he keeps them a while, abusing and torturing them for days before he finally kills them. After he murders a girl, he carves a CD on their forehead, like he branded them as his property."

Travis saw the color drain from Belle's face.

"Yes," Fury said softly, her eye's glazed over in a blank stare as she remembered. "I saw one of the girls' bodies. I was in Livingston when it happened. The sheriff asked me to come with him when news came about the murder. Jean, that was her name, just nineteen. What he did to her..." Fury wrapped her arms around herself, trying to hide the shiver crawling up her spine and throughout her body. A cold weight settled in her gut.

"Oh, honey, I'm sorry." Travis reached for her, but she jerked away from his grasp.

"What you got ta be sorry about?" Fury stood up, regaining her false toughness. She hated pity. "He kills women, so there is a large bounty on him, and I want the money."

"You can say that if you want to, Belle, but I don't believe you just want money. You want to bring him in for some other reason, but you are too bull-headed to admit it. You, a small little girl, wants to go after a vicious murderer; a man who even a ranger won't hunt alone. Sorry, Belle, but it ain't happening."

"I ain't Belle. I'm Fury, and I ain't a little girl. I'm—"

"A woman," Travis finished for her.

Fury growled at him, "I hate you!"

"I know." Travis grinned. "You done told me that."

"On our way back to your home, I will send a telegram to my boss. He will send men to Langston to look for Dan, so don't worry. Justice will catch up to Cutter Dan."

"You idiot, he's not *in* Langston."

"What? Weren't you headed to Langston to get him?"

Fury chuckled. "You gotta be the dumbest lawman ever. Do you think a man like Cutter, with a huge bounty on his head, would ride into town and stay there amongst all the townspeople?"

Travis's face became rigid. "No, I suppose you are right. He might go into town for some supplies, but he would hightail it out of there and be on the road again, or he would go to a hideout." Travis' stern eyes locked on to Fury's. "You know where his hideout is, don't you?"

Fury cocked her head back. "Seems whoever gave you your information left out some important details."

Travis walked up to her and grabbed her upper arms and gave her a shake. "You know where his hideout is, and you were going there alone. Oh, you are a little idiot who is too big for her britches. Belle, don't you understand? You woulda gone to his hideout without any help and not tell anyone your plan. You, against an insane murderer who is three times your size, and on top of that, he targets young girls like you!"

Travis let her go and walked a few feet away from where Fury stood. He removed his hat and dug his fingers through his hair. Then he replaced his hat and turned to face her. "I ought to spank you for having such an idiotic plan."

Fury squirmed.

Travis knew he had shaken her up as she worked to regain her defiant composure.

"I've been in tough situations before; I know how to take care of myself."

Travis shook his head. "Well, I don't have to worry about you and your harebrained plan, because you ain't traipsing after some cold-blooded murderer. I'm taking you home. Now, tell me where he is hiding out, and I will telegraph it to my boss."

Fury stretched herself to her full height, squared her shoulders, and tilted her chin back. "I ain't tellin' you nuttin'."

Travis paced. His heartbeat pulsed in his temples and his hands turned into white knuckled fists. "Listen here, Belle Alston." Travis released a trapped finger from his fist and jabbed it toward her. "Enough of your stubborn defiance. I'm giving you until morning to tell me where Cutter is hiding out, so if you want to sit your saddle in comfort tomorrow, you'd better be ready to talk."

"Ain't happening." Fury sat back on her log.

"We'll see."

FURY BROODED, trying not to lock eyes with the ranger. The sun disappeared behind the treetops, followed by the swirling purple and orange clouds of the sunset. Cool air blew against her skin, causing her to shiver.

"You cold? Damn, I'm out of coffee. I forgot to buy more before I left Serenity."

"Some ranger you are, always prepared," Fury sniped.

"I was in a bit of a hurry when I left," Travis retaliated.

The corners of Fury's mouth lifted. She looked at the ground so Travis would not see—a plan formed in her mind.

"Well, I always go out prepared. I've got coffee in my saddle-bags; I can brew some."

"I'll get the coffee."

"I don't like strangers poking about my stuff." Fury raised the palm of her hand. "I will get the coffee, you," she said, picking up the empty coffee pot and ramming it into Travis' hands, "can fill this with water."

Travis arched an eyebrow. "You'd better watch that sharp tongue of yours."

Fury smirked and left to retrieve the coffee. *Where is it?* She held the bag of coffee as she continued to search with her other hand, reaching deep into her saddle bag.

"Damn," she whispered to herself and plunged her hand into the other bag. A smile broke across her face as her hand grasped the small bottle.

"Did you get lost?" Travis called from the fire.

"I'm coming," Fury yelled as she hid the bottle of Laudanum in her pocket.

Laudanum, always handy to have around. Most people carried it as medicine, for pain and such, but Fury used it not only for medicinal purposes, but also found it helpful when trying to subdue a problematic prisoner. Over the years, she had learned the proper dosage to make even the most hardened criminal malleable.

A short time later, the smell of coffee filled the air.

"I think it's ready." Fury grabbed an empty cup and filled it with coffee. Travis reached for the cup she offered but stopped when he saw the concerned look on her face.

"What's wrong?" he asked, keeping his voice low.

"Did you hear that?" Fury's face reflected fake concern.

"Hear what?"

While Travis surveyed the area behind him, Fury signaled the dog to bark, warning them of some unseen danger."

"You stay put," Travis ordered as he stood and drew his gun, walking in the direction the dog barked.

"What is it, boy?"

Fury popped the top off the medicine bottle and poured the Laudanum in Travis' cup.

"I can't find anything," Travis said as he walked back to the campfire.

"It coulda been a rabbit or a man; you never know with that dog. Here, drink your coffee."

Travis' fingers wrapped around the warm cup. "I don't know," he said, looking at the cup in his hand. "This may keep both of us up all night."

"Suit yourself," Fury said. "All I know is it smells good and it's hot."

"As exhausted as I am, I suppose I'll drop off anyway." Travis sipped the warm drink. "Good coffee."

"Yes, it is." The corners of her mouth turned up.

"Well, you seem to be in a better mood."

Fury shrugged.

Travis sat by the fire. He put his cup down and yawned. "I drank a full cup of coffee and I'm still tired."

Fury was silent.

Travis stretched and then stood up. "Let's get our bed rolls," he ordered. "We can spread them out by the fire.

Fury found her bedroll and beat Travis back to the fire. Travis retrieved his and staggered back with it tucked under his arm. In his other hand, he carried two small, flimsy ropes.

Fury sat on her bedroll trying not to laugh as he staggered back to the fire. "Whata ya plan on doing with that pig-string?" Fury asked, seeing the worn sections of rope in Travis' hand.

"Well, you're too small for my handcuffs; they'd slip right off those tiny wrists. I can't take any chances." He yawned. "I know as soon as I'm asleep, you'll run."

Well, damn. "You ain't tying me up, Ranger."

Travis knelt in front of her and grabbed her hands.

Fury fought, but even in his drugged state, he was quick, and before she knew it, her hands were tied in front of her.

"You no good, son-of-a-bitch." Fury kicked as he attempted to tie her ankles.

Travis rolled her on her side, laying three heavy smacks on her bottom. "Watch your language and be still," Travis scolded. He returned her to her back as she continued to fight but lost the battle. He struggled to stand. His body swayed before he staggered back to his bedroll and then plopped himself down. He groaned as he stretched out his long body. His eyes slammed shut.

Damn it. Fury pulled and twisted her bound wrists. *They're not as tight as I thought; guess he was too doped up to check and see if they were snug.* A warm, furry body curled up next to Fury. A triumphant smile grew across her face.

She lay still until the heavy breathing and snores from Travis convinced her he was out. Time to act. She wiggled herself to a sitting position. "Max," she whispered to the dog lying next to her.

Max sat up.

"Bite," she ordered and held up her bound wrists. "Bite," she said once more as the dog cocked its head. Fury shoved the rope in front of his face. "Bite."

Max began to chew on the loose, worn rope. The warm wetness of the dog's mouth covered Fury's hands as he worked to free her. Every few seconds, her eyes darted to where Travis lay, to confirm he was asleep. After what seemed like forever and a day, the rope loosened.

"Stop," she ordered, and Max sat back on his haunches.

Fury pulled the loose, wet rope apart, freeing her hands. She rubbed her wrists then patted the dog's head. "Good boy," she whispered, then she untied her ankles.

She crept over to where Travis slept. Fury took a deep breath, carefully sliding her gun from where the ranger had tucked it into his belt, stopping once when he moved about.

In the dark silence, she saddled her horse and led her animals down the deserted road. When she figured they were far enough from the ranger, she mounted Swift and motioned for Max to jump up to her. With Max situated across her saddle, she tapped the horse's sides and galloped away. Fury laughed at the thought of the ranger waking to find her long gone.

Too bad I didn't think to tie him with his own rope. But the more distance she put between her and Travis, the more a twinge of sadness stirred in her. Damn. Did she miss him?

Fury did not try to hide her tracks. She knew when he woke, he would trail her, so the best thing to do was ride; time and distance were her friends.

She rubbed her eyes. Fatigue was winning, and she knew she needed to rest but only for little while. Fury figured it was close to midnight, and she did not want to lose the lead she had on the ranger. But she needed to stop, only for a quick rest. There was enough moonlight to spot a small clearing.

This will work. I'm gonna rest my eyes for a bit.

A few minutes later, she lay on a blanket, not wanting to

unpack her full bed roll. Max coiled next to her, sharing his body heat. Something warm and moist slid across her face. Fury brushed it away. Once again, the warm, moist softness slurped across her face. She batted her eyes open, blinking them until the image before her came into view.

A wet nose sniffed her face as she tried to swat him away. Max assaulted her entire face with his sniffing, wet nose. He paused at her ear, blowing out moist puffs of air, causing her to giggle.

"Cut it out, boy, that tickles." Fury stirred, sending Max into a dancing jig. "All right, all right, I'll get up and get you something to eat."

She sat and yawned, stretching off her sleepiness. "Oh, no, it's morning; the sun is up. I didn't mean to sleep until sunup." Her heart thumped. She didn't know what bothered her more, over-sleeping or her worry that a certain ranger would catch up to her. *What's wrong with me? I'm never this careless. What if I did it on purpose?*

"What the hell?" she said, reacting to her own thought. "Why would I want to get caught by that irritating man? Must be all this Fury-Belle talk he keeps giving me; he is making me loco. Let's go!" Fury ordered the dog as she grabbed up her blanket.

She mounted her horse. "Come on, Max, we gotta go." The dog whined. *Hell, he's hungry, and so am I.* "Come on, boy." She looked down at the dog. "Come on—up," Fury commanded as she patted her leg.

The dog bent down on his front legs then sprang up to Fury. She caught him, sitting him in front of her. Fury reached into her saddlebag and produced some jerky. "This gotta do until we are far enough away to set up a camp." Fury tapped the sides of her horse with her heels. They continued their journey with her sharing her jerky with Max, whose wagging tail thudded against the saddle.

TRAVIS YAWNED and scrubbed his hand across his face. "Dang, I haven't slept like that in years. How about you, Belle? Belle?"

His vision cleared. "Damnit. Belle, Belle!" Travis knew he called out in vain. Her bedroll was gone. He took a quick survey of the camp. No horse. No dog. No Belle.

He found the tattered remains of the rope he'd used to tie her. "Well," he said as he examined the frayed ends of the rope, "looks like she had help."

Travis tunneled his fingers through his hair. How could he not hear her leave? As a ranger, he had learned to sleep lightly. What happened this time?"

Travis glanced at the cold campfire. "The coffee!" He slapped his palm to his head. "She put something in my coffee. No wonder she was so eager to make some."

She had outsmarted him, and Travis hated to be outsmarted. "Come on, Chief," Travis said to his horse. "We got to get going. That little girl is gonna be very unhappy when I find her and roast her butt."

HOW FAR AHEAD WAS SHE? Fury wondered. Maybe three hours, she hoped more. Three hours was not enough if she ran into trouble; there would be no slowing down. Well, not until she saw the large man in the middle of the road frantically waving his arms.

Fury considered riding around him, but the mammoth of a man seemed to occupy the entire rode. As she drew closer, the more frantic he became, as along with his flailing arms, he began to jump, quite a feat for such a huge man.

Fury stopped a few feet in front of the giant. Her hand rested on her gun.

Blocking the road, loomed the largest man Fury had ever seen. She thought Travis was big, but this man was at least six inches taller, with broader shoulders, hard muscular arms, and biceps she would have sworn were as thick as her thigh. Blond hair peeked out from under his hat, and his baby blue eyes pierced right through her.

"Please. Please. Sir. I am Lars. I need help."

Fury cocked her head. "You gotta be kidding me," she said. "*You* need *my* help?"

"Yah, yah. I do."

He spoke with a strange cadence to his voice.

Max, who followed alongside the horse, raised his hackles and growled.

"Quiet," Fury ordered. The dog stilled but remained vigilant.

"You ain't from around here, are you?"

"Lars. I am Lars. I am from Sweden."

"Sweden? You're shitting me?"

The large man's face went from worry to confusion. "Shitting you?" he repeated.

"You know, you gotta be joking."

"Yoking? No. No. Lars no yoking. Lars need help."

Fury relaxed. "I just don't see how someone like you," Fury's eyes scanned the behemoth, "would need help from me."

"Yah, yah. I will tell you, sir. I yam Lars Hansen. I yam a Swede."

"You mean you are from Sweden?"

"Yah. Me and Gretchen stopped here to rest." Lars pointed to his wagon on the side of the road." I say to Gretchen, you no go far. I go and get food from back of wagon and call Gretchen. But Gretchen no come. I call. Gretchen, Gretchen, but no Gretchen." Lars shrugged his massive shoulders. "Please, sir, if you can help find Gretchen?"

The pained look on the large man's face tugged at Fury's

heart. Everything in her told her she needed to keep going, but she could not look at his desperate blue eyes and refuse.

She took a deep breath. "All right. I will help you." Fury got off her horse and stood in front of Lars. On the ground, he loomed over her.

"How long has Gretchen been gone?"

"I do not know," answered the Swede. "Maybe tirty minutes. Yay, I tink maybe tirty minutes."

"Do you have anything that belongs to her?"

She saw the question in Lars eyes.

"A piece of clothing, something like that would work."

"Yay," Lars answered and ran to the wagon. He climbed to the seat and retrieved a small pillow and rushed back to Fury.

"Gretchen's pillow."

A few feathers hung from the worn blue pillow. It was so dirty, Fury did not think any lady would want to sit on such a nasty pillow even if it did offer some comfort.

She shrugged and turned to Max. "Come," she ordered. The dog moved toward Fury.

"If anyone can find Gretchen, this dog can." Fury smiled as she looked at Lars.

She turned her attention once more to the scraggly mutt. Fury held the pillow to the dog's nose and said, "Find."

The dog sniffed every inch of the pillow, his wet black nose huffing and puffing with each breath. He stopped, raised his head, and his nose twitched as it searched out the scent. Max froze then barked. In seconds, he was running, with Fury on his heels and Lars close behind.

The mutt stopped and sniffed the air. He barked once again, and the race was on once more. Down a bank, across a small field, and finally he dove into a group of reeds growing by a nearby pond.

Fury came to an abrupt stop, and somehow, Lars kept his large body from careening into her. The reeds shook and shimmied. A few growls and yelps then one long honk as a goose ran from under the shelter of the reeds. The goose's wings spread wide, and it honked as its feet padded the ground when it attempted an ungraceful run from the biting teeth of its pursuer. Feathers and fur flew.

"Gretchen!" Lars yelled.

"Gretchen?"

"Yah. Please. Gretchen." The Swede's eyes pleaded with Fury.

"Stop." The dog slowed his pursuit. "Heel!" Fury commanded. Max obeyed and sat on his haunches.

Gretchen dove into the pond, but Lars waded in after her. He picked her up and whispered comforting words to the fowl. He walked out of the pond, to where Fury stood watching. He was soaked to his knees.

The mutt whined and cocked his head. Fury looked at his confused face and chuckled. "I don't understand, either, boy."

Lars continued to pet and coo at the nervous goose.

"So, this is Gretchen."

"Yah. Yah. This is Gretchen."

Lars turned to Fury and gave her a broad, innocent smile. "Tank you, tank you."

Fury wanted to be angry, to rail at the giant idiot for wasting her time, but the sight of this gentle giant hugging his goose touched a part of her she had not felt in an awfully long time. She smiled. "I'm glad we found your Gretchen," Fury said as she petted the goose. I must go now. I am late."

"I yam sorry me and Gretchen caused trouble. Can we help?"

"Naw, naw," Fury said as she walked away. She stopped and turned. "Well, maybe you can help me after all."

"Yah. Lars help you."

"Good," Fury said with a devious smile.

"Lars, I have trouble."

"Yah. What trouble? Lars help."

"Lars." Fury removed her hat, hoping the man would notice

her more feminine features, even though her hair barely reached her chin.

"Lars," she forced her feminine voice, "I'm not a young man. I am a woman."

Lars' face scrunched up.

"Look," she said as she removed her jacket and pulled her shirt close to her body. Fury hoped there was enough woman on her that he could tell her gender.

Lars nodded.

Fury rolled up her sleeves, thinking he needed more convincing. "See, my arms are not hairy like a man's." She reached down to roll up her pant legs.

"Yah. No need for that. Lars see you are a lady."

"Lars," Fury batted her sweeping eyelashes, trying to call up some fake tears, "a man is following me."

Lars stretched out his frame. Anger darkened his face. "No man will hurt my new friend."

The image of an ogre from a fairytale crossed Fury's mind. "Lars, I dress like this to hide from him."

"You stay with Lars. I will protect you."

"No, thank you. I need to get to Langston; there is someone there who will help me." She was surprised how easy it was to lie. "All I need you to do is slow him down. Now, Lars, he will tell you he is a ranger, a lawman. But don't believe him; it's a trick."

Lars nodded as he rolled his thick hands into fists.

"His name is Travis, and he is almost as tall as you. He has brown hair and green eyes, oh, and a dimple when he smiles, on his right cheek."

Where the heck did that come from? She was surprised she had not only noticed the dimple, but that she thought it necessary to add to his description.

"Dimple?" Lars questioned.

"Oh, that's not important."

"Lars will stop this man."

"Good." Fury smiled and began to walk away. She stopped and turned. "Lars, don't kill him or hurt him badly. I just want him slowed down."

Lars nodded. "Yah."

Fury and the dog sprinted back to her horse, and in moments, they were back on their trek to Langston and away from the irritating ranger. *Hopefully, I will never see him again.* She smiled. Her words repeated in her mind, *I will never see Travis again.* Her smile faded; her earlier twinge of sadness grew to a heavy ache in her heart.

～

ANY GOOD LAWMAN would notice the trampled grass by the side of the road.

"Whoa, Chief."

"You see here, Chief." Travis pointed to a small patch of grass plastered to the ground. "Someone slept here, and I'm bettin' that someone is a certain little girl named Belle."

She had set out in the middle of the night. Travis was relieved to see her tracks on the main road, glad that she did not risk riding across country, trying to avoid him. He knew she was heading for Langston and Cutter Dan, and that meant trouble.

"Come on, Chief."

How far ahead is she? I gotta find her before sunset. His thoughts were interrupted by the honking sound of a goose. Travis spied a wagon coming toward him. The wagon stopped in the middle of the road, and a mountain of a man climbed down and walked toward Travis.

"Hello, neighbor," Travis greeted the giant. "Can I help you, stranger?"

"Yah." The mountain spoke. "What is your name?"

"Who wants to know?"

"I do. Lars." Lars thumped his chest with the palm of his hand.

"Well, Lars, not that it is any of your business, but I am Ranger Travis Parker—

Before he could finish his sentence or draw his gun, Lars pulled him from his horse as if he were a ragdoll. Travis tumbled to the ground. He stumbled to get on his feet, but before he could get his bearings, the goliath grabbed him by the collar.

"You will not hurt my friend," Lars said, still holding Travis by the collar of his shirt.

"Your friend? Wait, do I know your friend? Look, I don't want to hurt anyone. I'm looking for someone."

"Yah. You are looking for my friend. She saved Gretchen."

Travis heard a goose honk. "What?"

"Gretchen." Lars let go of one side of Travis' collar and pointed to the goose on the wagon seat.

"Gretchen," repeated Travis as he nodded in the direction of the goose.

"Yah."

"Now, I stop you." Lars drew back his massive fist.

"Wait, wait," Travis pleaded, before he was pummeled into next week.

Lars stopped. "Why. You try hurt the girl. I stop you."

"No, no," Travis continued, "you don't understand; she is lying to you. I don't want to hurt the girl."

"Yah. She say you would tell me this."

"Oh, come on, Lars," Travis said. "Don't tell me a woman never lied to you before."

Lars stopped. Travis watched the hulk's face as he searched his memory.

"One did, am I right?"

"Yah. My wife."

Lars tightened his grip again. "But this do not mean the little woman is lying."

"No. you are right. But look, you appear to be a fair man. At least hear my side, then you can decide whether to pummel me or not."

Lars thought for a moment then nodded. "All right. Lars listen."

"Good, I need to reach into my pocket."

Lars nodded.

Travis drew the handbill from his front pocket and unfolded it.

"Here," he handed the handbill to Lars, "does this girl look like the one who helped you?"

Lars studied the picture. "It is hard to know. The girl in this picture is dressed as a girl; the one who helped Gretchen was dressed as a man."

"I know, but look around the eyes. Do you see anything?"

"Maybe? I don't know," Lars said as he shoved the handbill back at Travis." It best I hit you and help the girl. Just in case."

"Wait, wait," Travis said. "What about the description? Can you read English?"

"Yah." The large Swede answered, "I read English."

Travis handed the paper back.

Lars brought it closer to his eyes and studied the words.

Travis breathed a sigh of relief when he saw Lars' face brighten.

"Yah, yah," he said as he pointed at the writing. "The mark on her arm. Yah. I see the mark on her arm." Lars stopped and handed him the paper. "You do not lie; the lady does. I will not hurt you."

"Good," Travis said with a sigh of relief, "but, Lars, could you tell me how long ago you saw her?"

Lars scratched his head with his bulky fingers. "Maybe two hour ago; she said she was going to Langston."

"So, she is a few hours ahead of me. It will be dark before I can catch up to her."

Lars smiled. "No, I know a shorter way. I didn't take it because too rough for wagon, but I know way you get at crossroads in hour; maybe you catch her there."

Lars gave Travis the shortcut directions.

"Thank you, friend," Travis said as Lars climbed onto his wagon.

"You welcome, friend," Lars answered. "What you do when you get her?"

"I'll spank her backside, friend."

"Yah." Lars picked up the reins and drove away.

"THE CROSSROADS," Fury said to her furry companions. She thought about Travis meeting Lars. A pang of guilt ran through her as she hoped Lars wouldn't hurt him but only detain him long enough for her to get away.

She studied the road signs in front of her. The road to her right was marked with a sign for Langston, the one on her left said Clarksville. Her eyes lit up with mischief. All right, it was an old trick, but it might help slow Travis. She smiled and dismounted her horse.

Fury walked to the sign for Langston. She wiggled it back and forth until she yanked it from the ground. Then she did the same with the sign for Clarksville. With a little effort, she succeeded in switching the signs. She laughed thinking of Travis making it this far, only to go to the wrong town. She walked back to Swift with a triumphant spring in her step.

The cool evening air blew across her face. She rubbed her sandy eyes. *Damn, I hoped to get closer to Langston before I stopped for the night.*

Hank's training came back to her. 'Sleep when you can. You don't want to face any bad guys without a clear mind.' She nodded as if to agree with the memory.

The evening light was dimming when she found a campsite.

Fury unsaddled her horse, leaving her to graze. She pitched her saddlebags against a tree then went in search for firewood. It didn't take her long to start a fire. She placed a pot of beans on the fire, sat back, and warmed herself.

"Nothing like a crackling fire to warm an achy body, huh, Max? Max?" Fury whistled a few times then shrugged. It was not unusual for Max to go off on his own. Why, one time, he was gone for two days, but he managed to find his way back to her. However, it was not like Max to miss a meal.

She ate her beans, contemplating her next day and how to capture Cutter Dan. Thoughts of Travis made concentrating difficult, but she credited her inability to think clearly to fatigue and not the troublesome ranger. Fury rubbed her heavy eyelids; the sun had yet to set, but she struggled to stay awake. She decided to surrender to her exhaustion and got her bedroll.

THE BIG SWEDE did not fail Travis. He made it to the crossroads while there was still enough evening light to see which way to go.

Well, Miss Belle, I'm closing in on you. Fifteen minutes into his new path, Travis stopped, thinking he heard something. He strained his ears to hear then shrugged. *There it is again. Sounds like barking.*

Travis turned to see the dim outline of a familiar shape coming his way. The barking grew louder as Max came into full view.

"So good to see you." Travis smiled at his floppy-eared friend. "Did you get yourself separated from Belle? Not to worry, friend, follow me. We will find her."

Travis nudged the sides of his horse, taking the road to Langston. He had traveled a few feet when the dog began to bark once more. Travis stopped.

"What are you trying to tell me, boy?"

Once again, the dog began to bark, but this time he ran a few feet and then turned and barked.

"You want me to follow you, don't you, boy? But Belle went this way. The sign pointed—oh." Realization washed over Travis. "That little—she changed the signs, didn't she, boy?"

The dog barked as if he understood.

"Go on, boy, lead me to your mistress."

FURY LAY with her back to the fire, her gun resting by her side. She struggled to sleep, even though her body begged for rest. Thoughts of Travis, her life as Belle, her parents, and Cutter Dan all competed for her attention. The battle ended when she heard the snap of someone stepping on a stick. Fury grabbed her gun. A large hand grasped her forearm and rolled her over. Her mouth hung open when she was eye to gun sight with Travis.

Travis grabbed her gun and tucked it into his belt. He pulled a stunned Fury to her feet. His eyes smoldered like the fire. "I told you not to ever point a gun at me again."

Before Fury could utter a word, Travis hauled her over to a large rock. He sat down and flung her over his knee.

She yelped at the first smack on her backside and cursed with the second.

"No cussing," she heard Travis order as he continued the assault on her pant covered bottom.

Fury fought with everything in her, her legs scissored as she twisted and turned, desperate to throw herself off his lap. The sting of his large hand set fire to her backside, but she refused to concede defeat and beg for mercy, and she sure as hell was not going to let him see her cry.

"Belle Alston, do you realize the worry and work you've put me through today, girl?" Travis scolded as he rained down burning pain on her backside.

Belle let out a guttural scream as she beat his hard calves with her fists. She continued to kick and jerk and wiggle, doing anything to get out of this man's grip. "Go to Hell," she screamed.

"Cursing now. Can't have none of that, Belle; young ladies shouldn't curse."

He picked up the pace, and Fury bit down on her lip fighting off the tears welling up in her eyes.

"You run from me. You drug me. You run from me again. Oh, and yes, you send a huge man after me." Travis punctuated each phrase with a hard smack on her bottom. The spanking stopped for a moment as Travis drew in a breath. "And," *smack* "you think you can bring Cutter Dan in alone." Travis was infuriated by his own words and spanked harder.

Fury hated the show of weakness when her hand instinctively went to her backside to protect her burning bottom.

"Oh, I see I may be getting through to you," Travis said as he trapped her hand in the middle of her back and continued spanking. He slowed his pace when Fury became quiet and stopped struggling. "Have you learned your lesson?" Travis up righted her, only to have her give him an angry scowl.

Fury opened her tight lips to speak. "I. Said. Go. To. Hell!"

"I see," Travis answered and flipped her back over his knee. "This time, you lose your pants."

"What the hell!" Fury screamed and fought. "You can't do that."

She barely finished her protest when she felt his hand undo her pants and push then around her knees. Fury bucked and tried to bite his leg.

"Bite me, and you lose your drawers."

Fury froze. "You won't dare!' she screeched.

"Try me and see."

Confusion and panic swam in Fury's head as his hand made contact with her thinly clothed bottom. The spanks to her bottom scorched, and her resolve was caving.

Travis continued to spank and scold, but the burn in her

backside and her internal fight to remain in control blocked out much of what he said. She heard words, *never, never, again and do you hear me. Also a few young ladies.* But the words she heard clearly, the words that put a dent in her walled-up emotions were, "What do you think your parents would want? Do you think they would want your life at risk.? Do you think anyone who loves you would want you to risk your life—do you think *I* would want you to risk your life?"

Those words pierced the center of her heart, and a few tears broke through. "I'm sorry," she sobbed.

"What?" Travis said, still raining punishment on her backside.

"I'm so sorry," he heard her softly say.

He stopped and gently sat her up on his lap. He knew he'd freed her emotions; he knew he had reached Belle.

She hung her head, hiding her face.

Travis gently raised her chin. Tears ran down the curves of her face. He half smiled at the sad little face. As his gentle hand brushed her hair away from her cheeks, he tucked a stray strand behind her ear and lovingly kissed her tears away.

"My," he said, his voice warm and tender, "have I found my Belle?"

Her sniffles were replaced with silence. Travis steadied himself, ready for another attack of foul mouthed anger. Instead, Belle buried her head in his chest and sobbed out her pain. Her hand rolled into a fist, clenching his shirt like she was holding on so she would not come apart. Travis wrapped his strong arms around her, kissed the top of her head, and whispered, "I got you, honey, hold on to me and let it all out. You're safe in my arms."

He held her close, listening as her sobs turned to soft sniffles. "Belle?" he asked her as she quieted. She tilted her head, red eyes gazing up at him. "Belle, you know you are my girl, don't you?"

"Yes, I am," she whispered.

Travis kissed her forehead. "You're exhausted. Go to sleep, baby girl, I got you." Travis watched her as she drifted off to sleep.

CHAPTER 10

"Ew." A warm, wet slurp slid across Belle's cheek. She lifted her groggy eyelids to an eager dog's face looking down on her.

"Trying to make up after being a traitor?"

Max cocked his head.

"Oh, all right." Belle rubbed the dog's ears. "I forgive you. Go on and let me get up."

Belle yawned and stretched. She warmed in the memory of being wrapped in Travis' strong arms. Never had she felt so safe and secure, even—did she dare to think it—loved, and just maybe, she pondered, she felt something for him.

"Ouch!" Belle's backside came in contact with the ground. The stinging brought back the memory of the spanking, burying her warm feelings for the man who had set her bottom on fire.

"Oh, I am so gonna shoot him." Belle rubbed her aching bottom as her eyes scanned for Travis. "Lucky day, no lawman in sight." She rose to her feet, ready to make a run for her horse.

"Ugh." Belle found herself on the ground. "What the hell?" Belle spit dirt out of her mouth. Her eyes widened as she looked at her feet. "That no good idiot put his cuffs on my ankles—my boots, where are my boots?" Belle heard a humming coming toward her.

"Good morning, Belle." Travis smiled as he walked by with an armload of firewood. He added the wood to a small fire. "Did you sleep well?"

Belle's stomach tightened.

"I saddled the horses. After breakfast, we will start back to Faulkner."

Belle sucked in a deep breath." I ain't going to Faulkner or any other place with you, Ranger Travis Parker. Get these damn things off me and give me my boots and my gun."

Belle watched as Travis retrieved a frying pan and some bacon from her saddle bag, walked to the fire, and began to cook. "Did you hear me?" Belle screeched.

"Well, I guess that sweet girl who fell asleep in my arms last night is hiding again."

"You held me until I fell asleep?" she half whispered then squelched the warm tingle she felt at the thought of sleeping in his arms.

"Yes, I did, and I put you to bed and covered you with a blanket. Can't have my baby girl getting cold."

"Well, goody for you," she sniped, "and I ain't a baby, and I definitely ain't *your* girl."

Travis brushed his hands together then stood up.

Belle swallowed hard, worried there might be a repeat of the night before.

Travis tilted his hat back with a push of his thumb and crossed his arms.

Belle quivered as she felt his stare.

"I couldn't hear very well, but did I hear a cuss word?"

Belle's hands flew to cover her backside.

"Worried, Belle?" Travis chuckled.

"Shut up." She removed her hands and placed them on her hips. Her lips tightened. "What I'm telling you—no, ordering you

—to do is take these cuffs off and give me my boots and my gun."

Travis gave her a dimpled smile. "You *order* me?" Travis pointed at himself. "Ah, Belle." He shook his head. "You, little girl, ain't ordering anyone."

Belle's insides churned as a warm glow of anger spread across her face.

"Now," Travis added as he bent down in front of her, "I'm going to undo the cuffs and give you your boots. Then you are going to come over by the fire and sit and eat breakfast before we start for Faulkner, and there will be no gun for you."

Travis unlocked the cuffs, straightened up, and smirked. "Thanks for not kicking me in the face."

"Wipe that grin off your face, Ranger. You are going to pay for this, just you wait and see."

Travis stretched his mouth open to yawn. "All right. Come by the fire like a good girl and eat some breakfast." He extended an inviting arm in the direction of the fire and waited for Belle to pass by, but she didn't budge. Travis moaned and grabbed hold of her hand.

"Let me go!" Fury shook and twisted her arm, trying to loosen the ranger's steel grip.

"All right, Belle, we'll do it the hard way."

Before she could protest, Belle found herself draped over Travis' muscular shoulder. "You son of a bitch. Let me down." She kicked and beat his back with her fists."

Three searing smacks reignited the flame on her backside. "I said no cussin'." Travis plopped her down on a log by the fire.

"Ow!"

"Sorry, Belle." He grinned.

"You no good, low life, bast—

"Watch it, Belle."

Belle tightened her lips and locked her jaw, forcing her mouth shut. In quiet defiance, she crossed her arms over her chest.

"Now," Travis said as he filled a plate with bacon and shoved it in front of her, "eat."

Belle reached out with her hand as if she would take the plate, but instead, she flipped the plate out of Travis' hand. The plate and its contents landed on the ground in front of her. Her eyes glared at Travis.

"Suit yourself, Belle," Travis said, "no breakfast for you."

Travis loaded his plate with the remaining bacon as the dog gobbled up Belle's mess.

Belle sat quietly, smug in her victory but also hungry.

Travis cleaned up after breakfast, put out the fire, and grabbed his saddle bag.

"Come on, Belle, pick up your gear and let's go."

Belle froze, looking like a statue sitting on the log.

"Belle," said an exasperated Travis, "get up off that log. Get your gear and let's go."

Still, she didn't move a muscle.

"All right, Miss Stubborn, either you get up, or you'll be one sorry young lady."

"Fine!" Belle huffed and rose to her feet.

"But the first town we come to, I'm having you arrested for kidnapping."

"Kidnapping?"

"Yes, kidnapping. You are taking me against my will; that's kidnapping."

Travis laughed. "Sorry, honey, you already tried that argument, remember? You're a witness to a double murder, and I have the authority to bring you in."

Belle's stomach tightened at the mention of her parents' murders. The world began to spin like the last time he had spoken to her of their deaths.

"Belle, you all right? You're white as a sheet." Travis was at her side in seconds. "Sit down, baby girl, before you faint. I'm making you something to eat."

"I don't need food," Bella murmured. "I need you to stop talking about my parents' murders."

"Oh, Belle, I'm so sorry. I didn't mean to talk about your parents like I didn't care." He attempted to place his arm around Belle's shoulder, but she shrugged it off. "What's wrong? I only wanted to comfort you."

"I ain't in no need of support or comfort, especially from you."

"All right, all right." Travis backed up a few steeps with his hands up. "I am sorry, but, Belle, you are going to have talk about it someday."

"Talk about what?" Belle snapped.

"You need to talk about what happened, let all that pain out."

"Not likely." Belle avoided his eyes.

Travis shifted his weight as Belle continued to avoid his glance.

"Come on, Belle," Travis broke the silence, "let's go."

"Get this through your thick ranger head. I ain't going to Faulkner with you. I have a murderer to bring to justice."

"No, the only thing you have to do is come with me."

"Some lawman you are, standing in the way of catching a murderer like Cutter Dan. I hope while you are wasting time taking me to Faulkner, no other woman is butchered. If another woman is killed, it will be your fault." Belle jabbed a finger in the air toward Travis.

"And what makes you think you can find Cutter Dan? There is an army of lawmen searching for him, and they can't find him. What makes you so special?"

Belle squared her shoulder and raised her chin. "Remember, Mr. Ranger lawman, I know where he is."

"And if you do know where about his hiding place is near Langston, you should tell me, and I'll pass on the information."

"And someone else get my bounty. I don't think so."

"Come on, Belle." Travis dragged a struggling Belle to her horse. "Mount up."

Belle crossed her arms. "I ain't getting on no horse."

"All right then, I'll put you in your saddle."

In seconds, Belle felt herself whisked off her feet and plopped down on her saddle. "Ow!" she screeched, pushing herself up in her stirrups. "Let me off. I would rather walk."

Travis pushed her down on her saddle.

"Ow! I told you that hurts."

"I know, little girls who get spanked hurt when they sit."

"Exactly, you fool. Now, let me down."

"Nope, it's part of your punishment. You are gonna live with that sore bottom for a few days. Now, sit, or I'll relight that sting on your backside."

Belle gently sat on her saddle. "I hate you."

"No, you don't," Travis answered. "Now, Miss Alston, put your hands on the saddle horn."

"What?"

"Put your hands on the saddle horn so I can tie them to it."

"H-how can I ride with my hands tied?"

"You don't need to worry about that, Belle. I can't have you getting' a notion to gallop away."

Belle slapped her hands on the horn. "One of these days, Ranger, I'm gonna—

"Shh, Belle." Travis held his hand up. "I hear something."

Belle's hunter's instinct caused her to quiet down and listen.

"It's a rider," Travis said, "and he's coming fast. He's either running from something or to something. Either way, I've gotta stop him and find out. You stay put."

Belle began to open her mouth, but Travis threw her a glare that told her she'd better be quiet.

Travis walked to the center of the road. He held up a hand and kept his other on the top of his gun. The rider did not slow down.

Belle bit her lip. *That idiot is going to get trampled.*

The rider's horse stirred up a cloud of dust as it stopped only a few feet in front of Travis.

"Calm down," Travis said to the gangly young man. "I'm Ranger Travis Parker." Travis pointed to his badge. "If you don't mind me saying, you look frightened, son. What's happened?

The youth cleared his throat. "I am scared and don't care if anyone knows. There was a murder in our town, and I'm on the way to Clarksville to fetch their sheriff."

"Where are you from, son?"

"N-name's Bobby, Bobby Nelson."

"Bobby, where are you from?"

"Langston."

THE PIT OF TRAVIS' gut turned cold with remorse. *Belle was right. This death is on me.*

"Langston? Don't you have a sheriff?"

"Y-yes, sir, we do, 'cept'n Sheriff Hayes fell a couple of days ago and broke his leg. He ain't in no shape to chase a murderer."

"What about your deputy?"

"Deputy went back east to visit family a week ago, and no one will take his place. Sheriff's afraid, without a lawman, he is gonna have ta deal with vigilantes. You see, it were a young girl who got killed. Meg Jackson, the mayor's daughter, and they say she was all cut up; he even cut letters into her forehead."

"Cutter Dan," Travis sputtered and shook his head.

"Yes, sir, that's what they are saying."

Travis looked at the ground and took a deep breath. *Time to switch, Travis, gotta put this away and be a lawman.* He straightened his body. "Bobby, you go on to Clarksville and tell the sheriff about the murder. I will go into Langston and meet up with your sheriff."

"Ya gonna catch the man who butchered poor Meg?"

"Yes, I am."

The boy galloped off toward Clarksville.

Travis remained standing in silence.

"It wasn't your fault," Belle said as he came back from the road.

TRAVIS MOUNTED HIS HORSE, and Belle saw a rigid resolve in his eyes as he looked at her. He took the reins of her horse and started toward Langston.

After riding in silence for what seemed like an eternity to Belle, Travis stopped and turned toward her. "Don't think this will keep me from taking you to Faulkner, and don't even think of running away."

"Oh, I wouldn't think of running, Ranger." Belle raised her chin. "After all, Langston is where I want to be, and I think you will need the help of a good bounty hunter." Belle smirked.

"No thanks."

"Why? Are you afraid a girl is a better lawman than you, Ranger?"

Travis shook his head, grabbed the reins of Belle's horse, and headed for Langston.

Belle noticed his slumped shoulders as she followed behind him. *I'm an idiot. Why did I tell Travis he would be responsible for any girl getting killed?*

"It ain't your fault," Belle said.

"What ain't my fault?"

"You know—the girl—it ain't your fault the girl in Langston was killed."

Travis stopped and pulled Belle's horse up beside him. "It's all right, Belle. I know it ain't my fault, but it's sweet of you to worry about me." Travis leaned over and brushed her lips with a kiss.

The kiss rushed through her like a bolt of lightning; why did this man have such an effect on her? "I ain't worried about you,

Travis Parker," Belle huffed. "I don't want to get killed because you are feeling guilty and not paying attention."

Travis smirked, "Sure, Belle."

"Don't make fun of me, Ranger," Belle fumed. "I told you I ain't worried about you."

"All right, Belle, whatever you say. But you need to understand something."

Belle's ears pricked.

"Don't think going to Langston means you won something. I still plan on taking you home, so don't even think of running away."

"Oh," Belle grinned, "I already told you I wouldn't think of running away. Besides, Ranger, you will need the help of a good bounty hunter to capture Cutter Dan."

"No thanks."

"Why, Ranger Travis, I think you *are* afraid a girl is a better lawman than you."

Travis pulled Belle's horse closer. "Look at me, Belle," he ordered.

Belle studied her hands.

"Belle Alston, you look at me right now, or I'll throw you across my saddle and make you wish you'd listened to me."

"All right!" Belle answered through clenched teeth. Her chin flicked up and her eyes locked onto his smoldering look.

"Listen to me, Belle Alston. You are not to do anything when we get to town. You are to stay put. If you try to go after Cutter, I will find you and take my belt to your cute little bottom, then I'll lock you in a jail cell. Do you understand me?"

Anger boiled in the pit of Belle's stomach. "Just one minute, Ranger Travis Parker," Belle fumed. "I have tracked and captured many dangerous criminals over the past three years, and I think I know what I'm doing."

"Maybe so, but even if I call you 'Fury' while we are in town, it's only to protect your identity. Fury the bounty hunter is gonna sit this one out or not sit at all."

"But," Belle said with a smug look, "Fury the bounty hunter knows where to search for Cutter Dan."

When they reached the town, Travis stopped at the outskirts. He pulled Belle's horse alongside his. "Now you listen to me, Belle—

"Fury. You idiot. It's Fury."

"All right, Fury. When we get to the sheriff's office, I'll do all the talkin'. If they've heard of Fury—

"Oh, they've heard of Fury." Belle grinned.

"As I was saying, *if* they know about Fury, you're gonna tell them you're sick and can't help with the man hunt."

Belle looked Travis in the eyes. "Whatever you say, Ranger." Belle spoke in a sing-song voice. A satisfied smile stretched across her face.

"All right, Miss Belle." Travis crossed his arms. "What's up?"

"Fury. Remember, the name's Fury."

"All right, Fury, but if you're conjuring up some devious plan, you might as well forget it. I'll be watching you. Do you understand?"

Another wide smile bloomed on Belle's face. "Why, Ranger Parker, don't you trust me?"

"No. Listen, Belle, whatever you're planning, forget it."

"I'm not planning a thing," she replied, her voice veiled in innocence. She found Travis' uneasy stare entertaining. "Ranger Parker—

"Don't you go all prim and proper with me, Belle. That's more worrisome than you smiling."

"Ranger Parker, I need my gun."

Realization washed over Travis' face. "So that's it. You think you're getting your gun back. Are you aiming to shoot me before we get to town?"

"The thought crosses my mind about every fifteen minutes,

but that can wait until another day. I, Fury, can't ride into town without a gun."

Travis was silent.

"Come on, Travis, you know I'm right. So, you gonna untie my hands?"

Travis removed his knife from its holster and cut through the rope. He scowled then reached into his saddlebag and dug out a holster and gun.

Belle smiled and reached for the prize that dangled before her, only to have it jerked from her grasp.

"Hold on there, girl; we gotta set some rules."

"Rules? Rules? I know you're addle brained, but you must not remember who I am. I know how to use a gun, and I also know how to take care of myself."

"You want your gun back?"

Belle locked her jaw and nodded.

"No pulling a gun on anyone, especially me, unless someone is threatening you."

"Travis, is this necessary? You know—

"Do you understand?"

"Yes," Belle answered through her teeth, "I understand." She grabbed the gun and wrapped it around her waist. Then she looked at Travis with a triumphant smile.

"So, you think you have won?"

"Well, yes, I have my gun after all."

"Don't get uppity. I will do all the talking when we meet the sheriff; you'll be quiet."

"Yes, Ranger." She batted her eyes at him.

"Let's go."

"Wait," Belle said, "I have a rule too."

"Oh, you do, do you?" Travis crossed his arms. "Well, what is it?"

"Remember to call me Fury, you dope." Belle kicked the sides of her horse and galloped toward town with Travis close behind.

She slowed her horse's pace when they reached the edge of town. "Why the sour face, Ranger Parker?" Belle giggled.

"Very funny, Bel—

"Fury!"

"Yeah, Fury. Come on; let's find the sheriff's office."

"Just follow me, Ranger. I know where it is."

Belle trotted up to the sheriff's office with Travis close behind.

"Here we are." Belle dismounted and tied her horse to the hitching post. She headed for the sheriff's office.

"Hold up there." Travis was off his horse in seconds.

"What is it?"

A few strides of his long legs and he was at Belle's side. "Listen up Bel—Fury."

Belle shifted the bulk of her weight to one leg and placed one hand on her hip. "I'm listenin'."

"Well, that's a first." Travis grinned.

"Get on with it."

"I do all the talkin', and you keep your mouth shut."

Belle sighed.

"Fury is not going to have anything to do with hunting Cutter Dan."

Belle shot him a piercing glare.

"I mean it. If I catch you doing anything about Cutter Dan, well, you know what to expect, young lady."

Belle bit down on her lip.

Travis crossed his arms. "I'm waiting. Answer me; are you gonna do what I say?"

Belle gave a conceding nod.

"Good, now come on."

"Wait," Belle said as she reached down and scooped up some dirt. She scanned to make sure no one was watching then proceeded to rub the dirt on her face.

"What the hell are you doing?"

"Trying to hide the fact that I don't have a beard, you idiot."

"Watch the mouth, Belle."

"It's Fury; let's go."

The hinges on the door gave out a tired groan as it slammed shut. The small jail smelled of tobacco, stale coffee, and body odor. A man sat behind a gnarled wooden desk with a splinted leg propped up on a stool. Two other men hovered over him as they exchanged a heated debate.

Belle walked through the threshold, but Fury emerged at the other side. With her hat tilted in Fury fashion, she rested her back against the cold wall. She pulled a cigar from her pocket and guided it her mouth. Then she raked a match against the rough wall and lit the cigar that hung on her lip. She laced a thumb through a belt loop and took a slow drag.

Travis stood in front of the desk, but he might as well have been a ghost to the men who were locked in a tense argument.

"It will take too long, Sheriff," argued a rotund man with a boisterous, quivering voice. "We can't wait until Bobby finds a sheriff. Meg is dead, and the folks are scared. They are locking up their daughters and loading their rifles."

"Mr. Tate is right, Ed. With you laid up and Deputy Sims back east, the men of this town need to take over and ride out after this killer."

"And when you find him, what then?" the sheriff asked. "Do you have a trial right where you find him, then convict and find a convenient tree to hang him. No, there will not be vigilante justice in my town."

Travis cleared his throat." Gentlemen—

The combative voices drowned him out.

"Gentlemen," Travis tried once more but was again drowned out. He rubbed the back of his neck, then he straightened his body, took in a breath, and let out a sharp whistle.

Silence. All eyes focused on the tall man standing in front of them.

"Now that I have your attention, let me introduce myself. I am Texas Ranger Travis Parker."

"Did you say ranger, young fellow?" asked the sheriff.

"Yes, I did, sir. I met Bobby Nelson on the road, and he told me about the murder and your need for a lawman."

"Welcome, welcome," said the rotund man. "Allow me to introduce myself, name's Stewart, Ben Stewart." He extended his thick hand for Travis to shake. "This here is Wilus Beasley."

"Nice to meet you," said the mousey man.

"And, of course, this is our sheriff, Ed Hayes."

"Good to have you here, son. You don't mind if I don't get up? Had a bit of an accident with my horse."

"I can see. Well, gentlemen, there is no time to waste. Tell me what you know about the murder."

"Wait a minute, Ranger, who's your friend?"

"Never mind about him, Sheriff, he's not—

"Come on out of the shadows, stranger," the sheriff coaxed Fury forward.

"I'll be." Fury saw recognition on the sheriff's face." If it ain't Fury! Look, boys, it's Fury. Ain't it like you, Fury, to show up right when we need you? Come on up to my desk; let me take a look at you."

Fury swaggered her way to the desk, stopping for only a moment to blow smoke in Travis' face.

"Look here, men, now we have Fury here to help the Ranger. I'm certain we will find that poor girl's murderer now." The men nodded their agreement, and the atmosphere of the room lightened.

"H-how," Travis interjected, "how is it that you know Fury?"

"Ranger, surely you know the reputation of the man you are traveling with. Why, I would say it would be hard for anyone around these parts not to know about Fury, the bounty hunter."

"Sheriff, I think what the ranger is asking is how come you ain't afraid of me."

The sheriff chuckled. "Ranger, ain't no one in Langston afraid of Fury. Why, to us, he is a hero."

Fury delighted in Travis' confusion.

"A year or so back, Fury was in town. Back then, most folks gave Fury a wide birth, if you don't mind me sayin' so, Fury." The sheriff glanced at the bounty hunter.

"No, go on, Sheriff."

"One day, word came that three-year-old Carrie Milner fell into an air shaft to an abandoned mine. The menfolk dug a parallel shaft, hoping to reach the girl, but whenever they tried to get near her, the walls would crumble. We knew we needed a smaller shaft and a smaller man to crawl down and get her. We about gave up when, out of nowhere, Fury showed up and said he would try to reach the little girl. Well, he rescued little Carrie, and he is a hero to the people of Langston."

"Imagine that," Travis said. "Fury, a hero."

"What of it?" Fury snapped.

"Nothing, Mr. Fury, it was lucky you were small and could fit in the hole, that's all."

Fury tightened her fist, holding back her anger. "Tell me, Sheriff," Fury asked, as she continued to glare at Travis, "what happened to the murdered girl?"

The mood darkened; Sheriff Hayes stumbled for words. "H-horrific, the only word to describe what happened to poor Meg, horrific."

"Where was she found?" Travis asked.

"Behind the livery, at about five in the morning. Old Amos heard the horses in the back stalls whinnying. When he couldn't find anything wrong in the stalls, he stepped out back. He found her lying in a heap, covered with her own blood. They say animals can smell blood; I suppose that's why the horses were riled up. Doc figures she was killed around midnight."

"Do you know the last person to see her alive?"

"I reckon her ma was the last one to see Meg. Poor woman said she told her daughter good night around ten."

"Was she taken from her home, or did she leave on her own?" Fury added.

"We think she left on her own. The window of her room was open, but there were no signs of a struggle. We found one set of small footprints under the window, and we figured they were Meg's."

"Anything you haven't told me about the murder?" Travis asked.

"Yeah, the letters cut into her forehead."

"C. D.?"

"Yes."

"Cutter Dan. Anything else you can tell me?"

The sheriff scratched his head. "No, don't think so. Oh, wait, don't know if it's important, but she was missing a silver earing. Looked like he pulled it right off her ear. What kinda animal is this man? I heard of him, but his other murders were twenty miles from here or better. Why would he be in Langston?"

"I suppose," Fury answered, "he came here to lay low for a while then move on to new hunting grounds."

"But why kill Meg?" the sheriff asked.

"Because he needed to," Travis answered.

"Why do you say that, Ranger?"

"Just something I'm working on in my head. It ain't all come together yet, but I'll figure it out."

"Why don't you and Fury get a room and some food at the Grand Hotel. We can meet here this evening. By then, the posse will be back."

"No." Fury said. "The longer we wait, the more chance Cutter will get away."

"Now, Fury," Travis added, "I don't think it's a bad idea to get some rest and food. After all, you haven't been feeling well. It would be a shame if you couldn't help with the man hunt."

Fury knew Travis' ridged face and stern voice meant business, so she decided to concede.

∾

"WHY IN THE hell are you putting off going after Cutter? What kinda lawman are you?"

"Quiet," Travis said as they continued their quick pace toward the hotel.

"No, no, I won't be quiet. We are losing precious time."

"Listen to me." Travis slowed his pace enough to ensure Fury heard his words. "You can't go off halfcocked when you are after a man like Cutter. You need to gather as much information as you can, and you need to plan."

"What information?"

"Information, like him taking the girl's earring. I heard he took things from the other girls."

"So how does that help you find Cutter?"

"It tells me now that we ain't dealing with an ordinary murderer."

"I coulda told you that. Don't make this complicated, Travis. It's simple; the plan is to find him and bring him in," Fury railed under her breath. "He kills women; that's all the information I need, and since when are you an expert on Cutter Dan?"

"I'm warning you, drop this until we can talk in private."

"All right, you win for now," Fury said as they stopped at the hotel entrance. "But I warn you, I only have so much patience, and when that is used up, I'm going out on my own."

"I wouldn't advise that," Travis fixed his stone gaze on her, "or else."

Fury's insides wobbled at his words. His effect on her body confused her. How could she both love and hate when he spoke to her with steel in his voice?

CHAPTER 11

*I*ridescent streams of angelic sunlight drifted through the open window, illuminating his treasure displayed on the table. Cutter Dan sat on a crude, hewed chair admiring his mementos: a cameo, a locket, a blue hairbow, they were the first of his keepsakes. To his treasure, he would add the silver earring in his paw of a hand, the newest member of his morbid collection.

Pinching it between a meaty thumb and finger of his free hand, Dan held the earring up to the light and watched it sparkle. The dancing silver glimmers gave him momentary satisfaction.

He slammed the trinket on the table, something he would never do to such a coveted prize if he had not messed up. He jerked his body up from the chair, scraping the legs against the wooden floor. The creaks and moans of the floor planks followed him as he paced. His trembling hand dragged his fingers through thin, greasy black hair, stopping to cup the back of his gritty neck. He paused.

"Damn! I never shoulda listened to you," Dan railed against his inner demon.

"Supplies, that's why I went to town, to steal supplies." At least that is what the demon told him. But he knew it was not so, because he knew the demon well and it was hungry.

The demon's appetite had won that night, but it could not again. He needed to be in control. In the beginning, he'd controlled the demon, at least he thought he did. Now the terms had changed. Dan didn't care about the murders; he relished them. But now his life was threatened, and he cared about living —did the demon care about his life?

"Why? Why did I have to kill in Langston? Damn, it's the closest town, and now they are after me. I don't make mistakes. No, wait, there was the girl, the one with the blue bow. Shoulda waited to kill her."

I remember, the demon cooed, *the pretty little thing—long brown hair, bright blue eyes, just like you want them. She shouldn't have laughed at you.*

Dan remembered. "Yeah, yeah, that's right; it was her fault. I worked for her pa, and she thought she was better than me. She shouldn't have laughed at me," he repeated. "I woulda waited, but I couldn't. I had to kill her, right then, in that alley, but someone heard me. I ran. Never ran that fast in my life. I didn't know she didn't die right away. She told them about me, even my name. Because of her, they got them wanted posters." Dan slammed his fist into his hand.

Don't worry, the demon's words slithered around his brain, *no one will find you here.*

"Yes, that's right. I'm hidden. This is a secret place, and if someone accidently finds it, then I'll kill him. There's only one way in. That's what I wanted, so no one can sneak up on me. Yeah, that's what I'll do, kill him—no big deal."

"WHAT DO YOU MEAN, you only have one room!" Fury grumbled at the desk clerk.

"Y-yes, Mr. Fury, sir. Just the one room. But it's a very nice room."

Fury cut her eyes toward Travis, who tried to suppress a grin but failed.

"What the hell you smiling about?" Fury snarled at Travis.

"Oh, nothing, Mr. Fury." Travis chuckled.

"Yeah, right, don't you have anything else? At this point, I'd sleep in your office or a broom closet, anywhere but with him." Fury jerked her thumb toward Travis. She rubbed her temples. The burn across her cheeks assured Fury her face was blazing red, and her head began to thump, a sure sign of a threatening migraine.

"M-Mr. Fury," the clerk's voice squeaked, "I'm sorry, but I need the office and we can't have a person of your stature in our community sleeping in a *broom closet.*"

"Listen here." Fury lunged for the clerk's lapels, but Travis intercepted her.

"Fury, put your hands down and stop clowning around; you're intimidating Mr.—

"Peterson," the wide-eyed clerk responded.

"I'm sorry, Mr. Peterson." Travis leaned on the desk and motioned the clerk to lean toward him.

"You see," he said in a hushed tone, "Fury here, well, Fury's very tired. I mean very, very tired." Travis cut his eyes to meet Fury's gaze. "I suppose he needs a long nap."

Shoot him—yep—definitely need to get that done. Fury gave Travis a mercenary glare. "Not likely," she interjected.

"Fury, if you please." His voice held a tinge of playfulness, but his eyes were stern, sending her a message to back down.

Fury's shoulders slumped in defeat. She tried to convince herself that she hated the authority he wielded over her, but part of her loved it, even craved it. Damn that man.

"As I was saying," Travis patted Fury's back, "well, you see, it's not so much as he wants a room to himself, it's just that Fury is so damned considerate." He smiled at the confusion on Fury's face. "You see, Mr. Peterson, Fury here," Travis gestured for the man to lean in closer, "Fury snores."

"Oh, I didn't know that," the clerk said.

"Well, of course, you didn't, you jackass," Fury fumed. "And. I. Do. Not. Snore."

"Fury, come on; be nice. You know you do so, and it doesn't bother me one teensy bit. So, Mr. Peterson, one room will be fine for me and my friend."

"Good, good." The nervous clerk turned to retrieve the key from its peg.

"You, dirty, good for nothing, son of a—

"Here you go, sir." The clerk presented Travis with a key, number seven. "It's upstairs, toward the back of the hotel. I'm sure you will like it; it's a very quiet room."

"Thank you." Travis smiled. "Come on, Fury, let's find *our* room."

Fury cast one more killer glare at Mr. Peterson.

"And you call this the Grand Hotel?" she sniped then turned and stomped after Travis.

"What's that, Fury?"

Travis stopped at number seven. "I can't hear you; you're muttering. In fact, you've been muttering and moaning all the way to our room."

Fury slogged the rest of the way to the room. "I keep my muttering to myself."

"Good idea; I would really hate to hear you cursing."

Travis opened the door and stepped in.

The shock on Fury's face made him chuckle as he tossed his saddle bags on the dresser along with his hat and then plopped his large frame on the wrought iron bed.

The only bed.

"Come on, Belle, lie right here next to old Travis." He patted the empty side of the bed and gave her a wink.

"Very funny," she answered. "And it's Fury, remember."

"I prefer Belle when we are alone."

"You would." Belle crossed the room to the pale green chair by the window. She sank into the chair and surveyed the room. It was a nicer place than some she'd stayed in, but no palace. "This room looks like a woman's room." She pointed to the wallpaper with its pink roses.

"Eh, they're just flowers, Belle."

"Just flowers! How about that quilt? It's pink and green and has lace on the bottom. And look here," she held the edge of the curtain, "more lace."

"What's your point, Belle?"

"You should leave and go sleep in the livery; you don't belong in this room," she sneered.

"And you, *Mr.* Fury, do *you* belong in this *lady's* room?"

Belle paused. "Point taken, but you should go anyway."

"Sorry, honey, I like this soft bed. You really should try it." Travis winked once again.

"Ha, ha." Fury stood and picked up her saddle bag. "Fine. I'll go to the stable. I sure ain't sharing a room with you. By the way, I think there is something wrong with your eye."

"You move one step toward that door, and you will be one sorry girl."

"Damn it Travis, I'm not sharing anything with you—not this room, not that bed—nothing, understand?"

Travis jerked himself off the bed so quickly, it made Belle jump. She dropped back on the chair. "Fine then, I'll sleep here in the chair."

Travis stood with his hands perched on his hips as he studied her.

The power of his gaze made her quake inside. She cleared her throat. "Travis," she held up her hands in a weak attempt to slow his advance," I didn't move toward the door, and look, I-I'm sitting here in the chair."

A few steps, and he was looking down at her.

Belle swallowed—hard.

He grabbed her hands and pulled her to her feet, he half turned her, and gave her three stinging swats. "That's for cursing, and next—

"Travis, I haven't done anything wrong." She jerked her hands from his grasp, blushing when she realized her hands flew behind her to cover her backside.

"Belle," he said in an even tone. He removed the hat from her head and laid it in the chair, then he pulled her hands from her backside and gently pulled her toward the bed. "Belle, sweetheart." His voice softened. "You're exhausted."

"I am not." Belle straightened her stance and planted her feet firmly on the floor.

Travis smiled and cupped her face in his large hand. He lifted her chin, so his eyes met hers.

Belle dropped her gaze to the floor.

"Belle, look at me."

She sighed and brought her eyes up just short of an eye roll.

Travis smirked at the defiance in her tired eyes. "Yes, you are, stubborn girl."

The gentle touch of his finger traced the curve of her jaw, stopping at her chin with a soft tap. There it went. That zap she felt when he touched her or spoke to her in that voice.

"You said we were gonna talk about Cutter Dan when we got to our room."

"Later. Now, you sleep."

"I don't need to sleep."

"Belle, don't fight me on this. Aren't you the girl who ran away from me in the middle of the night?"

"I slept on the side of the road."

"Yes, I'm sure that was restful."

"All right then, I slept last night."

"Well, the dark smudges under your eyes say you didn't sleep enough. Now sit down and I'll take your boots off."

"I can take my own boots off, thank you very much."

"Belle, sit!" he ordered, and she plopped down on the bed. "Fine!"

Travis kneeled. "Foot, Belle."

She hesitated.

"Now!"

"All right," she huffed and jerked one foot up.

"Thank you," he said as he pulled the boot off her small foot. "Next."

Up went the other foot, and off went the boot.

"Let's wash some of the dirt off your face." Travis poured some water in a basin and wet a cloth. He reached out to wash Belle's face.

"Hey, I need that dirt to hide the fact I don't have a beard."

"Belle, honey, I don't think you will have any trouble finding more dirt." He ran the wet cloth over her face, removing as much dirt as he could. "That will have to do." He tapped her nose and smiled. Then he stood and tugged her back on her feet. He drew back the quilt.

"Travis, you don't have to do any of this. I can take care of myself."

"Let me take care of you, sweetheart."

She melted at his words.

He turned to face her. "Pants," he said as he held out his hand.

Her eyes widened as she shook her head.

"Pants, Belle. You take them off, or I will."

Her warm feelings for him faded. Belle sighed her defeat and removed her pants and gave them to his waiting hand.

"Shirt," he ordered.

One minute, he's sweet, and the next, he's ordering me around. Oh, I so need to shoot him. She tossed her shirt to him.

Travis bunched her clothes in one hand and held up the quilt with the other. "In."

Belle stood in her undergarments with her arms folded across her chest, not moving a muscle. "No, Travis, you don't get to tell me when to sleep. I ain't five years old."

"Sometimes I wonder. You're mine, Belle. I might be a bit overprotective and possessive, but I take care of what's mine, so I do get to tell you when to sleep. You need a nap. Now, you can get in the bed with a sore bottom or not, it's up to you."

Belle stomped her foot. "I don't remember giving myself to you," she sniped.

"Don't worry, darling, you did. Don't you remember the night I spanked you?

Belle blushed, remembering that night and how he had held her in his arms. She thought it was a dream when he said she was his, recalling she'd agreed with his declaration.

"Memory coming back, Belle?"

She huffed.

"Now get in this bed."

"Damn you, Travis," she said as she crawled into the bed.

Smack.

"Ow," Belle hollered.

"I told you, no cussing. Lie down."

Belle flopped down on the bed. "Hey, what are you doing with my clothes?" Belle propped herself on her elbows as she watched Travis cram her clothing into his saddle bag. He picked up the bag and slung it over his shoulder.

"They're coming with me, can't have you sneaking out the window again."

"You son of a—

"Belle, do I need to come over there and add a few smacks to that last one, cause I'm thinking I do? Or maybe you would prefer I wash your mouth out with soap." He moved next to the bed.

"You wouldn't." Belle's voice softened.

"Honey, you know I would, so what is it, sore bottom, soapy mouth, or nap?"

"Nap," Belle surrendered.

"Good girl." Travis bent down and kissed her forehead. "And don't think you can get up after I leave. I'll know if you do."

"How?"

"Oh, I have my ways." He pulled the door open.

"Where are you going?"

"Sleep," he said as he closed the door.

"He'd know, huh." She sat up and placed one foot on the floor. "He would know. I don't know how, but the jackass would know." She jerked her foot off the floor and lay back in the bed. "Damn man."

TRAVIS CHUCKLED to himself as he walked to the sheriff's office. He was quite pleased with his plan to keep Belle from participating in the hunt for Cutter Dan.

Belle Alston, I might be a possessive bastard, but you are mine, and I'm keeping you safe.

He walked into the jail. It was silent, different from a few hours ago. Sheriff Hayes was the only person in the room.

"Come on in, Ranger," the sheriff said.

Travis approached the sheriff's desk. He gazed at the poor man in front of him. He sat in the same position as when Travis had first entered the jail; his broken leg remained propped up on a stool. Travis could tell the man was in pain by the way he winced.

"Glad to see you are a dedicated lawman, but shouldn't you be at home resting your leg? I expected one of the gentlemen from this morning to be watching the jail for you."

"Can't do it," the sheriff said. "I've known Meg since she was a baby. My duty is to this town, to Meg, to find her murderer."

"Has your posse returned?"

"Not yet. Should, before too long. I'm hoping they found him."

"Me too, but don't count on it. This Cutter Dan is smart. He won't be found easily."

"Well, for our sake, I hope you are wrong."

Travis nodded. "Any news on why the girl was out of the house?"

"Yes." The sheriff shook his head. "A boy, Tommy Jameson, to be exact. They were going to meet near the livery."

"So, what happened to the boy?"

"He got caught by his ma, trying to sneak out. Poor boy, I hear he's blaming himself."

"Poor kid, it's not his fault, it's Cutter Dan's."

"So, where is Fury?"

"Oh, well, you see, Fury, he's not feeling well. I told him I would leave him to rest at the hotel and come down here and see if there were any new developments."

"Fury's not well? We got a doctor can go over and check him out."

"Not necessary, I think with some rest, Fury will be back to his old self."

"Good, we can't do this without him."

"Well, I best get back and check on Fury."

"You think he'll make the meeting?"

"It will be hard to keep Fury from it," Travis said with a smirk. *Hard, yes, but I can do it. No, Belle's not getting involved in this, even if I have ta hog tie her to the bed. Which, come to think of it, isn't that bad of an idea.*

"GET AWAY FROM ME," Belle grumbled. She was half asleep when she swatted at the fly attempting to land on her nose. Again, the fly attacked, and this time she moaned and rubbed her nose.

"Belle," she heard her name cutting through her groggy haze. Her eyes fluttered open.

"What the hell?"

Her vision focused on Travis who was chuckling and holding a feather in his hand.

She rubbed her eyes with the back of her hands. "Where'd you get that da...that feather?"

"It was sticking out of the side of your pillow, just begging me to pluck it out." Travis chuckled.

"Well, my, ain't you the clever one?" Belle sniped.

"Get up, Belle, it's almost suppertime."

"I wasn't sleeping." Belle shot up and swung her legs over the side of the bed.

"Belle, you know I don't hold with lying. You fell asleep and don't want to admit I was right about you needing a nap."

"So what if you were right?" Belle rubbed her sweaty palms across her thighs. "But I still have the right to make that decision for myself."

"Sure you do, Belle," Travis raised an eyebrow, "as long as you are willing to take the consequences.

Belle's face burned. "I want my clothes. Now."

Travis sat in the overstuffed green chair. He steepled his fingers. "You can have them back, but you have ta ask nicely."

Belle seared him with her eyes and sucked in a deep breath. Her hands rolled up in fists. "May, I have my clothes, please?" Her words hissed from her mouth.

Travis stared at her for a moment. "I suppose that's as nice as you can ask. Here." He tossed his saddle bags to the bed. "If I wasn't pressed for time, and if I didn't need to get some food in you, I would make you ask again in a kinder tone."

Belle huffed and began to yank her clothes from the bag. She sat for a moment clinging to the bunched clothes that lay in her lap. "Well?"

"Well, what?"

"Aren't you going to turn around so I can dress."

Travis laughed." Belle, I saw you in your undergarments when I took your clothes, and don't forget I saw you when you were taking a bath, and then I saw every—

"So, I don't deserve any respect. You keep reminding me, I'm Belle, a woman. Oh, never mind, just shut up, I shoulda known you weren't no gentleman." Belle was confused at her own outburst. Why should she care if he treated her like a lady or not?

Travis leaned forward and smiled. "Honey, since when does Fury care about gentlemen?"

Belle let out a guttural sound, followed by a string of muttering.

"All right, all right." Travis stood up. "I'll turn around, but I admit I kinda like this more ladylike side of you."

Belle stuck her tongue out at Travis when his back was turned then proceeded to jam her legs into her pants. "All right, turn around." She sat on the bed, shoving her feet into her boots. "Let's go," Belle said as she stood.

Travis nodded as he made his way to the door. When he got to the door, he paused and turned to look at her. "Oh, and don't stick your tongue out. It's not very ladylike." He turned and went out the door.

"How did you know?" Belle asked as she followed him out the door.

"Belle," he said as he paused in the hall, "the washstand in the corner has a mirror on it."

"Oh. Hey, wait a minute; that means you watched me get dressed." She crossed her arms and waited for a reply.

Travis smirked, "Hmm, maybe I did at that."

"Oh, why can't I just shoot—

"What were you going to say?"

"Never mind." Belle stomped past him.

TRAVIS SMILED and shook his head. *Travis, old boy, you're going have a heap of trouble with this one, but you know you'll love every minute.* He sighed and followed Belle down the stairs.

The restaurant in the Grand Hotel was simple and clean. Tables with gingham tablecloths were scattered throughout the room.

"Welcome to our restaurant, gentlemen," said the large woman with dark hair and a bellowing voice. "As you can see," the woman held out her hand to the room, "ain't got many customers tonight. Reckon all this ugly business with poor Meg got people scared. Just sit wherever you want, and I will be right with you."

Travis nodded and led Fury to the tables near the big front window. He always sat where he could see what was going on around him.

"Can't we just skip this and get right to the sheriff's office and get on with this. Ranger, you have got to be one of the slowest lawmen in the state."

"Calm down, Fury. You can't hunt the bad guys on an empty stomach. Plus, ain't no one gonna be there until after supper time."

"Well, don't try and trick me, Travis," Fury huffed under her breath. She leaned toward him. "I know you want to keep me from all this, but I'ma telling ya now," she thumped the top of the table with her finger, "no one is keeping me from getting Cutter Dan." Fury tightened her lip and glared.

Travis' cool eyes met Fury's fixed gaze. "Don't bet on it, little girl."

"Well, then," the waitress's bouncy voice broke into the battle of wills. "What will you gentlemen have?"

"I'll have fried chicken, but my friend here," Fury snarked, "he will be eating crow."

Fury and Travis walked into the jail, now occupied by a small group of men.

"Remember, the only reason you are here is because the

sheriff wanted you in on the meeting," Travis said to Fury. "But you and I know Fury isn't going to be well enough to join the posse."

"If you think, for one minute, you can tell me—"

"Fury," the sheriff called from his perch behind the desk. "You and that ranger fella come on in here." The sheriff motioned for them to come closer.

"Good to see you again, Ed," Fury said as she extended her hand, ignoring the gruff man at her side.

"Well, we can finally get started, been waiting for Fury to get here."

"Thanks, Ed. I'll do my best."

"You mean you will do your best if the sickness don't come back on you," Travis tried to interject. "In fact, Fury, you're still looking poorly; why don't you sit down here in this chair and rest a bit?" Travis guided Fury over to the chair nearest the jail cell.

"Trying to hide me here ain't gonna change a thing, Ranger," Fury whispered. "I'm still gonna get Dan."

"I wouldn't bet on it." Travis gave her a stony look before he turned away. He joined the group of men gathered around a map that hung on the wall.

Fury's stomach boiled with anger. *You are stupider than I thought, Ranger Travis Parker. Ain't no way I'm gonna stay behind and lose the most important bounty of my life. I'll get away, but how? Think, Fury, how can I get away from that ass of a man?* Fury listened as the men droned on.

"Roger, show us where on the map the posse searched today," the sheriff asked the lanky, sandy haired man closest to the map.

Roger pointed his bony finger to the upper side of the map. "Me, Alvin, and Sam searched up here, just north of town. We went as far up as the Upton ranch and as far east as the McClellan's place. Didn't see or find a thing. It was getting dark, so we didn't search the north east side of town."

"You boys need to cover it tomorrow," the sheriff said.

Roger nodded.

"Martin, where did you and Clem search?"

"We covered this side of the Spiny River. Didn't think we would find much; the banks are pretty much open space, no real place to hide out."

"Sheriff," Travis spoke up, "are there any rocky places around, with caves where someone could hide in or abandoned shacks?"

"Well, there are a few caves around the McClellan's place, but we searched them; they ain't well hid. And we searched any abandoned shacks and some old mine shafts."

"I knowed where he could be."

Fury almost jumped when she heard the drunken voice speak out from behind her. She looked over her shoulder to see a withered old man standing in the cell with his gnarled hands wrapped around the bars.

"Geez, mister," Fury said, "if you're gonna talk, don't do it in my direction. You smell like a whiskey still."

The old man chuckled. "I'd could find him, if'n I wanted to, or if'n someone give me a bottle." He smiled a broad toothless grin.

"Ike," the sheriff bellowed, "shut up and sit down."

The old man muttered and shuffled back to his cot. "No one listens to an old man."

But someone was listening. Fury's years of training told her not to ignore any information, and she planned to find out what the drunk could tell her. She needed a plan.

The men plodded along, revisiting the same topics and answering the same question with numerous interruptions by Ike. Fury would have relished the sight of Travis rubbing his face if she weren't trying to come up with a plan to talk to the old man —alone.

"Ranger, you've been mighty quiet; you got anything to add?"

"I think we all know where we want to search, but I believe we should be prepared to camp out. Coming back to town every evening and going out again in the morning wastes a lot of valuable time," Travis answered.

Everyone agreed until Clem spoke up. "I can't do that, Ranger, I got to go home in the morning and help the wife with the livestock. She is expecting our first any time now, and she can't do all the work by herself."

"I agree with Clem," said Sam. "I need to be here in the evening, to check the store receipts. Can't trust my clerk, he's a good man but can't add a column of numbers to save his life."

"Well, I'm in agreement with the ranger," Alvin added.

"I'm a thinkin' all of ya are crazy. He ain't gonna be where you lookin'," Ike spoke out once again.

The room broke out in rumbles; everyone spoke, but no one listened.

"Ike, you ain't helping none." The sheriff reached into his desk and removed a large ring of keys. He limped to the jail cell and unlocked the door.

"Ike," he said, "I'm letting you out early. Last thing we need in here is another opinion."

"All righty then, Sheriff, I'm a goin'." Ike picked his hat up and a small bundle of his belongings from where they lay on the cot and walked back to the door. He stopped for a minute and looked at the sheriff. "But I'm a tellin' you I knowed where to look."

"Go on, Ike, we don't have time for this."

Ike nodded and shuffled out the door.

The room broke out in a rumble once more.

Fury looked at Travis. He was trapped in an argument with two of the men as the others watched. This was her chance, while he was distracted. She slowly rose to her feet and made her way to the sheriff, who was back in his chair nursing his aching leg.

"Ed," Fury said in a low voice.

"Yeah, Fury?"

"Ed, I'm a gonna head back to the hotel. Ain't feeling all that spry. Want to rest up so I can go with the posse in the morning."

"Yeah, want me to get that ranger fella?"

"No, no," Fury said with a slight crack in her voice. "No need, from the looks of it, he's pretty busy."

Ed glanced at the purple-faced ranger locked into a useless debate. "Poor guy, you go on, Fury, we're gonna need you."

"Thanks, Ed." Fury strolled out the door and into the cool evening air. *Damn I'm good.* "Now, where the hell did he go?" Fury asked herself as she looked up and down the street. *How can an old man move so fast, and where was he going? Dang, Fury, you're losing your senses. You know where he's heading; he's heading for a saloon. He's headed for the Silver Dollar.*

Fury quickened her pace. She passed the dressmaker's. Surely, she would see him soon; the Silver Dollar was a few doors down Main Street. Then she spotted an old man tottering his way down the walkway, rocking back and forth on his bow legs. He stopped in front of the Silver Dollar to panhandle for money.

"Please, mister, could you spare some money for a thirsty man?" Fury heard him ask a man in a black hat.

"Get away from me," the man answered as he walked into the bar.

Fury watched as Ike's eyes scanned for another mark. He walked toward another prospective victim, but Fury interrupted him. "Ike," she called but no response. She scurried up behind him and tapped his shoulder.

Ike turned. "Can I help ya, mister?"

"Ike, I think so, and there's a bottle for you if you do."

Ike's eyes twinkled. "Well, friend, what kin I do fer ya?"

Fury noticed they were getting some attention from the patrons entering the bar. She tugged on Ike's sleeve. "Let's go somewhere and talk."

Ike nodded and followed Fury to the alley next to the saloon. The lights from the saloon were bright enough to illuminate parts of the alley.

"Well, young fella, where's my money so I kin git my bottle?"

"Wait a minute, Ike, I want to give you the money, but first I gotta ask you for your help."

"You want help from old Ike?" Ike tapped his chest with the palm of his hand.

"Sure do."

Fury watched as the old man's expression went from astonishment to pride. "Been a long time since anyone wanted my help."

"Well, I'm asking."

"Say?" Recognition lit up Ike's grey eyes. "Ain't ya one of the fellas from the jail?"

Fury nodded.

"I thought so; guess you're a smart one. You want to hear what old Ike has to say about whereabouts that killer might be a hidin'."

"Yes," Fury added, noting Ike's thinking was clearing. Maybe not as sure of a sign he was sobering up, but his shaking hands were a sure giveaway.

"That's right, Ike, I will get you a bottle if you tell me where you think he might be hiding."

Ike rubbed the back of his neck with his hand. "You know it gives me a lot of satisfaction knowing someone believes me. Most folks don't give us old folks much credit for knowing things. Specially if'n they nip at the bottle a bit." He chuckled.

"I know, Ike, but I'm really in a hurry. Could you please tell me what you know?"

Ike looked into Fury's eyes. For a moment, Fury did not see a bleary eyed drunk. She saw wisdom, sense, and sadness, and she knew he was once a man people respected. Fury wondered what happened to bring him to his current state. Surely, a story lived behind those tired eyes, but she did not have time to hear it. Maybe, she hoped, when all this was behind her, she could come back and find Ike and listen to his story, but now was not the time.

"Crouch down here, mister."

Ike laid his bundle of earthly belongings on the ground; he stretched out a boney finger and drew in the dirt.

Fury watched as he traced a winding line.

"This here is Spiny River."

"The men searched there; they said the land around the river was too open to hide anywhere."

"Yeah, that's what they said." Ike cut his eyes toward Fury and gave her a sly grin. "Be patient, young man." He continued creating his map. "Over here, on the east side, there is a small forest." Ike drew crude trees in the dust. "And beyond these trees, the land gets rocky and the rocks get bigger and bigger as you go. And I'm not saying a little bit rocky but very rocky, too jagged for horses to climb, but a man on foot could make it. He would have to be a good climber, because after a while, the big rocks turn into boulders and then you come up on a rock face, and that rock face gets steep."

"And you think Cutter Dan was able to climb that rock face?" Fury rubbed her chin.

"I didn't say that. Ya young'uns, always in a hurry."

"I'm sorry, Ike, please continue."

Ike smiled at the use of his name. Most people called him old man or drunk. "When you pass the rock face, you gotta be careful, because there is an Indian burial ground." The man added small crosses to his map, showing the location of the burial ground.

"You don't need to go through the burial site, just skirt around it. Most folks wouldn't go near it, afraid they'd get killed. Stay on this side of any warning markers, and eventually, you will find an old mining shack."

Hope lit up Fury's face. "So that's where you are, Cutter. How do you know this for sure, Ike? How do you know about the burial ground and the shack?"

"I weren't always the town drunk, ya know."

Fury could hear the regret in his voice.

"Many years ago, when this town and I were young, I knew a man named Jed Ashland. Old Jed, he was set on finding gold and he thought the Spiny was a good place to search. One day, he was at the river panning for gold, when he heard a ruckus. He followed the noise down river and spotted an Indian boy in the river. The boy was drowning. Jed jumped into the river and saved the boy. Turns out, he was the chief's son. The chief was so grateful to Jed, he said he'd reward him with anything he wanted. Jed thanked the old chief, but he wanted nothing. Well, time passed, and other folks decided to pan the river. Jed got real mad over it. He wanted to find a spot where no one would bother him or jump his claim. So, every day, he searched. One day, he was searching the rock face when he came up on an opening in the rock. It was so narrow, a horse could just go through it without a rider. Jed went through and found the burial ground. He was spotted by some braves and taken to the chief. He sure was glad when he saw the man whose son he'd saved. The chief gave him permission to pass by the sacred ground. Jed knew the river ran close to the burial ground so he took a chance and asked the chief if he could build a shack there. The chief agreed, so Jed built his shack there and started panning. He never did find anything to speak of, died a few years back."

"And you think Cutter Dan is hiding there. How could he even know about the shack?"

"When Jed got older, he began to drink too much." A tinge of self-recrimination crossed Ike's face.

"And then he started talking about the shack and the Indians. Most folks didn't believe him, but some did. The rumors said outlaws used it as a hideout when they needed to lay low fer a while. If'n outlaws knew about the shack, I believe Cutter heard about it, and he's hiding there."

"He might have, but what about the Indians? Wouldn't they kill him?"

Ike shook his head. "The Indians moved on as the town grew,

and some ended up on the reservation. But folks around here, them that knowed there is an Indian burial site, won't go there. They either think its haunted or maybe a stray Indian might show up and kill 'em."

Fury nodded. "I think you might be right, Ike; that would be a perfect hiding place, and I intend to check it out. You have any idea where the opening is in the rock face?"

"Nah, mister, not for sure, but," Ike squinted his eyes as if he was trying to force a memory out of the back of his mind, "seems to me I heared Jed say sumpthin' once about two oak trees growing outa the same stump. I seem to recollect him saying he carved J.A. on one side, but not big soes anyone could see, he did it kinda hidden like. The opening is across from the trees."

A broad smile stretched across Ike's face. "Can I have my money now, mister?"

"Yes, but first I have a couple of other small favors to ask."

"Go ahead, mister."

"First, do not tell anyone about this."

"Why, don't you want the posse to look there?"

"No," Fury answered," I hunt alone."

"All right, I won't tell."

Fury stood then helped the old man to his feet.

As Ike picked up his bundle, Fury's eyes scanned his small, frail frame, and a thought crossed her mind. "Good. Ike, what do you carry in that bundle?"

"Not much." Ike shrugged. "I ain't got much. Just some clothes and this and that things."

"Ike, I want to buy your clothes. Sell them to me, and you will have enough money for two bottles. But, Ike, I would like you to consider buying yourself a decent meal and a nice bed in the hotel."

Ike laughed. "I ain't got much use for good food and soft beds, but you got a deal, mister. I'll sell you my clothes."

A little later, she was on her way back to the hotel. *Damn, I wish these folks would get a move on. I gotta get back to the hotel before Travis.*

Fury clutched the wad of clothes in her hands as she weaved her way through the pedestrians, making her way to the hotel. She pushed through the heavy wooden doors of the Grand Hotel. Her pace slowed so as not to draw the attention of Mr. Peterson, who was perched behind the desk. Luckily, he was busy with other travelers and she slipped by unnoticed. Fury shuffled up the stairs and down the hall to her room.

She paused and took a deep breath. Her heartbeat bobbed in her throat as she turned the doorknob. *Good, no Travis.* She lit the lamp on the nightstand and yanked open the last drawer of the small dresser, shoving Ike's clothes into their hiding place, then she stripped off her clothes, got in bed, and blew out the lamp. She lay in the bed, trying to sleep, her ears perked to the sound of the turning doorknob.

He's here. Fury slammed her eyes shut and did her best to fake sleep.

TRAVIS OPENED THE DOOR. He was surprised to hear a low mumble come from the bed and the sound of rustling bedsheets.

So, Belle, you're here—sleeping. I don't buy this for a minute. I know you're up to something, but what?

Travis fumbled his way across the room to the green chair by the window. He lit a small candle. Once again, he heard a murmur from the bed as the occupant turned away from the light.

All right, Belle, I'll play your game. I know you're not asleep. Whatever you are planning, young lady, it doesn't include you hunting Cutter. I can promise you that.

Travis pulled off his boots and tugged his shirt out of his pants. He settled into the chair and gazed at the feminine form lying in the bed. He imagined himself lying next to her, cradling her in his arms, feeling her warm, soft skin against his, hearing her gentle sighs. He dreamed of kissing her luscious lips and tenderly loving her with his body. *Stop torturing yourself, son.*

Travis shifted in his chair, trying to control his arousal. *She's yours, it will happen soon enough. Got to get Cutter and get her home. Then I'll marry that girl. Well, if she don't shoot me first.* He blew out the candle, closed his eyes, and dreamed of Belle.

The rustle of movement drew Travis from an uneasy sleep. Although, sleeping in a chair almost guaranteed an ill night's sleep, it was not the cause of his restless slumber. He focused his eyes on the cause of his fatigue, the slip of a girl standing by the bed buttoning her shirt.

Travis sat up and smiled, noticing the quilt from the bed spread over his lap. "Well, now," he said, "looks like someone doesn't hate me as much as she pretends to."

Belle whipped around to face him. "Don't flatter yourself; I would give a dog a bone if he was hungry."

"Ouch!" Travis said as he placed his hand over his chest. "Bull's eye, right to the heart." He chuckled, rose to his feet, and tossed the quilt onto the bed. Travis crossed his arms over his chest and walked to where Belle stood. "I see you helped yourself to the contents of my saddle bags."

"They're my clothes, you big oaf, and you stole them. I got what is rightfully mine."

"Oh, you did, did you? And just what do you think you're doing?"

"I'm getting dressed, and if you were any kind of a gentleman, you would turn around." Belle proceeded to yank up her pants.

"Pants," Travis demanded and held out his hand.

"You can't be serious."

"I can't? Try me, Belle." He saw the flare of anger in her eyes as she tightened her lips.

Belle pulled off her pants and threw them at him. "Travis, you can't keep me a prisoner. I have a right to go where I please."

"Uh huh. Shirt."

Belle growled, "Fine." She lobbed the garment toward him, slapping him in the face.

"Funny." Travis attempted to sound stern, but there was a speck of amusement in his voice.

Belle plopped down on the bed. She sat looking at the floor, her foot tapping at an angry pace.

"Belle, look at me."

His request went unanswered.

"Belle, I don't have time for one of your tantrums. Now, look at me."

Belle's eyes shot up to meet his gaze. Defiance sprang from her eyes.

"I know you are mad at me, but I mean to keep you safe and get you home."

"I ain't your responsibility," Belle sniped.

Travis bent down to her eye level. He took her chin in his hand. "You are my responsibility, professionally, and," he kissed the tip her nose, "personally."

He read the confusion on her face. "Yes, Belle—personally."

"What does that mean?" Belle asked. "Do you mean you own me?"

"No, Belle, I don't own you, but you are mine because you belong to my heart."

"I-I belong to your heart?" A quivering thrill zapped through her body. Oh, what he did to her when he spoke sweet words. Maybe she did belong to his heart, and he, she did not want to admit it, belonged to hers.

"You think on it while I'm gone."

"And while you're gone, am I supposed to sit here and starve?"

"No, Belle, I'm leaving Mr. Peterson instructions to leave your meals at the door until I return."

"And how long is that supposed to be?"

"Belle, you know how this works. If we don't find him, we will come back in three days to get more supplies."

"Three days, are you crazy? You expect me to stay here for three days, in nothing but my—my underthings? What if something happens? What if I need something?"

"Leave Mr. Peterson a note on the door; he will get you what you need."

"Oh yeah, well, what if, what if I need…to go?"

"Go where?"

"Oh, Travis, you can't possibly be that dumb, what if I have *to go*, you know, personal needs."

Travis laughed. "I suppose I'll have to get you a chamber pot."

"For three days!"

"Don't worry; Mr. Peterson can take care of that too."

"What!"

"Sorry, Belle." Travis stooped down and kissed her pouting lips. "Now be a good girl, Belle."

He turned and walked out the door, leaving her with her mouth hanging open.

When the sound of Travis' footsteps faded, a conquering smile crossed Belle's face. "I did it! I beat you, Ranger Travis Parker!" She danced around the room.

Don't get so cocky; you're not free yet. How long should I wait? Damn, why did he get a room in the back of the hotel? I can't watch the road to see the posse leave. I'll have to guess. He needs to get his horse and meet up with the posse. What else would he have to do? Maybe eat breakfast and get supplies, Oh, I don't know. I know how long it would take me; that's another good reason to go at it alone, I don't have to wait on others.

Belle heard a soft rap on her door, followed by quick footsteps.

"What the hell?"

She cracked the door open and peered out. No one. Her eyes searched the long hallway but saw nothing. She shrugged. The door creaked as she began to close it, but she stopped when she glanced down and spied a tray on the floor, covered with a small gingham cloth.

Peterson, with Travis' damn breakfast tray. Belle rolled her eyes. *Smells good. Might as well eat before I leave.*

Belle picked up the tray and carried it to the small table by the window. She sat in the overstuffed chair and removed the cloth covering the food. She inhaled the pleasant aroma of eggs, bacon, biscuits, and wonderful coffee.

The welcoming warmth of the food and the homey smell of fresh coffee stirred memories of homecooked meals her mother prepared with love. She missed feeling loved and the peace that came from knowing someone cared for her. Other people cooked for her, but she never felt loved by them. She missed feeling loved and cared for by someone. But now there was no one, well, there was Travis. He wanted to take care of her, even this meal was him caring for her. Travis, he made her feel safe, secure, and loved, at least when he was not making her furious. But how did she feel about him? Maybe she cared about him. Maybe she even loved him. For a moment, she entertained the thought of her and Travis together. A serene happiness rested in her at the thought of being with him, but it was short lived as the reality of her life came back into focus. A life with Travis could never be, and she refused to let him know her feelings for him.

Stop dreaming about Travis and get Cutter, and then you can find Mama and Papa's murderers.

"Ugh," Belle recoiled at the smell of the clothes she held in her hands. "Stop being a ninny and put them on; focus on the job." Belle winced as the rancid shirt touched her skin.

"Come on now; you can do this," she ordered herself, cringing as she jammed her arms through the sleeves of the whiskey and sweat stained jacket.

The pants were a might big, but not so much so to cause worry about them falling. Luckily, Travis had left her boots.

Belle picked up her saddle bags and opened the door. She almost tripped over a chamber pot sitting on the floor by her room. She shook her head and stepped over the offensive item and made her way down the hallway.

"Mr. Fury."

Fury sighed. She had hoped she would make it past the desk without being noticed.

"Yes, Peterson, what do you want?"

"I-I'm sorry, Mr. Fury, sir, but that ranger said you were sick, and I was to watch out for you. You're not going to the doctor, are you? I can send for him to come here if you wish."

"No, no. I'm fine. Feeling much better, so you don't have to worry about me."

"Oh, well, that's fine, Mr. Fury. So glad you are well."

Fury nodded and turned to go out the door.

"Oh, Mr. Fury."

"Yes," Fury answered through tight lips.

"May I ask where you are going? Just in case the ranger or someone wants to find you."

"My business is my business; ain't no one needing to know where I am." Fury walked out, feeling in charge of herself once more.

Swift and Max were glad to get out of the livery, and after one quick stop for a few supplies, the trio were on their way to hunt down their prey.

CHAPTER 12

*T*he warmth of the sun and the gentle breeze should have lifted her spirits, but something was off, something was missing. Where was the adrenaline that fueled her hyper focus and energy for the hunt? Her senses were clouded, not sharp. *Come on, Fury, get yourself together; where is your mind?*

Fury would not admit it, even to herself, but she knew exactly where her mind was, and it wasn't fully on finding her bounty— the image of a tall, handsome ranger was invading her thoughts. *Damn it, I miss the ass of a man. How did I let this happen? How did I let him get to me?*

She needed to bury these thoughts, these feelings, these distractions. Distractions led to mistakes, and mistakes can get you killed. *Travis, I gotta get you out of my mind, but how?*

Her troubles vanished when she heard running water. "The Spiny." Fury rode to the edge of the river.

"Whoa, Swift." She dismounted. "Might as well take a short break here," she said to her companions, "don't have any idea how long we will be riding today."

Fury sat on a large rock by the river. The water glided over a smattering of rocks, filling the surroundings with a hypnotic babbling echo. The Spiny was not as wide as most rivers. Fury pondered why it was even considered a river, but calling it a stream or a creek did not seem to fit. River or not, it was serene, a place perfect for reflection or a beautiful place for lovers to meet.

Her imagination snapped to an image of Travis, but she caught herself before she was lost in a dream. *None of that thinking,* she reprimanded herself.

"Max," she said to her friend as he lapped at the cool water of the Spiny. "How about something to eat?"

The dog's ears perked up at the word 'eat'.

"Jerky, it is." Fury went over to where Swift munched on a patch of grass.

"Sorry to interrupt you, girl, but this will only take a minute." She patted the horse's side and then pulled some jerky from her saddle bag.

"Max," she said to the dog who trotted up beside her. "Wait, Max, you know how this works; you gotta earn it." Fury smiled; she missed training Max.

"All right, boy, let's start easy. Sit." She accompanied the command with a hand signal.

Max's quick, obedient reply rewarded him with a small piece of jerky.

"Good boy!" Fury patted his head.

"Lay." Again, Max obeyed and earned another morsel of jerky.

Fury ran through a few more basic commands, then she decided to try a difficult task. This trick required more preparation, and Fury warned herself not to waste time, but something in her spurred her to continue.

She found a small sapling. "This might work." She took off her jacket and wrapped it around the tree. She stepped back and studied the figure. Fury cocked her head, studying her creation, then removed her hat and placed it on the top of the sapling. Again, she studied her work.

"Well, it kinda looks like a person. Now for the hard part." Fury drew her gun from her holster. She hated removing the comfort of her gun and using it as part of Max's training, but this element required reality. Fury used a small segment of rope she found in her saddle bag and tied her gun to a sturdy branch of the tree.

She stepped away from the make-believe bad guy and looked at Max. For this trick, there would be no word command. The hand gesture would be subtle, and Fury hoped Max could remember his training; it had been a long time since they'd practiced. Max's eyes fixed on Fury, a good sign that he was waiting for her orders. But Fury knew she needed to lock on to Max's eyes with one quick glance. It may be all the time she would get, so it had to work. Her eyes met the dog's, and Fury splayed out the fingers of her right hand, a simple gesture, one most people would not notice.

Max transformed. The happy go lucky countenance of a dopey dog was gone, and in its place, a snarling wild thing. Max growled and bared his teeth; he drew up his hackles and pounced on the tree man, dislodging the gun from his branch appendage.

The dog continued to ravage the tree's fake arm as Fury scooped up the gun.

"Max, heel," Fury commanded.

Max returned to her side and returned to his old self. Fury tossed him the last bit of jerky, showering him with praise. She made a quick meal of a few pieces of jerky and then mounted Swift. Her eyes scrutinized the area.

"East, Ike said head east." Fury tapped Swift with the heel of her boots and headed east, with Max following close behind.

"So, exactly why are we headed back to town? I thought we were supposed to stay the night then meet up with the rest of the posse tomorrow," Zeke asked the two men with him.

"Zeke, this is the second time we've searched the riverbank, and me and Sam gotta go back. I gotta go home and check on the wife, and Sam here's got a business to check," Clem explained to the new member of the group.

"But what about the other end of the riverbank? We ain't checked there."

"You're welcome to go check it out, if'n you want," Clem added, "but we're headed home."

"Hey, lookie there," Sam motioned to a figure at the opposite end of the bank.

"Ain't that that Fury fella?" Sam asked.

"Yep, looks like him anyhow. And that looks like his horse and dog. What you figure he's doing?"

"I reckon he's searching for Cutter. Ain't much use in searching there with the rocks and the Indian burial site folks say is thereabouts," Clem added.

"Indian burial site?" Zeke asked.

"Yep, some folks say it's haunted; others say you'll get killed if an Indian finds you there. Hey, you want to do more looking, Zeke, why don't you go join Fury?"

"Nah." Zeke's voice quivered. "I don't think that Fury fella likes company. He's supposed to be a great bounty hunter. I say let him look by himself. I'm heading up to where the others are and help with the search there."

"All right, you do that, Zeke. We're headed home; we'll meet up with the rest of you when we are done with our business."

"This is the most unorganized, chaotic group of yokels I've ever seen in a posse," Travis muttered under his breath. He rubbed his forehead, hoping to squelch the pounding anvil in his head. *Calm down; you gotta take control of yourself and this band of idiots.*

"Listen up!" The rumbling debates concerning the search stifled at Travis' command.

A group of empty, confused eyes fixed on the tall ranger.

"Here is what we will do." Within minutes, Travis had divided up the men and assigned them to search areas. "All right men, let's get going; remember we meet up here tomorrow and—

"Rider coming," Rodger shouted.

The group focused on the rider.

"Whoa," Zeke ordered his horse.

"Has Cutter been found?" Travis asked.

"Nah, not yet."

"Then why are you here? Is there a problem?"

"No, Clem and Sam didn't want to search the river anymore. They said they needed to attend to some business at home. I wanted to search more, so I came here to join the rest of the posse."

"Damn them," Travis fumed, "I thought we'd settled that argument. Damn it. Zeke, I need you and a volunteer to go back and finish searching that riverbank."

"No need, Ranger; we saw that bounty hunter, Fury, there. Looks like he's searching the river. And we figured he wanted to work alone so—

"What! You saw Fury, oh hell, never mind. Rodger, you're in charge here; I'm going to the river."

Travis bumped Chief's sides and was gone before anyone could ask any questions.

"Great," Fury said, "it's starting to rain."

She pulled a rain slicker from her saddle bag and hoped the

rain would slack off. She'd spent most of the day wandering through the thick woods, hoping she would not get lost and wishing she had a compass. Finally, the woods thinned, and the ground grew rocky. She knew she was on the right track.

"Damn rain, it's gonna slow us down." Fury bowed her head to keep the driving rain from slapping her face and blinding her eyes.

The rocky path grew into jagged stones and boulders. Fury dismounted, leading Swift through the treacherous stones. She tripped and landed face down in the mud. She rose to her knees and wiped the mud from her face. "Well, at least it's just mud and not a rock in my skull."

She grabbed at Swift's lead and rose to her feet. Her vision cleared. "The rock face. Swift, Max, we found it!"

Like a blind man making his way through an unknown room, Fury felt her way along the rock face. Their movements along it were slow and tedious; a wrong step or a slip on wet stone could prove disastrous. The rain pelting her face seemed to slack off, but Fury still heard the pounding downpour. She realized she'd found shelter, a shelf of rock to huddle beneath protected from the driving rain. Wiping her eyes with the back of her hand, her sight focused. "Fury, your luck is changing; you found shelter."

The small haven supplied by the overhang was shallow and provided minimum cover. Max and Fury crouched down but only half of Swift's body fit in the limited space.

"Sorry, Swift girl, but at least you're half dry."

TRAVIS GRILLED Peterson for details concerning Fury's whereabouts. He knew she was seen at the river, but he had no clue where along the river she was headed.

"So, you did see Fury leave?"

"Ranger, I told you he left here this morning, not too long after you rode out with the posse."

"Didn't you know he was too sick to leave?"

"Ranger," the hotel clerk sighed," Fury is a grown man. I think he knows if he is too ill to leave his room."

"You don't know Fury like I do," Travis mumbled.

"What?"

"Never mind, thank you, Mr. Peterson." Travis turned to leave.

"Wait a minute." Travis turned back to the clerk. "What was he wearing?"

"Oh, those awful clothes." Peterson's face scrunched.

"What about his clothes?"

"They were not the clothes he usually wears. They were dirty and smelled of whiskey, not that I think Fury was drunk, but he sure smelled like he'd dumped a bottle on himself."

"Whiskey?" Travis rubbed his chin." Tell me. Mr. Peterson, is there anyone in town who, um, well, who drinks too much, someone like a town drunk."

"Yes, a few, but the worst by far would be old Ike."

"Ike?"

"I don't know his last name. I just know him by Ike. He's usually at the Silver Dollar if he's not sleeping it off in an alley."

"What does this Ike look like?"

"Old man, kinda frail, balding, grey beard stubble."

"Thanks," Travis said as he took off to find Ike.

A few minutes later, he found him. "You Ike?" Travis asked the old man standing at the bar.

"Who's askin'?" The old man turned to look Travis in the eye.

"He's Ike," bellowed the bartender, "why don't you run him out of here? He keeps trying to get a free drink from me."

Travis recognized the old man from the jail.

"I ain't hurtin' no one," Ike pleaded.

"Ike, I ain't here to run you in. I need your help."

"My help?" The old man's tone rang with disbelief. "Last night, someone wanted my help, and now you do. Most folk don't even notice me." He gave Travis a toothless grin.

"Come, let's sit down and talk." The last thing Travis wanted to do was waste time, but talking to Ike might help him find Fury.

"Ike, the person you talked to last night, was his name Fury?"

"My throat's kinda dry; I think a bit of a drink might help."

Travis motioned to the bartender. "A glass of whiskey for Ike here."

"A bottle will do me better." Ike's eyes brightened.

"Ike, I think the last thing you need is another bottle of booze."

Ike hung his head.

Travis did not mean to shame the poor man. In fact, he wanted to help him, but right now there was no time; he needed to find Fury and find her fast.

"I'm sorry, Ike, that was uncalled for. I'm concerned for my friend, and I'm taking my frustration out on you."

"No one has apologized to me in a long time. Thank you, son. How can I help you?"

"Did you talk to Fury last night?"

"Fury? Well, I can't recollect his name, but he was the fella that sat by my cell at that meeting in the sheriff's office."

"Ike, I need to know what you talked about. It's very important; Fury's life could be at stake."

Ike pondered his words. He had promised not to tell, but he didn't want anyone's life in his hands. He believed the ranger was sincere. "I'll tell you, but you gotta keep Fury from shooting me if'n he finds out I told."

"Don't worry; I'll take care of Fury."

"All right, young fella, I'll tell ya about Jeb and his shack."

Ike tried to tell the entire story, but Travis did his best to keep him to the highlights.

"Thank you, Ike." Travis added, "Here." He pulled some money from his pocket and handed it to Ike. "Spend this on some food or a room."

"That's what that Fury fella said when he gave me money."

She would. Travis smiled.

"Oh, and, Ike, I just want to know, did you give him some clothes?"

Ike nodded.

"Thought so."

Travis mounted Chief and headed for the river. Now, he was not hunting blind; he knew where she was headed and prayed he would not run into trouble finding her. He scowled when he saw the rainclouds forming. *Damn rain, it will wash away her tracks and slow me down.*

"Stop it, Max."

Fury woke to Max licking her face as usual.

"All right, all right, I'm awake."

Fury stretched and groaned as her sore body felt the dent of every rock and rough spot she slept on. She rubbed her eyes. The rain had cleared and was replaced by the rising sun warming her damp, cold body.

"Good, no more rain. Let's eat something and get going. I gotta find that passage today."

Fury led Swift thorough the rocky ground as Max ran a few feet ahead of them. Her head turned from side to side as she searched for the marked oak trees and kept an eye on her footing. Success as a bounty hunter depended on patience, but she was weary of the slow pace and lack of progress.

Get a grip, Fury, this isn't different than any other bounty hunt. Haste can get you killed. Hank's words rang in her ears. But this really was not like any other bounty hunt. This bounty was the most important of her life and the tedium bred frustration. She needed to stop, to regroup, to get a hold of herself before she made a deadly mistake.

Fury leaned on a boulder. She removed her hat and wiped the beads of sweat from her forehead with the sleeve of her coat. "Ew!" The smell of the rancid coat filled her nostrils and made her nauseous. "Just what I needed," Fury huffed.

How long have I been searching?

Fury raised her gaze. The sun was high, almost noon, she reckoned.

She downed a gulp of water from her canteen then poured some in her hat, giving the animals a drink. She returned the cool wet hat to her head and scanned the area. There were spots of grass and small clumps of trees, but the rocky terrain was still too treacherous to risk riding Swift.

"Well, Swift," Fury stroked the horse's nose, "we best get back at it. Where's Max?"

Fury surveyed her surroundings for her wayward dog.

"Damn, Max, you picked a fine time to wander off."

Max always came back after he went off on his dog adventures, but she wanted him close; she might need his tracking skills.

"Max," Fury called out, trying not to be too loud. Last thing she needed was for her bounty to hear her. She walked a few steps.

"Max, you dope, where are you?" Fury growled.

"Umph!" Fury hit the ground. Max jumped and danced around her. "Max," Fury scolded, "this is not the time to play."

But Max was caught up in his happy dog moment. He danced a doggy jig and took off running once more.

"Oh, come on, Max. I don't have time for this."

Fury sprinted after him. Of all the complicated commands that Max knew, 'come' was the one he selectively obeyed. Every now and then, she would catch sight of him as he darted in and out of the trees. Fury stopped and leaned against a tree, panting, trying to get her breath.

"All right, Max," she puffed. "I guess we'll go on without you, and you will have to find us."

Max stuck his head out from behind a tree a few feet from her.

"No, Max, I ain't biting. I gotta go find that double oak tree." Fury's eyes fixed on a tree a few feet from where Max stood. "H-holy crap."

"Nah, it can't be." She walked toward Max. "It can't be." She quickened her pace. Fury stood before the tree and stretched her hand out. She slid her hand down the rough bark and to the junction of both trees. "Two oak trees coming out of one stump."

Fury circled the trees, searching, searching. "There," she jumped and pointed up the bark, "there they are. J. A., Jed Ashland's initials. Max, you old rascal, I know you didn't intend to, but all your silly playing led us right where we want to be. I gotta go get Swift, then we can search for the opening in the rock face."

Fury led Swift through the rocks, and they found Max lying next to the double oak tree. "Well, now you want to lie around. Did all that playing tire you out?" Fury smiled at the dog as he thumped his tail against the ground. "Come on, Max, we got to find that entrance."

Max rose from his comfortable repose, his tongue curled as he lowered his front paw and jutted his back side up in a satisfying dog stretch.

Some brush and a few scrubby trees failed to hide the opening in the rock face, and in a matter of moments, Fury was leading Swift and Max through the narrow entrance to the other side.

I'm getting closer to Cutter. I feel it.

TIME'S A WASTIN', *damn rain slowed me way down, washed away her tracks.*

"Whoa, Chief." Travis took off his hat and wiped the sweat from his brow with the back of his sleeve. He rubbed the back of his neck. "Chief, we gotta find her soon." He ran his fingers through his dark hair and took a long swig of water from his canteen. "Boy, it's hot today."

He dismounted and scanned the area with tired eyes. "I'm sure we are in the right place; it's pretty rocky here. I've got to find that damn tree. Come on, Chief." Travis grabbed his horse's reins. "Time for me to walk, boy, and you to follow."

THE SUN WARMED Fury's face as she emerged from the passage. She searched the area, looking for any sight of the Indian burial ground. She saw none.

"Come on," she said to her companions. "I hope Ike wasn't full of sh—" Fury stopped when she came across the first warning marker that signaled the Indian burial ground. Her heart fluttered as she covered her chest with her hand.

"It's here; it's really here. What did Ike say? Oh, I remember, you don't have to go into the burial ground, just skirt the edge and you will come up on a small patch of trees. You can see the shack from there."

But how far was it from the burial ground to the grove of trees? She'd forgotten to ask Ike.

All right, Fury, you gotta be careful; you are getting close to Jeb's shack, which means you are getting close to Cutter Dan. Too bad she didn't know how close.

CHAPTER 13

*D*an woke with the demon pounding in his head. Last night's rain had cleared, but a storm still raged in his mind. The hunger returned, and Dan tried to ignore the need that filled him.

"Don't bother me," Dan screamed at the voice within. "I ain't going anywhere; they'll find me and hang me."

He banged his fists into his temples, trying to dislodge the urge to kill, but not for anyone's well-being but his own. Dan tried to distract himself. He admired his treasures once more, but that only increased his desire to obtain another trinket.

"I gotta think, gotta make plans. How long do I hole up here? The plan is to go to Mexico, but when? I can't go now. There's a posse looking for me. Damn, why did you want to go kill that girl in Langston?" he railed at his demon.

Restlessness overtook him as his cravings grew.

"I gotta get out. Need food. I gotta go hunt. Ain't going to town for supplies, just gonna hunt, maybe get a deer," Dan lied to himself.

FURY LEFT Swift in the meadow at the edge of the woods and she went ahead with Max. They hid behind a clump of trees and watched the shack.

"Look, Max, a horse." Fury pointed at the animal grazing a few feet from the shack. "He's gotta be there; that's gotta be his horse."

Max raised his paw and dragged it across Fury's arm and whimpered.

"Quiet, Max, and be still; we can't play now." She misread his warning.

Max's whimper became a growl. His body recoiled, ready to leap at an unknown threat.

Then Fury heard a gunshot. Her ears filled with the piercing scream of a wounded animal as she turned her head to Max. A searing pain dug into her skull as bright lights exploded before her eyes, then her world went black.

∾

"KILL HIM LATER," Dan said as he plopped the unconscious intruder in the chair. "Gotta find out how he found me and if anyone else knows where I am. Then I can kill him."

Dan crossed the intruder's arms across his chest then began to bind them at the wrists. He studied the face of the unconscious man. The intruder had lost his hat when Dan clubbed him with a branch, but this was the first time he truly looked at his face.

Sweat and blood covered hair clung to the face in front of him. His hair reached just past the chin, the features delicate.

I wonder? Nah, couldn't be.

Dan finished binding the intruder's hands. His curiosity led him to reach under his captive's coat and feel the shape of his body. He released a guttural laugh. Dan relished the tingling surge of adrenaline at his discovery that the intruder was a woman.

"Now, they're sending little girls after me."

The demon reveled at the discovery. *Kill her, kill her now!*

"No, can't do that now, gotta know if anyone else knows, then kill her."

TRAVIS FOUND SWIFT IN A MEADOW. Finding the two oaks and the opening in the rock face proved aggravating as Travis swore he'd passed the tree three or four times before he recognized it. Travis cursed himself, knowing if he could control his feelings, he would have found it sooner. Adding to his anxiety was the muffled sound of a gunshot he had heard as he passed through the opening in the rock face. What direction did it come from? Did he really hear anything? *Travis, you can't help her if you panic.* But what could he do? He loved her, and his desperation clouded his mind.

"Stay here with Swift, Chief." Travis spotted Fury's trail and followed. It led him to a clump of trees. He could see the shack from where he stood, but seeing Fury's hat on the ground made his heart sink.

He picked it up. "Blood! Belle's blood!" The air seemed too thin as a thickness developed in his throat and a cold, dark dread spiraled into the pit of his stomach. He dropped her hat then wiped the sweat that erupted on his forehead with the back of his hand. "Come on, Travis, get a grip; you can't help her like this."

The sound of rustling brush reached his ears. Travis drew his gun and spun in the direction of the sound.

"It's you," he sighed and re-holstered his gun.

Max limped toward him, saliva dripping from his panting tongue.

Travis bent down and patted the dog, hoping to calm the poor animal.

"Good boy, Max." He ran his hands along the dog's body. Max

whimpered when he touched his right side. Travis drew his hand up—*blood.*

Damn, you're shot. You gotta hang on, Max; we gotta save Belle.

∼

A STINGING PAIN ignited the side of Fury's face, drawing her out of the darkness. As her eyes focused, the slamming pain in her head intensified. She heard herself moan.

"Girl!"

Another burning pain met the other side of her face. Someone had slapped her.

"Wake up, you bitch!"

Fury's eyes fluttered and her vision cleared. Nausea settled in her gut as the monster of a man came into view. "Cutter Dan," she mumbled.

"How'd you find me?" Dan snarled.

Fury fought to ignore her pain and fear. She needed to keep her wits.

Dan walked across to her and yanked the hair on the top of her head, raising her face to meet his. A blinding light crossed Fury's vision as the pain in her head reignited. The smell of his hot, moist animal breath on her face made her want to vomit.

"You heared me, gal, how'd you find me?" Dan jerked on the hair clasped in his thick hand and shook her head once more.

"I ain't a girl, you hideous, rancid breath monster." Through the pain and fear, Fury's defiant temper still managed to surface. She braced herself for another stinging blow, but none came.

Dan's crazed eyes danced as he chuckled. "I like them sassy; makes killin' 'em exciting." He jerked back on Fury's hair, making her head swing backward, then he released his grip.

"Oh, I knowed you're a girl. Ain't no boy or man feels like a woman."

His lust sent a creeping cold down her spine, spreading its chill throughout her body. *Did he touch me? What did that pig do to me while I was out? I'm gonna kill this bastard.*

"I know you're thinking how to kill me, but forgit it; you ain't getting out of here. The only reason you are still alive is so I can find out how you found me and who else knows I'm here."

"I don't know how anyone so stupid could not have been caught yet. You tell me you're planning to kill me if I tell you how I found you, or if anyone else knows your whereabouts, so it's to my advantage to keep quiet." *Damn it, Fury! Think. You just gave him a reason to kill you.*

DAN TROMPED UP TO HER. He leaned down, his face close to hers once more. "Well, I guess then I need to go ahead and kill you." His thick hands wrapped around her throat. He squeezed, gradually tightening his grip. She strained to breathe.

I like to see their pleading eyes. I love the terror. The demon spoke to Dan.

Cutter bent down until he was eye to eye with Fury. Her gaze locked onto the dark void of his eyes, and she knew she looked straight into death. The darkness began to overtake her as she felt her life draining from her.

"Cutter Dan!"

Dan quickly released his grip.

Fury sucked precious air into her lungs and began to cough.

"Who the hell came with you? How many men are out there? Answer me?" Cutter raised his hand once more to strike Fury.

Fury winced in anticipation of the blow, but Dan stopped when he heard his name called once more.

"Dan, come on out. You are surrounded. You ain't got a chance!"

Travis?

Hope sprung in Fury when she heard Travis' voice, but it quickly turned to fear, not for herself, but for the man she loved.

Dan stormed toward the window. He leaned against the wall to avoid being shot. "Who the hell are you?"

"I'm Ranger Parker. Come on out, Dan."

TRAVIS' hand shook. He hoped he'd made the right decision by calling out Dan. Nothing but open space was between him and Dan, so there was no way to rush in on the cabin. He didn't know if Fury was in the shack, or if she was still alive. *God, please, let her be alive.*

"You and your men need to back off," Dan's voice boomed. "I got me a hostage."

She's alive! Think, Travis, what's your next move? Travis contemplated his options. Never had he questioned his decisions, but never had he loved someone like he loved his Belle. The cabin door swung open and there stood Belle, her hands tied at the wrist. *She's all right. But that damn bastard hurt her.*

Travis steeled himself to ignore Belle's beaten face. He watched as she stumbled coming out of the cabin. Cutter Dan stood behind her with a gun in his hand.

"Hey, you, lawman, you know this fella, or should I say girl?"

Damn, Cutter knows her secret.

"Give it up, Dan. If you hurt your hostage, I guarantee you will die." Travis could hear the despair in his own voice. He scrubbed his hand over his face.

"Max, you got any ideas. Max?" Travis looked over to where he thought Max sat. "You sure picked a good time to wander off."

"What do you want?" Travis asked, hoping to stall for time.

"What do you think I want? I want to get out of here. I want to get to my horse and leave with my hostage."

⁓

FURY'S MIND GALLOPED. *Think, think, oh if I didn't have this pounding in my head.* "It ain't happening, Dan." Fury's voice cracked.

Dan pulled on the back of her hair. His mouth was next to her ear. "Shut up, gal. Dan and you are gonna have a good time together." His thick, slimy tongue dragged along the side of her face. Her stomach clenched. "Well, until I gotta kill you." He released her hair.

Fury shook her head, trying to fight the pain. It was only a quick glance. Were her eyes fooling her? Was that Max she saw peering from the woods? *Oh, please be Max, please be Max.*

She took a deep breath to steady herself for what she hoped to come.

Fury raised her bound hand. Then she spread her finger out, hoping Max could see and remember. *Max, where are you. Come on; I need your help.*

"What the hell?" she heard Dan's pathetic screech as he fell to the ground.

Fury watched the screaming man. Max clenched to his wrist, swinging, twisting, and ripping at the hand that held the gun. The gun flew to the ground, just out of Fury's grasp. Crawling, she tried to get to the weapon. Once again, she heard the pained cry of an animal.

Dan flung the dog off his arm and got to the gun before Fury. He aimed the gun at her.

A shot rang out, and Dan crumpled to the ground.

Belle slid down into the dirt.

"Belle, honey, are you all right?" Someone was holding her, cradling her in strong arms. She opened her eyes to a blur.

"Belle, please, be all right, say something."

Her sight cleared. "Travis."

"Yes, it's me."

The strong arms that cradled her now pulled her close to his chest. "Thank God, you're all right." He gently swept the matted hair from her face and brushed his lips against hers.

Her eyes widened. "Cutter?"

"He's dead. I gotta get you to a doc." Travis lifted her into his arms. He walked toward Dan's horse.

A faint whimper reached Belle's ears. "Max? Where is he?" she pleaded.

"Honey, I'm worried about you, I need to get you to a doctor."

"No. Please, Travis. I can't leave Max."

"I'll come back for him," Travis lied, knowing the dog would not survive.

"No, Travis." Tears streamed down Belle's face. "He saved me, Travis, please." Her voice hitched. "He was the last gift my parents gave me."

Travis stopped. Everything in him knew he should ignore her, but he could not bear to see her in this state. "All right, darlin'," he said as he carried her to where the dog lay in the dirt."

Max's breathing was labored.

Travis gently placed Belle down next to her dog. "It's all right, boy." Belle cried and petted his head.

Max lifted his head and whined.

"Shh, shh, shh, Max, it's all right. I'm here." Belle looked at Travis, who was crouched beside her. "He will be all right, won't he, Travis?"

Travis sighed, "I don't know, darlin'. He's lost a lot of blood, but right now, I need to get you to town."

"And Max, too?" Belle implored.

"And Max, too," Travis conceded.

And soon, they were on their way. "Come on, you loping old nag." Travis kicked Cutter's old horse as he galloped through the woods. He was relieved to see the trees disappear as the meadow opened up to him. There, not too far from him, grazed Chief and Swift.

Travis whistled. Chief's ears perked up as he lifted his head.

"Belle, honey, you need to stay awake." From Cutter's shack and throughout their ride, he repeated the same words to her as she struggled to stay with him. "Belle, I need you to sit up and hold on to Max. I'm gonna switch us over to Chief."

Travis whistled once more, and Chief trotted over to his side with Swift in tow. He reached up to get Belle but stopped when he heard the sound of pounding hooves. He drew his gun. Knowing he was out gunned, he tried to think fast. His worries vanished when he recognized Rodger and the rest of the posse.

"Hey, Ranger, is that you?"

Travis re-holstered his gun. He saw worry wash over Rodger when he saw Fury.

"What the hell happened?" Rodger asked. "Did he find Cutter?"

"Yes, Cutter's dead, out by his shack. Go through the woods, and you'll find him. I gotta get B-Fury back to town to a doc. One of you men help me with him."

Travis mounted Chief as Rodger got Fury off the old nag.

"You ridin' with this dog too?"

"Yes, he's important to Fury." Travis arranged Fury in front of him then retrieved Max from Rodger. "How'd you know where to find us?"

Roger chuckled. "Seems like old Ike grew a conscience."

"Good," Travis said as he kicked at Chief's sides.

Their pace slowed when Travis led Chief through the rocks. When the path cleared, he mounted his horse, concentrating on keeping Chief at breakneck speed and Belle awake.

$\mathcal{A}$ dust cloud whirled around Chief as they stopped at the doctor's office.

"Hey, you," Travis called out to a young man on the road. "Come here and help me. Take this dog and follow me." Travis ran up the walkway to the small white house where the doctor lived and worked. He kicked the door open.

"What the hell,?" Doc. Johnson leapt from his chair. "You wrecked my door."

"Never mind your door. I'll fix it. I-I need you to help my friend."

Doc looked at the crumpled young man. "Good Lord, what happened to him? Quick, follow me into my office."

Travis trailed the older man into his small office.

"Lay him on the exam table," Doc ordered.

Belle moaned as Travis carefully laid her down.

"Hey, mister?" the youth asked. "Where do you want the dog?"

"What?" Doc looked surprised to see a young man holding a gravely injured animal. "I am not a dang animal doctor. Get him out of here, so I can attend to my human patient."

"No," Travis commanded, "the dog stays. Put him over there." He pointed to a bench next to the wall.

The doctor opened his mouth to protest but pulled back when he saw the determined look on Travis' face. "All right, but you need to put some pressure on that animal's wound. Wrap a bandage around it." He tossed Travis some bandages and turned to the youth. "You can go, son."

"Thanks, Doc."

"Tell me what happened."

"That's Fury."

"The bounty hunter?"

"Yes, he was searching for Cutter Dan."

"I take it he found him."

Travis nodded. "I wasn't there when Dan found Fury, but he musta hit him with something."

"Yep." The old man examined Fury's wound then checked his eyes. "The wounds on the face will heal, but he's got a concussion." He placed a stethoscope in his ears. Before Travis could think to stop him, the doctor unbuttoned Fury's shirt and reached in to listen.

Travis looked at the doctor's face, waiting for a reaction.

"Well, you mind telling me why this girl is pretending to be Fury?"

"She ain't pretending, Doc. She is Fury."

"You don't say." The doctor sounded more amused than surprised.

"Please, Doc, you can't tell anyone, or someone might kill her."

"Don't worry, son, as a doctor I don't reveal anything personal about my patients."

"Good," Travis said, "I would hate to have ta shoot you."

The doctor grinned. "Not as much as I would. Now let me tend to my patient." The doctor finished his exam and turned to Travis. "Bad concussion."

"And what about the concussion?"

"It's not good, and the next few hours are critical; we need to keep her awake. She needs a lot of looking after."

"Don't worry, Doc, I'll take care of her. I'll keep her awake."

"And who's gonna keep you awake?"

"Don't worry. If Fury needs me awake, I'll stay awake."

"It's all right, Ranger, I'll be in and out, keeping a check on her. Ranger, if you can't stay awake, I can sit with her or get someone to help."

"I'm staying with her," Travis insisted. "You couldn't make me leave, even if you wanted to."

"I thought as much." Doc smiled. "I know love when I see it."

Travis bent down and kissed Belle's forehead. "Belle, you need to wake up, sweetheart."

Her eyes fluttered open in response to his kiss.

"Shh, honey, you stubborn girl." Travis gently stroked Belle's forehead. "You're going to be all right. I'm going to see to it."

Belle moaned. "Travis." Her voice quivered.

Travis leaned closer to hear her.

"Max, how is Max?"

"Belle, don't worry about Max; the doc is gonna to do all he can for him, aren't you, Doc?" Travis' eyes flashed a warning gaze at the older man.

"I'll do my best, but I ain't an animal doc."

"Please, doctor, please don't let him die." Tears spilled over Belle's eyes.

Travis gritted his teeth. He'd made his Belle cry; he could pummel the doctor if he did not need him. "Belle, darlin', don't cry. The doc is going to do the best he can for Max, aren't you, doctor." Travis felt the blaze of anger rise to his face and stiffen his body. *You better give the right answer, Doc.*

"Sure, I will." Doc patted Belle's hand. "We need to get you situated in the other room."

"Where is it?" Travis asked, already lifting Belle into his arms.

"Next door down. Oh, and Ranger." Travis stopped and looked

at the doc. "She will need to be cleaned up, and there is a night-shirt in the dresser. I suppose that will be better than a gown if she needs to be seen as a man. I will get Mrs. Mason to help."

"No. I'll do it; I'll take care of Belle."

"Are you her husband?"

"Not yet, but I will be. Don't worry about her reputation. I would do nothing to sully her, but I will be the one caring for her. The less people who know who Fury really is, the safer she will be."

Doc nodded.

THE COMFORT of the warm washcloth skimming her body and massaging her sore muscles helped Belle relax.

"I gotta lift you up a little, honey," she heard Travis' voice. "Go slow, can't have you gettin' dizzy."

A soft cloth slid down her body. Travis guided her back into the downy pillows. Her mind began to clear as her thoughts roused. "Travis?"

His image cleared. Belle tried to sit up. "Where am I? And what is this?" Her hand swept over the surface of the nightshirt.

"Belle, lie back," he said as he adjusted her pillows.

"You're in the doctor's office in Langston. Don't you remember Cutter Dan?"

Her memories rushed back—the shack, the pain and dark-ness, a gunshot.

"Y-yes, it's coming back. I found Cutter. He hit my head." Her hand rubbed the tender lump on the back of her head. "He held me hostage, a-and you came, and Max… Oh, my, Travis, where is Max?" she wailed.

"It's all right, darlin', lie back. The doc's looking at him right now."

"And?"

"And what, Belle?"

"I-is he gonna make it, Travis? Will Max be all right?"

Travis hesitated.

A stray tear slid down her cheek. "Oh, Travis," she moaned, "please tell me he will be all right."

"I don't know, Belle. The doctor will come talk with us when he is done. Right now, you need to calm down and let me take care of you."

"He saved me, Travis."

"I know, but you have a concussion, and you getting' worse ain't gonna help Max."

Belle wiped the tear from her eye with the back of her hand. "Where's Cutter Dan?"

Travis wanted a change in subject, but he didn't want it to be about Dan. "He's dead."

"Good." She winced as she brushed her hand against her bruised face.

"Does it hurt, sweetheart? I'll get doc to get you something for the pain."

"No, I'll—"

The door squeaked open.

"Doctor?" Belle asked the large old man who stood at the door.

"Yes," Doc Johnson answered.

"How is my dog?"

Doc pushed his spectacles up the bridge of his nose. "Well, I'm not a vet." He brushed his finger across his bushy grey moustache and walked over to Belle's bedside. "The animal lost a lot of blood."

The little color in Belle's face faded, the room spun, and she steadied herself, trying to prepare for bad news. "I-is he gone?" the words sputtered out of her mouth.

"No, dear, he is still with us. As far as I can tell, the bullet did not hit anything major."

"Then he will be all right." Belle's heart lightened.

"I didn't say that. The dog—

"Max," Belle interjected, "his name is Max."

"Yes, well then, Max lost a great deal of blood."

"Max is strong." Belle shook her head, her voice agitated. "You'll see; he'll pull through."

The doctor gave her a compassionate look. "I hope so."

"He will, just you see." Belle's body shook.

"Right now, miss—

"Hey!" Belle's eyes fixed on Travis. "Did you tell him? How does he know?"

"Calm down, Belle," Travis said. "I told him nothing; he examined you."

"Oh." Belle unconsciously pulled the sheet up to her neck as if she were shielding her body from prying eyes.

"Don't worry, miss, as your physician, I cannot divulge personal information. Your secret is safe with me."

"Good, but you need to call me Fury, not miss."

"All right, Fury it is. Now, Fury, I am glad to see you are more responsive. Right now, I want you to rest, but you cannot go to sleep."

"I'll keep her awake," Travis added.

"Good, I'll be back to check on you."

"I can't sleep, anyhow. I need to go see Max; he will get better if I'm around. Then I need to go to the sheriff's office and see about my bounty."

"You most certainly will not."

Belle's eyes darted to Travis.

He stood over her with his arms crossed over his chest, the steely firmness of his eyes burned on her. "You, young lady, will do exactly as the doctor says. Do you understand me?"

"But, Travis I-I—"

"Do you understand?"

She surrendered to his firm tone. "All right, I won't go to the sheriff yet, but please, could you bring Max in here with me?"

Travis rubbed his chin. "Doctor, what do you think?"

Doc Johnson took a deep breath and smiled at Belle. The smile removed the grim look from his face and put a twinkle in his eye. "I think that can be arranged if you remember you are not his nurse and promise to stay in bed."

"I-I—

"She will," Travis interjected

"Travis, I can speak for myself."

"Honey, I'm glad to see the feisty you. It lets me know you are feeling better, but while you are recovering, you will do what I say, and I say you need to stay in bed."

Belle scowled. "But, the doctor," she pointed at the old man who appeared amused by their interaction, "said that Max could come in here."

Travis sucked in some air. "All right, I'll get Max, but then you gotta rest."

"Fine," Belle snapped and crossed her arms.

Travis raised a warning eyebrow, and Belle knew she'd better remain quiet.

For the remainder of the night, Travis told Belle stories of when he was younger and stories of being a ranger, anything to keep her awake. The doctor checked on her numerous times, and it was early morning when he decided she had improved enough to get some sleep. Travis still refused to leave her, and he slept in a chair as she slumbered in the bed. When he woke, he gazed at the sleeping Belle. He kissed her on the forehead. "Be right back, gotta go get my girl some food."

A NIGHTMARE WOKE BELLE, causing her to jut up in bed, and a searing pain cut through her head. "Damn." She rubbed her forehead as scraps of her nightmare came rushing back to haunt her mind.

Hideous images of Cutter Dan's face morphed in and out of proportion as insane laughter danced from his mouth. Dan pointed to cloudy images of women standing behind him, each bloody, with his initials etched into their foreheads.

"Won't you join us?" Dan motioned to his harem, and his laugh echoed through Belle's mind.

"Come on, ladies; let's welcome our newest member."

Belle's hand went to her chest. Her heart pounded as she recalled the group of victims drawing close to her.

Then she woke. She tried to slow her breathing, but the images were still with her, then she heard a whimper.

"Max?" Belle turned toward the sound. There, across the room from her on a pile of cushions, lay her dog.

"Max!" Belle threw the covers off and slung her legs to the floor, her head spinning as she rose to her feet. "Slow down, Belle, or you'll pass out," she admonished herself.

She took a few moments, letting her head settle, then she padded over to where Max lay. She crouched down beside him. "Oh, Max." A tear trickled down her face as she gently stroked his head. His body felt cold as Belle's hand trailed down to his bandage and stopped.

"Oh, Max, I'm so sorry, boy; this is my fault." Belle cupped his chin and brought her head down to rest on his. "Max," she sighed, "you saved me, boy."

Her gaze met his gentle eyes. Max gave a weak thump of his tail.

"Shh, boy, you rest; you will be fine. I'll see to it."

The door creaked open. Belle looked up to see Travis holding a tray of food, with the look of thunder on his face.

Uh oh.

Travis strode across the room and placed the tray on the nightstand. In moments, he was back to where Belle sat crouched with her dog. He helped her to her feet, turned her sideways, and gave her two sharp swats to her bottom. They didn't sting as much as others he had administered. She supposed he wanted to get her attention but held back because of her injures.

He then lifted her into his arms as if she were weightless.

Belle avoided looking at him; she did not want to face his scolding glare.

"Belle Alston, you look at me. I want to make sure you hear what I say."

Belle sighed and inched her face up toward the angry man.

The purple-faced man spoke. "You know you were not to leave your bed, young lady." He carried her to the side of her bed. "And you are adding to the big punishment you have coming. You, my love, will not sit comfortably for a long while." He laid her in bed and tucked the covers around her.

Belle's head hurt, and she could not keep a lid on her temper. "You got no right, Travis Parker, no right at all. You don't own me. I'm a grown up, and I'm a bounty hunter. I was doing my job, and you got no right to interfere or to punish me for doing what I am free to do." Belle shot her eyes at Travis, and if they were arrows, he would be mortally wounded. She crossed her arms and snorted hot air, like a bull ready to fight.

"Are you done?"

Her lip quivered. *Damn, I ain't crying again.* She threw her gaze down at her lap, hoping to gain control of the impending flood, but it was too late, and the tears cascaded down her face. Once again, she felt herself lifted by his strong arms.

Travis took her place on the bed. He arranged her on his lap and leaned back on her pillows. His strong arms were firm and tender around her as she felt the warmth of his hand gently guide her head to his chest. "Aw, darlin'."

Belle listened to the low rumble of his firm yet tender voice as her head rested on his chest. Somehow, the deep, raspy tones comforted her. "It's all catching up with you now." He stroked her hair. "Just let it out, honey; you're safe with me."

Those words, full of love, along with his tender touch, were like a healing balm to her heart. Belle buried her head in his chest. Her small hand clasped onto his shirt as she held on to him and cried. Her petite frame shook with each sob. Travis held her close as she released her pain and fright. Her sobs lessened and were replaced by gentle hiccups, then soft breathing. Finally, she surrendered to peaceful sleep.

Over the next few days, Belle improved, but Max did not. His condition remained the same, his breathing labored at times, his body weak, his eyes dull except when Belle spoke to him. At those times, a small spark of affection shone in his eyes. And that spark was enough to give Belle hope. Travis and the doctor were not as hopeful as Belle. They even spoke of how to break it to her when they thought it was time to put the dog down.

Travis spent his days and nights at Belle's side. Eventually, with the help of the doctor, Belle convinced Travis to go to the hotel and get some sleep.

"Son," the doctor said to him," I know you want to be here with your girl, but she needs you well, not sick from exhaustion."

"All right," Travis conceded, "I'll go, but if anything—

"If anything happens, which it won't, but if anything happens, I will send for you," Doc answered.

"Now, I will leave you two alone." Doc winked at Belle. "You sleep well."

"I will, thank you, Doctor." Belle smiled.

"All right, Belle, you've won. I'm headed for the hotel. But if you need anything—

"I know, I know," Belle said as she picked up the small silver bell on her nightstand, "If I need anything, I'll ring the bell, and Doc will come a runnin', which, if you think about it, would really be something to watch." Belle grinned.

"Well, I can see you are feeling better, but you shouldn't disrespect the doc; he's done a lot for you."

"Geez, Travis, I ain't disrespecting him; it was a joke."

"At someone else's expense." Travis tried to give her a stern look but then chuckled. "Well, I suppose it would be funny, but still, Belle." Travis shook his head. "Sleep well, darlin'." He bent down and kissed her forehead.

"Good night, Travis," Belle answered, surprised at her disappointment at the friendly kiss.

Travis turned toward her as he opened the door to leave. "Belle, be good."

"I am always good," she huffed.

"Yeah, sure you are," Travis smirked and shut the door behind himself.

Belle waited to hear the front door close. "Oh, that man." She leaned back on her pillows. Her eyelids felt heavy, and sleep began to overtake her, but her eyes popped open when she heard Max whimper. She threw her blankets off and flung her legs over the side of the bed. She leapt to her feet and was surprised she did not get dizzy.

"Max," she said, her voice soft and gentle as she stroked his head. "You're going to be all right, boy. I know you are." Belle brushed a tear from her eye. "You gotta get better, Max."

She cupped his face in her hands and kissed his snoot. "Max, I'm not sure how to help you." Belle patted his side. "You're so cold. Well, I can do something about that, and I don't care what Ranger Travis Parker has to say. You're coming with me."

Belle lifted the dog and walked over to her bed. She laid him on the bottom of the bed and then crawled in herself. Belle drew Max up to her then tucked them both under the covers.

A WARM, morning breeze furled the curtains and danced across Belle's face. She moaned at the interruption of her sleep. She rolled on her side, trying to go back to her sweet dreams.

A warm, moist sensation flicked at her face. She tried to shoo away whatever disturbed her with a brisk wave of her hand. But it returned, and this time it felt decidedly warm, wet, and persistent. Belle tried to escape, but the flicking at her face followed her. She cracked open an eye and saw a black nose sniffing her. A pink dog tongue slurped the side of her face.

"Stop it, Max, she groaned. "Can't you see I'm trying to sleep?" The wet assault on her face continued. "Max! Stop!" Belle sat up and opened her eyes.

"Max, I told you to—Max!" Belle shrieked, "Max, you're better!" Belle rubbed behind his ears, and the dog leaned into her hand. "You're really going to be all right!"

Belle did not hear the door open.

"What in the world is going on here!"

Travis could not believe what he saw—Belle, in bed, petting Max. "Why is that dog in bed with you?" Travis moved to her bedside.

He was ready to scold, until Belle looked up at him.

Her face lit with joy. "He's gonna be all right, Travis. Max is going to be all right."

Travis melted, watching Belle kissing and hugging Max, making him slightly jealous of the dog. The happy mutt rolled on his back, and Belle began to rub his belly.

Travis bent down and joined Belle in rubbing the dog's underside. Max was in doggy heaven.

"Belle, I'm so happy Max is better, but you shouldn't put him in bed with you."

"Why not? He slept here all night, didn't bother me a bit."

"Oh, Belle," Travis scrubbed his hand over his face, "are you ever going to behave?"

"What do you mean, Travis? Max is better because he slept with me, so how could that be wrong?"

Travis huffed; he knew he had lost this argument.

Belle laughed. "Is it that hard for you to admit I'm right?"

Doc Johnson came in the room. "Well now," he said as he surveyed the bed, "both of my patients in the same bed?"

"Look, Doc," Belle squealed, "he's better, isn't he? Max is going to be all right." Belle beamed.

"It most certainly looks that way." Doc petted the animal on the head. "But right now, if you don't mind, I need Travis to move Max so I can look you over and see if I can get you out of this place."

If it were not for the fact that she might be released from his care, Belle would protest Max being removed from her arms. "Max, you go with Travis, then you can come back."

"We'll have to see about that," Travis said as he lifted the happy canine and placed him back on his cushions.

Doc's exam did not take long. "Well, everything looks good. You are free to go, but you still need to take it easy."

"Yippee!" Belle threw her arms in the air and jumped out of bed. "Get out, you two," Belle addressed the men. "I need to get dressed and collect my bounty."

"Belle, be careful, stop jumping around. You have got to take it easy," Travis scolded.

"I've taken it easy for days; I need to get my bounty."

"We need to talk about that," Travis said. "I'll be in the next room."

The door closed behind the two men.

"Don't know what the hell Travis wants to talk about, Max," Belle huffed as she jammed her legs into her pants, "but he better not get in the way of me and my bounty. I need that money." Just then, she noticed her clothes. They were her own clothes, laundered and clean. "That man," she muttered to herself as she smelled the fresh soap used on them.

Belle whipped on her shirt and fastened the buttons. She had one boot on when she heard the rap on the door.

"Everything all right, Belle?"

She rolled her eyes at the tinge of worry in Travis' voice. "Max, will he ever stop being overprotective?" *I hope not.*

"I'm fine; come on in, Travis."

Travis walked in as she shoved her other foot in her boot.

"Travis, you don't have to watch over me. I'm fine. I'm going to the sheriff's office to collect my bounty. You can do whatever it is you need to do. Why don't you go back to wherever you rangers go when you are done with a job?"

Belle's insides went cold at the thought of Travis leaving her, even though it was her suggestion. But she needed to push him away; she would not rest until her parents' murderers were caught.

"Uhm, Belle." Travis chuckled. "I ain't leaving without you. Did you forget, it's my job to take you back to Faulkner? Besides, you are mine, remember, and I ain't going anywhere without my girl."

Belle grabbed her hat from where it hung on the door and placed it on her head. "Oh yeah." She took a deep breath. "That ain't happening, Travis. I gotta collect my bounty and be on my way."

She headed for the door, but Travis cut her off. He leaned against the door and crossed his arms. "No, Belle, you're coming home with me."

"Damn it, Travis." Belle pulled her hat off and slammed it to the floor. "I have business to attend to—my own personal business."

"What business? Your parents' murderers?"

"I said it was personal. It doesn't concern you."

"Oh, honey." Belle saw his eyes fill with warmth as he reached out and wrapped his hands around her tiny waist. "There ain't nothing about you that doesn't concern me, and I'm not going anywhere without you. I don't ever want to leave your side, not because of a job, but because of you. I never gave up on finding you."

Belle's knees wobbled when he pulled her close. Her pulse raced as he leaned down, drawing her lips to his. His lips were soft and tender as they embraced hers. She closed her eyes.

"Belle."

She opened her eyes to his soft voice. "Uh?" She could not speak.

"Belle." He smiled at her innocence. "I love you, Belle. I think I always have." He went in for another kiss, and this time she met him halfway. The gentle kiss deepened. A charge rippled through her body, and she felt the pain of separation when he pulled back.

"Belle, honey, you gotta breathe." Travis chuckled.

Belle nodded. As she drew in air, her brain began to clear, and her fight came back to her. She batted his hands off her waist. "Don't you do that, Travis Parker." Her hands flew to her hips.

"What?" Travis smiled at her fluster.

"Don't you try to get around me with k-kisses and sweet talk. I got work to do and—"

"And what?" Travis pulled her toward him once more. She put up a weak fight but surrendered to one more kiss.

"Tell me, Belle." Travis rested his forehead against hers.

"Tell you what?" Belle panted.

"Tell me you love me, because I sure love you."

Belle's resolve collapsed. "I love you, Travis. *Damn it, I do.*"

He pulled her close and cradled her head against his chest. "Now, was that so hard to say?"

"Yes. Yes, it was."

Travis chuckled and squeezed her close.

TRAVIS' heart soared as he caressed Belle in his arms.

She loves me.

Contentment settled in his heart. Everything he wanted, all that was precious to him in this world, he now held in his embrace.

"Travis." Belle raised her head.

"Yes." He smiled down at her face.

"I-I still need to go."

"Go where, darlin'?" He kissed the tip of her nose.

"Travis, please." Belle tried to tug away from him. "Let me go, Travis. I still have to get my bounty."

Travis released her. His moment of ecstasy vanished as her words slammed him back to reality. "What?" he asked as he rubbed his brow trying to make sense of what she said. "After this moment we just shared, your mind is still on that stupid bounty?"

Belle's hands flew to her hips. "It ain't stupid to me. I need that money!"

Travis heard the desperation in her voice as tears gathered in her sad, violet eyes. She looked so little and fragile, he sensed her vulnerability, and protectiveness overtook him. He walked over to her and pulled her in his arms once more. "What's wrong, Belle?" He stroked her hair. "What's wrong, baby?" He could feel her body melt into his.

"I need the money, Travis. I need it to find the men who murdered Mama and Papa."

Her body trembled in his arms. She felt more like a frightened little girl than a feisty bounty hunter. He tightened his arms around her small frame and gently cradled her head against his chest. "Shh, shh, Belle," he kissed the top of her head, "tell me how is the money gonna help you find your parents' murderers."

Belle sniffled. He felt her take a deep breath. Travis loosened his grip so she could look him in the eye. He brushed a wet lock of hair from her face and curled it behind her ear. "Tell me."

Belle nodded. "Have you ever heard of Gentleman Jack Turney?"

Travis thought for a minute then nodded. "Yes, isn't he a gambler?"

"Yes," Belle answered, "and more."

"More?"

"He also sells information."

"Oh," Travis said as everything began to fall together. He released her from his grip and crossed his arms over his chest. "And I suppose he has information concerning your parents' murderers."

"Yes, I met him a couple of months ago, in Markle Springs. I was in the saloon doing my usual search for information. He overheard my conversation with one of the drunks there and sent one of his men to invite me to his table. He told me he couldn't help but hear me talk about the two men I was looking for, particularly the one with red boots, and he had information for me."

"Let me guess; he had information for a price."

"Yes, and it wasn't cheap. He wanted one thousand dollars."

"So, you decided the easiest way to get that much money was to go after a pricy bounty."

Belle nodded.

"Belle, you coulda gone to the law and told them."

"Told them what? That I knew someone who knew something about my parents' murderers.? Do you think Turney would just open up to them because they were *the law?*"

"Yeah, Belle, you're right." Travis shook his head. "Sometimes, I don't think straight where you are concerned."

"So, you understand why, Travis? Why I need that money and why I'm going to Serenity?"

"Serenity? Is he there?

"Not when we were there, but he doesn't stay in one town long. He mentioned he was going to Serenity in a few weeks, I figured by now he would be there." Belle looked at Travis as he stood in stoic silence. "Well?" Belle asked.

"Well, what?"

"Well, do I go get my bounty peaceful like, or do I need to fight you?"

Travis chuckled and took her hands in his. He raised them to his lips, giving each a gentle kiss.

"Darlin', as much as I would enjoy you trying to wrestle me, we don't have the time. We need to get to the sheriff's office and collect your bounty."

Belle gave a sigh of relief. "Glad you are seeing things my way. Maybe I can send you a telegram after I catch the murderers."

Travis laughed aloud.

"No, baby girl, you don't understand. I'm going with you to see Turney. Then we will give any information to the law."

"The hell we will. Those men are mine!"

"Belle, does it matter who brings them in, you or the law?"

"It matters to me."

Travis' frustration mounted. "Look, I owe you a hard spankin' for all that Cutter Dan business, but I didn't want to deliver it here. But I will, along with a spankin' for thinking about going after those men alone, if you don't do as I say."

He took two steps toward Belle. She backed up and held up both hands. "All right, all right, Travis, you win."

Travis stopped. "I win what?"

"You win; I won't go after Turney alone. You can go with me."

"And we will turn over any information to the law."

"Yes," Belle sighed. "We will turn over any information to the law."

"And they will bring in your parents' murderers."

Belle hesitated.

Travis raised an eyebrow.

"Y-yes, the law will bring them in." She crossed her fingers behind her back.

"Good girl." Travis smiled as he drew Belle into his arms. He kissed the top of her head. "Let's go get that bounty from the sheriff." He opened the door to let Belle by. "Oh, and Belle."

Belle stopped and looked at him. "What?"

"Don't think this gets you out of the spanking you already earned."

Belle bit her lip. "Fine. But don't call me Belle, you dope, remember it's Fury."

Travis and Fury found the sheriff sitting in his office with his injured leg propped up on the stool.

"Boy, am I glad to see you two," the sheriff said. His chair moaned when he shifted his weight to stand up.

"No, no," Travis said, "ain't no need for you to get up."

"We're here to get my money," Fury commanded.

"Fury, ain't you even gonna say 'hello' or 'how ya doin' to the man?"

Fury sighed, "Hello, how ya doin,' she mimicked Travis. "Now, where's my money?"

Travis glared at her.

"What? I said what you wanted me to say."

The sheriff chuckled. "It's all right, Ranger. I would think you would be more experienced with bounty hunters; they ain't much on manners."

"That's for sure," Travis answered, his disapproving eyes still locked on Fury.

The sheriff pulled a key from his vest pocket and used it to unlock a drawer in his desk. "Well, it ain't like having it in a safe, but it's the best I could do." The sheriff retrieved a stack of money from the drawer. "Here you are, Fury."

Fury yanked the money from the man's hand and began to count the bills.

"It's all there, Fury, but if you feel like you need to count it, then do."

Fury stopped. "Sorry, Sheriff, I'm sure it is."

"Oh, before you leave, I need you to sign for it."

The sheriff placed a receipt on the desk which Fury signed.

"Thanks for your help getting Cutter Dan."

Fury grunted and turned to walk out the door. She made it a few feet from the jail when she felt a tight grip on her arm.

"You mind telling me why you were so rude to the sheriff, young lady?" Travis whispered in her ear.

"Watch it, you idiot, remember I'm Fury," she sputtered.

"You're the one who'd better 'watch it'." He jerked her arm, making her stop.

"Stop it, Travis, you're making a scene."

"I can make a bigger one if you want."

"What do you want, Travis?" Fury sighed.

"I want you to stop being rude and disrespectful."

"To *that* sheriff?" Fury nodded her head in the direction of the jail. "Travis, I can tell you he couldn't care less how I speak to him; he is glad I found Cutter for him. I don't waste time on idle chatter and niceties when I have work to do."

"Are you done?"

"Yes. Can we go now?" Fury turned to walk away, but Travis pulled her back.

"I'm not finished."

Fury rolled her eyes.

"Fine, you want it that way, just keep it up, Belle. You're just adding to your tally."

"What tally? And I'm Fury, you idiot."

"That makes three."

"Three what?"

"Three times, you called me an idiot," Travis leaned closer to make sure only she heard him, "and that is going to make it even harder for you to sit once we take care of your punishment."

Belle figured she called him an idiot more than three times, but no way was she telling him. Butterflies, already, stirred inside her as a tingle danced across her backside. She gulped. "I have things to do," Fury said as she tried to gain control.

"No, not yet," Travis said as he pulled her arm once more.

"What is it now?"

"Breakfast. We are going to get something to eat and make plans."

"All right," Fury seethed.

But the only plans I'm making is to get away from you and do this on my own!

EXCEPT FOR THE decision that Travis would go buy some supplies and Belle would go get Max, breakfast was eaten in silence. They decided to meet at the livery.

Travis wanted to make sure Belle did not sneak off without him. He made a quick stop at the livery and paid the livery boy to find him if Fury came for his horse.

The thought would have crossed Fury's mind if she did not have to convince the doctor she and Max were fine to travel. She promised she would rest frequently and that Max would ride with her. She only intended to keep the latter promise.

CHAPTER 15

They rode most of the day in silence, stopping for a short rest and a quick meal of jerky and hardtack.

Travis kept a close watch on Belle. He looked for signs of fatigue; after all, she had just recovered from her injuries, and Doc did say she should not get overtired. He watched as she slumped in her saddle. "All right, it's time to stop for the night."

"What do you mean, stop? We still have some daylight left."

"Belle, you're about to fall off your saddle, and I need to get some food in you before you go to sleep." Travis grabbed Swift's reins from her hands and guided them off the road. He dismounted Chief and went to Belle's horse, where he lifted Max from where he lay across Belle's lap and carefully set him on the ground. He then turned back to Belle and reached up to help her down.

"I don't need your help." Belle crossed her arms and pouted.

Travis chuckled. "You look like an angry five-year-old. Come on, Belle, you are tired and hungry, and it's making you grouchy."

"Shut up, Travis, I ain't grouchy," she whined.

"All right, now you sound like a five-year-old." Travis reached up and clasped his hands around Belle's waist to help her down.

His touch only served to intensify her bad mood. She tried to kick him as she struck him with the ends of her horse reins.

Travis' patience was gone. His face looked like a thunderstorm. "I'll have none of that, little girl." In one forceful move, he plucked Belle off her horse, but she didn't give up her fight.

She kicked and screamed until Travis carried her over to a large rock. He sat on the rock and laid the struggling girl across his lap. "Belle, I ain't putting up with any little girl tantrum."

Belle continued to flail until one sharp *smack* landed across her bottom. She froze for a moment "No, no, no, Travis, please, no."

"Too late. I intended to wait until later for your punishment, but it looks like you'll get it now." Travis let his large hand land one more time over her pants covered bottom.

The sting on her bottom reignited her fight.

Travis stood her on her feet for a moment and unfastened her pants, dragging them down to her knees.

Before she could protest, she found herself, once more, dangling over his lap. She screamed when she felt his finger hook the back of her drawers and drag them down to meet her pants. "Travis, you can't do that," she squealed as the cool air brushed against her delicate skin.

"Looks like I did," Travis answered, restarting his assault on her bottom.

Belle's petite frame dangled over the large man's lap. The tips of her feet could not meet the ground, and her kicks were suspended in air. She could not brace her hands on the ground, so she clasped Travis' leg and held on.

Travis was not holding back. "I'm sick and tired of your attitude." *Smack! Smack! Smack!* "You have been rude and contrary, fighting anyone who wants to help you." *Smack!* "Especially me! You call me an idiot, numerous times. That ain't happening anymore."

Smack! Smack! Smack! "And now you want to have a 'little girl' tantrum—not happening." Travis did not slow his pace. The spanks were raining down a steady rhythm, turning her porcelain flesh to a nice shade of pink.

Belle fought not to give in to the pain, but her resolve broke with one woeful sob. "Please, please, Travis," tears spilled from her eyes, "please stop, I'm s-so s-sorry!" she wailed.

"I know you're sorry but not sorry enough. I say when we're done, not you."

The spanks continued. Belle could no longer form words as she dangled across her man's knee and wailed, her face drenched in tears.

Travis watched as the pink skin darkened, turning a light crimson red. "That's good enough for this part." He stopped and flipped Belle upright.

She buried her head into his chest and cried.

Travis rubbed her back for a few minutes then stood her up.

Belle gave him a confused looked. "Why aren't you holding me? You held me before when you finished spanking me," she sobbed.

"We're not done."

"W-what?"

Travis turned her and guided her over the rock. "That spanking was for your attitude, rudeness, and disrespect. We still have the matter of you going after Cutter Dan alone to take care of."

Belle tried to push herself off the rock, but Travis gently pushed her back down.

"But, Travis," she sobbed. "Can't that spanking take care of both?"

"That little spanking isn't hardly enough to make up for putting yourself in danger." *Whoosh.*

"What was that?' Belle turned to look over her shoulder and saw what she feared the most—*a belt.* "Travis, no," she cried.

Travis folded the belt and wrapped it around his hand, making sure he held the buckle in the palm of his hand.

"Oh, yes, young lady, you earned it, so you're gonna get it. Now turn around and lean over the rock. Do *not* move your hands, or I'll add spanks. I don't want to hurt your hands."

"You don't want to hurt my hands; what about my butt?" she wailed as tears flooded her face.

"You should have thought about that before you went after Dan. Now, enough arguing with me. Turn around, and let's get this over with."

Belle sniffled and turned around. The first contact with the belt and her skin sizzled across both cheeks. She wanted to cry out, but it had taken her breath away. She had barely filled her lungs when the second and third crisscrossed her bottom, causing her to scream as tears burst from her eyes.

"Belle, you are never to risk your life again. Do you understand?"

Another line of fire seared lower on her bottom, and Belle squealed in pain.

"Answer me, Belle!"

"I-I won't," she babbled.

A new stripe ignited across the previous one, sending her into fits of sobs. She was past being coherent.

Travis watched the angry red stripes as welts rose on her backside. He decided to quicken his strikes and end this punishment. Three more quick stripes and she danced on her toes. "Belle, you are far too precious to me to ever risk your life again." He lifted her higher on the rock then delivered two burning stripes to her sit spots.

Belle screeched and then went limp over the rock. A hiss escaped her lips when she felt him pull her drawers and pants over her throbbing, crimson bottom. She felt him lift her and carefully place her on his lap. Again, she hid her face in his chest and cried. His strong arms held her, and she basked in their comfort.

"Cry it out, honey," Travis said, "all is forgiven."

He continued to speak comforting words to her. Belle's head lay on his chest, listening to the rumble of his voice. The deep, graveled timbre lulled and calmed her. How could she feel this safe, this loved in the arms of a man who had just roasted her butt?

His hand rubbed her back. "Shh, darlin', I got you. I'll take care of you."

Those words filled a cold void inside of her with warmth and love. Her tears turned to hiccups. She looked up at him, her splotchy red face a mess of tears and snot.

Travis removed his bandana and wiped her face. "Blow," he said as he held his bandana to her nose.

"I can do that myself," she protested as she tried to snatch the bandana from his hand.

He drew back. "No, Belle. Mind me." He placed the bandana over her nose and nodded.

Belle blew. "That's icky," she said as she scrunched up her face.

Travis smiled. "No, it's not. I got to take care of my girl."

"Travis," she said softly as she played with a button on his damp shirt.

"Yes, Belle." He smiled down at her face.

"Why?"

"Why what, Belle?"

"Why the belt?"

"Darlin', I take no joy in using a belt on you."

"Then why use it instead of your hand?"

"Did the hand not hurt?" He chuckled.

"No, no, it did, a lot," Belle insisted, "but the belt, it's just so much worse."

Travis gave her a quick kiss on her forehead. "I know, but

putting yourself in danger is much worse than having a bad attitude, isn't it?"

"Yes. But I can take care of myself. I've done it for years."

"I'm not saying you are incapable of taking care of yourself, but you put yourself in an extremely dangerous situation. You knew that even lawmen would not go after a murderer like Cutter Dan by themselves. Besides, you're mine now. I take care of you, now."

Belle smiled at him.

"Belle, you know this country can be dangerous to live in, especially if you deal with criminals. I love you, Belle. I need to know that when I tell you not to do something that puts you in danger, you will obey me. Now, you've just got a whuppin' with my belt; do you want to experience that again?"

"N-no." Belle's head shook.

"So next time you think about putting yourself in danger, you will remember that belt and think twice, won't you?"

"Yes."

"Would my hand on your bottom be as persuasive as the belt, to keep you from doing something you were determined to do, like going after Cutter Dan?"

"No."

"So now, you will think twice about doing something dangerous because you know what you will get when I find out. Belle, your safety is the most important thing to me, and if it takes my belt to make you understand that, then I will not hesitate to use it."

"Because you love me?"

"Yes, because I love you."

"Well, I love you, so does that mean I can use a belt on you if you do something dangerous?"

Belle gave him an impish grin.

"Nope, doesn't work that way." He chuckled. "But I'd like to see you try. He tickled her side.

Belle cackled. "Stop it!" She tried to bat his hands away.

"Oh, are you ticklish?"

"Yes."

"Oh, maybe I should kiss you instead."

"Works for me." Belle smiled as he leaned down and kissed her.

THE SKY BEGAN to roll out the purples, pinks, and oranges of evening. Belle inhaled the homey smell of bacon frying and beans bubbling over the open fire. "Please Travis, let me help."

"No." The large man looming over the fire looked at her.

Every spot of empty loneliness inside her was filled by the love and warmth conveyed by his soft gaze.

"You just sit yourself down and let me take care of you. Remember, Doc said he didn't want you overdoing it. I shouldn't have let us ride so long today. I want you to eat your supper and then go to sleep."

"Travis, you know I can't exactly sit." She blushed as she sat on the side of her hip, trying to get comfortable.

"I ain't feeling sorry for you, little girl. You earned that sore bottom," he scolded.

A fat tear escaped and meandered down her cheek.

Travis stood up from where he crouched over the fire and went to her side. "Honey, I didn't mean to make you cry by bringing up your spanking." He sat on a log next to her and lifted her onto his lap.

"Ouch."

He wrapped his muscular arms around her, cradling her he kissed the top of her head. "Come on, honey, don't cry."

"I'm not crying about the spanking," she said in a small voice.

"Then what is it, sweetheart?" Travis tipped her head up to look her in the eye.

The worry in his eyes made her smile.

"I-it's just that, no one, at least since Papa and Mama, has taken care of me like you do."

"Oh, little darlin'," Travis smiled, "it's all I want to do. Care for you. Love you." He brushed a tender kiss against her rosy lips. "I love you, Belle."

She didn't answer.

"Belle, honey, don't you want to say something to me?"

She flashed him a mischievous grin. "Like what? I can't recall. What am I supposed to say, Travis?" Her grin grew into a giggle.

"Oh, so you think you're funny, worrying me like that? Seems to me, I remember someone is ticklish." Travis dug his wiggling fingers into her ribcage.

"Don't, don't," Belle screamed with laughter.

"Say it, little girl."

Belle caught her breath. "Oh, oh." She fanned herself with her hand. "Now, what was it again? I keep forgetting." Belle screamed with delight when his fingers attacked once more. "All right, all right, I give up."

Travis stopped moving his fingers but held them at her sides. He cocked up an eyebrow.

"I love you, Ranger Travis Parker."

He cupped the sides of her face and drew close to her lips, drinking once again the taste of her.

"Travis," Belle said when he withdrew his lips.

"Yes, darlin'."

"Um, the bacon's burning."

"Oh, oh, shit." Travis leapt to his feet, causing Belle to roll off his lap and onto the hard ground. He dove to the pan on the fire.

"Ouch," Belle yelled as her tender bottom hit the dirt.

"Ouch, damn it," he shouted as he pulled his hand from the scalding handle.

"Are you all right?" Belle's voice filled with concern.

"Yeah, I'm fine."

"Here, big man." She laughed as she watched him cradle his burnt digits. "Use this." She tossed him her bandana.

"Now I know what your bottom must feel like." He chuckled.

"That's not funny." Belle crossed her arms and pouted.

"Neither is burning your fingers." He filled her plate and handed it to her. "Sit up straight, Belle, and eat your supper."

Belle huffed.

"Belle," his voice turned stern.

"You know I can't sit up straight," she whined and took the plate he offered her.

"Belle, I've been easy on you. Sitting on that sore bottom is supposed to be part of your punishment. Besides, it shouldn't be as sore as it was right after your spanking. Do I need to inspect that poor sore bottom and make sure there isn't any permanent damage?"

A blush fired across Belle's cheeks. She opened her mouth but then thought better of it. She winced as her poor, punished backside touched the hard ground. She muttered a string of complaints to herself.

"What's that, Belle?"

"Nothing," she grumbled.

"Well, at least I didn't hear you offering to shoot me."

Don't be so sure.

"Good girl, now eat up."

TRAVIS ALLOWED Belle to help clean up after they ate. He did it to give her backside a break, not that he would ever tell her. "All right, time to spread out our bedrolls and get some sleep."

Belle took her bedroll and searched for a place near the fire to sleep.

Travis gently grabbed her arm. "Belle, honey, I want you to sleep next to me tonight."

The color drained from her face faster than a thermometer could drop in a blizzard. Butterflies thundered through her insides. Her eyes widened and she could not find words to speak. "I-I," she stammered.

"Tell me, Belle, what is it?"

She couldn't look him in the eyes and dropped her gaze to the ground. She mumbled a reply.

Travis placed a finger under her chin and carefully raised her face. She looked like a frightened fawn. "Belle, nothing happens between us that you don't want. So, tell me, darlin', what do you want?"

Oh my gosh, oh my gosh, oh my gosh! He wants me to talk about that!

"Belle, I'm waiting." There it was again, that rumbling, firm voice of his that made her weak in the knees.

"I-it's just that—

"What, baby girl? You can say it; you can say anything to me."

Belle nodded in agreement. She knew he was right, she *could* say anything to him. She swallowed hard. "I don't want to."

Travis gave her a confused look.

"Oh, that didn't come out right. I *do* want to. But not now." She shifted her weight from foot to foot and then spilled what was hard for her to say, "N-not until I'm married." There, she said, it. Belle chewed her lip and tried to read his non-descript face.

A few lengthy seconds passed before a smile stretched across his face and his eyes danced. "I agree, Belle, and I'm proud you want to save yourself for your husband. Who, by the way, better be me?" He chuckled.

Relief washed over her, helping her relax.

"But as hard as it is going to be, I want to drift off to sleep with you in my arms, nothing else, I promise." He held up his right hand as if he were swearing an oath. "I suppose part of me wants to feel you close, as hard as that is going to be, but part of me wants to protect you."

"But, Travis, you know you don't have to protect me. I can protect myself. Heck, I'm a better shot than you."

"I know, I know, well, except for the 'you bein' a better shot than me', but it's part of who I am. I protect what's mine."

Belle wanted to rebel against his protection and slight possessiveness, but deep down she felt a great sense of being valued, of being precious to someone, and she loved him even more.

"I want to feel you close to me." His mossy, green eyes glistened in the firelight and she tingled under his gaze.

"I would like that too, Travis."

TRAVIS COULDN'T HELP but grin as he watched Belle try to get comfortable in her saddle. They were up early this morning, thanks to Max's incessant licking, and were less than an hour from Serenity.

Belle moaned and shifted in her saddle. Every bump and dip in Swift's gait brought back the burning sting of her punishment. She gave up sitting in her saddle and tried standing in her stirrups in hope of relief.

"Belle, honey." Travis chuckled at her antics.

"Don't you laugh at me, Travis Parker. It's your fault I'm so miserable," Belle grumbled.

"Watch the attitude, little girl."

"Sorry."

"And, it's not my fault that you earned a spanking. You did that all on your own, young lady, didn't you?"

Belle steamed; she didn't want to answer.

"Belle, I asked you a question. I expect an answer."

"Yes," she whimpered.

"Yes, what?"

She stopped her horse and glared at him. "Yes, I earned my spanking," she choked the words out.

Travis nodded. "You certainly did. But I decided since you haven't complained, well, haven't complained much, you can get off your horse and walk or fold a blanket and sit on it, if you would like."

"How benevolent of you," she sniped.

"Watch it, Belle, or I'll reignite that fire and you can ride the rest of the way."

Belle's lip quivered. "I'm sorry, Travis," she said in a small voice.

"Thank you, Belle."

"May I please walk?" She chose her words carefully, hoping he would not retract his offer.

"Yes, you may, darlin', and thank you for asking nicely."

Belle wanted to leap from her saddle, but her soreness only allowed a slow dismount.

Max was happy to have her company; he danced around her as she walked.

"Well, Max, I'm glad to see one of us is feeling better."

She decided to ride Swift the last mile into Serenity. She was quiet, too quiet for Travis's liking.

"Belle, you all right, honey?"

She sat stoic, barely hearing Travis. As still and quiet as she appeared, a war of emotions churned in her insides.

"Belle?"

"I'm all right, Travis," she answered in a monotone voice.

Travis grabbed her horse's reins and stopped them. "Belle, you look at me."

Her eyes looked like dead voids, emotionless.

"Belle, snap out of it, you look like you are going to the gallows. Come on, Belle." He reached over and grabbed her shoulder, shaking her.

Her head began to clear as she reached out of her trance and concentrated on Travis.

"Honey?"

"Travis." She rubbed her forehead as her senses returned.

"What's going on in that pretty head of yours?"

She smiled, trying to alleviate the concern she heard in his voice. "I'm fine."

"No, you're not. Now, will you tell me what is going on?"

"I don't know, Travis. I-I was thinking how close I am to finding Mama and Papa's murderers. I suppose it sent me back to that evening, when I hid in the closet, and everything went numb."

Belle felt herself lifted from her saddle. Travis nestled her in his arms. Any leftover feelings of loss and emptiness where now replaced with his love and comfort and the feeling of safety that only he could give her. She dug her small frame into the warmth of his broad chest. She wanted so to melt into this safe, loving place and never leave, but she couldn't, not yet.

"Belle," she heard the low rumble of her name in his chest, "you don't have to do this. We can leave right now for Faulkner."

She looked up at his face. "No, Travis, I can't. I have to settle this so I can have peace."

"All right, Belle, if this is what you need, then let's go." Travis carefully lifted her and placed her back on Swift.

"Thank you, Travis, for always being there for me."

"Oh, darlin'," smile crinkles gathered around the edge of his warm eyes, "anything for you."

"I'm so blessed to have you." She leaned over and placed a delicate kiss on his lips.

"No," Travis said with a smile, "I'm the lucky one."

BELLE MADE out the outline of a small man as they rode up to the livery in Serenity. She wanted to gallop to the man but stayed at their steady pace so as not to attract attention.

"Miles," Belle called out as she and Travis stopped at the livery.

"Well, look who's here. Howdy, Fury, and you too, Ranger. Glad you found *him*," Miles said with a wink to the ranger."

"So am I," Travis answered the grinning man.

"As much as I hate to interrupt this touching reunion, I have business to attend to," Belle sniped.

"Sorry, Mr. Fury," Miles said. "Let me take your horses. You stayin' a while?"

"Don't know yet," Fury answered, still mounted on her horse. "Depends on if I find who I'm looking for."

"You ain't still hunting that Cutter fella?"

"No, found him already. I'm lookin' for someone else. A Gentleman Jack Turney, you heard of him?"

"Yeah," Miles answered, stroking the stubble on his face.

Fury beamed. "He's here!"

"Well, yeah, I mean he *was* here."

Fury didn't know if she could make it through another episode of Miles' meanderings.

"What do you mean, he *was* here?" Travis asked.

"I mean, he was here little over a week ago."

"Well, where is he now?" Fury snapped, losing her patience with her old friend.

"Calm down, Fury. I'm sure Miles will tell us where to find him," Travis added.

Fury took a breath. "Sorry, Miles. But would you please tell us where to find Gentleman Jack Turney?"

"Boot Hill."

Fury's heart crashed into a dark pit.

"W-what?" She struggled to breathe.

"What happened to him?" Travis tried to remain calm as he carefully watched Fury's reaction.

"He come into town a little over a week ago and got into a card game. One of the fellas he was playing with found out he

214

was cheatin' and he drew on him. They shot it out and Turney died. It were a fair fight, if'n you're a wonderin'."

A flood of emotions—horror, terror, anger—washed over Fury.

"No, no, no!" she screeched out a foreboding howl of pain and dug her spurs into Swift.

The horse bolted and Fury sped out of town.

"Hell!" Travis yelled and galloped after her.

Furious tears flooded her face as the dust Swift churned up choked her. She didn't know where she was going or what she was doing. Agony and darkness ruled her mind, and all she knew to do was run.

She didn't sense Swift was slowing to a stop. A muffled sound tried to break through but never reached her. She floated, someone lifted her from her horse, then came the warmth, the safety of strength surrounded her.

"I got you, I got you, Belle." The words broke through her darkness—Travis' words brought her back.

She looked up and locked onto his eyes.

"Shh, honey, I got you. I love you, Belle."

"Travis." She blinked through her tears. "Oh, Travis," she moaned, clinging to him for comfort."

"It's all right, love; you cry it out if that's what you need. I got you, Belle."

He kissed the top of her head and stroked her hair as he cradled her in his arms.

"No, no." Belle shook her head. She freed herself from Travis' arms and stood.

"Belle?" Travis' voice quivered.

"It can't be, Travis, it just can't be!" Belle hugged herself.

"Honey." Travis stood and walked toward her. He reached for her, attempting to take her into his arms.

"No, don't." Belle raised her arms to stop him.

Travis froze. "Talk to me, Belle."

Tears gushed down her face. "I-I can't." She shook her head."

"Yes, you can, Belle. It's me, Travis, remember, you can tell me anything."

She wiped the side of her wet face with the back of her hand. "Travis," she wailed as she reached out to him. Within an instant, she was wrapped in his embrace.

"Talk to me, Belle. What are you thinking, what are you feeling?"

Belle drew in a breath. "I failed them, Travis. I failed them again. It's all I do; I keep failing them."

"Failing who, Belle? Your parents?"

"Yes, and you."

"Honey." Travis lifted Belle in his arms and carried her. He sat on a log and nestled her in his lap. "Belle, you haven't failed anyone. Especially me."

"Oh, yes, I have." Belle bobbed her head. "I failed them today, just like I failed them that night."

"What do you mean, you failed them that night? Are you talking about the night they were murdered?"

"Yes, I didn't save them that night. I was having a grand time at the dance while they were home dying. If I were home, I could've done something—I could've saved them. And then when I did get home and I found them, I didn't do anything. I hid. I should've done something."

Travis sighed and rubbed his forehead. "Belle, darlin', if you had been home, you would've died too. Belle, tell me about that night."

Belle frantically shook her head.

"Please, Belle, you need to talk about it. You need to see that you are not to blame for anything that happened that night. Please, Belle, let me help you."

She hated the desperate, pleading tone in his voice. "All right," she whispered, "I'll try."

Travis' arms tightened around her. "Go ahead, darlin', I'm here. I'll keep you safe."

The security of his words and safety of his arms gave her the courage to speak her pain.

"I returned from the dance, the one where I met you." She gave him a small smile. "I knew something was wrong. The lamp in the foyer wasn't lit, but there was one upstairs and I could see that someone was walking around with it. I told myself that Mama or Papa was looking for something, but deep down, I didn't even believe myself. I snuck in, and, and…" Her body trembled as tears flowed.

"Go on," Travis encouraged her. "I'm here; I gotcha."

Belle sucked air into her raspy throat. "I-I found them. Travis, I found them." She shuddered, burying her face into the crook of his neck.

"It's all right, honey, you can stop if you want." He could not bear the pain she was in.

"No, no. Now that I started, I gotta finish."

Travis nodded.

"Mama," a small moan escaped her lips, "she was gone."

"And your father?"

"He was dying. But I spoke to him."

"You did? What did he say, Belle?"

"At first, he told me to run. The men were still there. They were upstairs. I-I didn't want to run. I wanted them to find me too, so I could die with my parents. I hid in the closet."

"Oh, Belle." Travis drew her tighter. "What made you hide?"

"I didn't want to leave them."

"Did your father speak to you?"

"Y-yes," Belle said as she squinted her eyes, attempting to retrieve something lost in memory. She rubbed her temples.

"I can't quite remember what he said. I mean, I know he told me to run, but he did say something else."

"Think, Belle, it must be something important he needed you to hear before he died."

"Yes, I'm sure it was." Belle rubbed her temples, trying to loosen the lost memory.

"I-I know he said he loved me, but what else? It's right there, Travis, right at the tip of my memory, but I can't pull it out."

"Belle, as hard as this is, I need you to relax. You can't remember anything if you try too hard." He began to rub her shoulders.

"What else, Travis? What else can keep you from remembering?"

"Well," Travis said, "hmm…guilt but, Belle, your guilt doesn't help."

"I don't think I can get rid of that by willing it away."

"I know. Lean back, Belle, try to relax,; don't talk, just relax. Let your thought drift by."

Belle worked on relaxing herself. She concentrated on the warm grip of Travis' hands as they kneaded the muscles of her shoulders. She focused on his deep, rich voice which lulled her into releasing all tension. She drifted in his warm, safe love. Then images of that night cleared in her mind, and she heard her father's voice.

"Live," she whispered.

"What, Belle?"

"Live. That's what he said, Travis." She sat up and fixed her gaze on Travis.

"He said, 'Live.'"

"Yes, yes, he said, 'Live, Belle, live. Don't live your life here, Belle, don't live in this moment, with us dying. Go, Belle, live.'" Tears streamed as she contemplated her father's words. "Then," she sighed, "we heard the men, and he told me, 'Run, Belle, you must live.'" Belle buried her face in her hands and sobbed. "I did it all wrong, Travis. I did it all wrong."

"Shh, shh, honey, what did you do wrong?"

"H-he didn't want this for me; neither of them did. They didn't want me to live like this, with their deaths defining my life. Oh, Travis, how could I get it so wrong?" She threw herself in his arms.

"Belle, honey." He drew her chin up to see her face and brushed the tears from her eyes. "You were eighteen and experiencing the most pain you have ever felt. Sometimes grief makes us behave in ways we don't understand. But you're free now, free to live like your parents would want you to live."

"I suppose so, Travis, but I don't know if I can."

"Why?"

"Because, knowing that my parents wanted me to go on with my life doesn't wipe this feeling in me that wants revenge. I don't know if it ever will. It may poison me forever."

"Belle, my love, you don't know that. The only way to find out is to live. For years, your life focused on vengeance; nothing else existed. Now, if you don't mind me saying," he smiled, "you have me, I should say us. Focus on us, Belle, focus on building a life together. Marry me, Belle."

"Marry you?" she whispered the words. She could see Travis' body tighten at her silence.

"Belle?"

"Huh?"

"You gonna answer me?"

"Y-yes...I mean, no...

Travis' shoulder's slumped.

"Oh, I'm not doing this well. I mean, yes, I will marry you but not right off."

Travis cocked his head like a confused dog.

"Travis, you are taking me back to Faulkner, back home. I need some time to readjust. I need time to be Belle again, and I need time with my grandmother."

"All right, Belle Alston, but it had better not be a long time.

219

And while you are being Belle again, I'll court you the old-fashioned way." Travis grinned.

"Oh, no, Ranger, not the old-fashioned way."

Travis rubbed his face in confusion.

"If you court me the old-fashioned way, then we can't do this." She drew close to him, and raising herself on her tippy toes, she drew him in to a kiss. She pulled back.

"To hell with the old-fashioned way." Travis smiled. He grabbed her shoulders, and pulling her into his arms, he met her with a deep, passionate kiss.

CHAPTER 16

*B*elle was terrified her grandmother would have a heart attack when she saw her the first time, but instead, she cried then insisted Belle get out of those "boy clothes", as she called them, and into a decent dress.

Belle did not know who looked more satisfied, her grandmother or Travis, when she descended the stairs wearing a lavender dress that brought out the violet in her eyes.

"Pretty as a picture," Grandma said. "Oh, Belle, why did you go and shear off all your beautiful hair?" The older woman drew her hand through the short, dark locks.

"Oh, Grandma, it's not that short; it will grow back."

The old woman smiled and threw her arms around Belle. "Short or long, it doesn't really matter, I've got my Belle back. And it looks like she has a young man of her own." Mrs. Alston smiled at Travis, who turned a rich shade of crimson.

Belle giggled at Travis, then she grabbed his arm and whispered, "Don't worry. I think she likes you."

Travis breathed a sigh of relief.

"Come on into the parlor; we can talk as we wait for dinner.

Belle, I sent for Hank Black Hawk and Little Dove to join us. They should be here soon."

Excitement stirred in Belle. "Oh, I would so like to see them, and I want them to meet Travis."

"Well," Travis said as he sat on the lush sofa next to Belle, "I have already met Black Hawk."

"You have?"

"Yes, I met him when I was searching for you."

Belle blushed when she recollected the day she was hiding in Hank's barn and watched as Travis questioned him. She hoped this meeting would go better. She turned to get up when she heard a knock at the door.

"No, Belle, you be still. Milly will get the door."

"Oh, Grandma, it's just that I'm so excited to see them."

"Well, then turn around," a booming voice said.

Belle turned to see Hank Black Hawk's form filling the entrance to the parlor, a large smile sprawled across his face. Belle didn't think she had ever seen such a smile on Hank. In fact, she couldn't remember ever seeing much more than a smirk on the large man's face.

"Come here, girl." Hank opened his arms to Belle, and she ran to them.

He picked her up and twirled her around as if she where a tiny girl. A baritone laugh echoed in the room. "Honey," he said, "it's good to have you home and all this Fury nonsense behind you."

"How about me?" Little Dove asked, her gentle voice contrasting with Hank's booming sounds. "I need a hug too."

"Little Dove," Belle ran into her arms, "I missed you so much."

"Stop that," little Dove gently scolded as she wiped tears from Belle's face. "If you begin to cry, then I will too, and we cannot celebrate with tears."

"Who is he?" Hank grunted as he caught sight of Travis standing by the window.

"Oh, oh," Belle beamed as she scurried to Travis' side. She tugged at his hand, pulling him over to meet her friends. "This is Travis Parker. He helped get me home."

"Looks familiar," Hank groaned.

"I'm Ranger Travis Parker, sir. We met when I came to your home searching for Belle." Travis extended his hand to shake Hank's, but the gesture was not reciprocated.

"Hank Black Hawk," Little Dove scolded, "you shake that boy's hand."

Hank extended his hand to Travis. "Don't much like lawmen, son."

"What do you mean, Hank? You were my father's deputy for years."

"Yep, I knowed; that's why I don't trust them."

Milly announced dinner served, much to Belle's relief.

The first few moments of dinner were tense until Hank asked about the capture of Cutter Dan.

Belle tensed as Travis told the story, hoping he would leave out the spanking he had given her, which he did. Hank began to warm up to Travis as they shared their stories of being lawmen. By the end of dinner, Belle was sure they would be friends.

The night ended on a happy note.

Hank and Little Dove said their goodbyes, and Belle's grandmother went up to bed, leaving Belle and Travis alone.

They sat on the moonlit porch and swayed in the swing.

"They love you," Belle said.

"I don't know about Black Hawk."

Belle laughed. "Don't worry. After telling him about saving me from Cutter Dan, I think you won him over."

"Maybe so." Travis chuckled.

"I'm just glad you didn't—

"Didn't what, honey?"

"Oh, never you mind." Belle blushed.

"No, what is it?" Travis teased.

"Stop it; you know exactly what." She stomped her foot and pouted.

"Watch it, little girl," he gently warned. "I won't tell anyone about your spanking. That's between us, but if you don't calm down, your grandmother might hear the next one you get."

"All right, all right," Belle sulked.

"Good girl. I need to leave in a bit, so let's not spend our time fighting."

"Leave?"

"Well, you can't expect me to sleep here?"

"Why not? My grandmother has plenty of room."

"Yes, and you will be in one of those rooms. I don't know if I can stand the temptation."

"But you slept by me at our campsite."

"Yes, and that was hard, but seeing you in that dress, well, now it's impossible."

"Oh, you." Belle smacked his arm.

"Ow." He clutched his arm, feigning a fake injury.

Belle laughed. "Then sleep in the shed out back."

"No thanks, there is a hotel in town. I'll stay there."

"Oh," Belle said, disappointed she would not have him close. "Travis, will you take me to my old home tomorrow?"

"Sure, if you are sure you want to go."

"Yes, I'm sure. I've got to see what it is like. I want to rebuild, Travis. I-I want us to build a home there."

"Are you sure? I mean, with all that happened there?"

"Yes, I'm sure. I know there are bad memories there, but there were many good ones before that night. I want to give that back to my old home. I want to refill it with good memories, Travis—our memories."

Travis leaned down and kissed her. "Those will be the very best memories, my love.

❧

AN ODD SENSE of familiarity hit the pit of Belle's stomach when she saw the barn and corral standing just as they were years ago. The crumbled remains of her home's foundation were all that served witness of that tragic night.

"Belle, honey, are you all right?" Travis' worried eyes watched as Belle scanned the remains of her home.

Lengthy seconds clicked by before she nodded her agreement. Travis stepped closer to her and slid his arm around her waist.

She drew from his strength. "Travis, it's odd; I feel nothing."

"Maybe it's not hit you yet. People react differently."

"Yes, I know, but it feels like I walked into a dream—into a place that used to be—a faded memory of what once was."

"Well, in a way, honey, you have. This used to be the happy home you shared with your parents, but that doesn't mean it can't be a happy place again."

A heavy tear fell from her cheek as Travis' words shook some emotions deep within her being. *No, tears,* Belle scolded herself. "You're right, Travis, this was a happy place. It was always meant to be. I won't let them win and take that away."

"Won't let who win, darlin'?"

"Them, the murderers, they took my parents, but they can't take the happiness and love that once thrived in this home. I'm not running this time, and I'm not hiding. I'll show them. We *are* going to rebuild, and we will live here and bring back the happiness and love. We will, won't we, Travis?"

"You bet we will." Travis picked her up and twirled her in his arms. "You bet we will!"

AFTER MONTHS OF WORK, Travis, with Hank's help, built a small house where Belle's old home once stood. The cabin was not as grand as the old house, but Belle loved it as much. Sometimes, she thought even more.

Everything in her world seemed right, but Travis held one concern, her parents' graves. They were buried under the oak tree, where Belle had fled, the night of their death. Belle knew they were there but could not bring herself to go to the graveside. She never even left as much as a flower where her beloved parents lay.

"I need to talk to her," Travis said as he and Black Hawk sat on the porch after a long day's work.

"Not yet, son," Hank said. "Give her time; let her work it through herself."

"I don't know. Sometimes Belle needs help talking it out."

"Son, all Belle is thinking about right now is you two getting married this Saturday. Don't ruin what should be the happiest day of her life by bringing up the saddest. It's already gonna be hard on her, without her parents there."

Travis nodded. "You're right. I won't bring it up, well, at least not until after we are married if I feel the need to."

"Good man!" Hank said as he slapped Travis' shoulder, "Now, you need any advice on being a married man?" The older man chuckled.

"Why, you know anyone I can talk to?" Travis smiled.

"Very funny, you just remember, you'd better treat her like gold." Hank wagged his finger at Travis.

"Always." Travis grinned. "Always."

BELLE AND TRAVIS married on a bright, beautiful spring day. She looked angelic in her white lace gown, with a crown of daisies in her hair. Travis wore his best clothes and quaked in his boots until he saw Belle walk down the aisle, her arm laced through Hank Black Hawk's. After a few precious words and shared "I dos", the preacher declared them man and wife. The party Belle's grandmother threw continued even after Belle and Travis said their goodbyes and sped away to their honeymoon.

The hotel was opulent, at least it was to Belle. Heavy velvet drapes and oriental rugs, with mahogany furniture decorated the lobby, while fine paintings hung on the walls. Their room was lush. The large bed, covered with a wine-colored duvet and piles of soft, satin pillows, dominated the room. Heavy drapes with a rose pattern hung over the window. The wallpaper shone with a delicate, golden pattern. She did not think a finer room existed than the one they were staying in. Belle had thanked her grandmother numerous times for the gift of the honeymoon but reminded herself to thank her again when they returned home.

Feeling shy, Belle decided to change in the water closet, another luxury of the room that she was thankful for. Nerves swirled inside her as she changed into her nightgown. Her gown, a pale blue, was trimmed in delicate white lace and appeared conservative, but she knew the scooping neckline skimming the top of her breasts and the sheer fabric would draw her husband's interest.

"Calm down," she told herself, "it's Travis. You trust him, you love him, and he loves you." She took a deep breath and entered their room.

Travis rose from the overstuffed green and burgundy striped chair, his mouth dropping open when he looked at her.

"Is something wrong?" Belle asked. "Are you all right?"

"I-I'm more than all right." Travis struggled to find words. "You are so beautiful, Belle."

Belle's wide smile made her cheeks hurt. "Thank you. What do you have there?"

"Huh…oh…umm." Travis looked down at the small table next to him. "It's champagne." He tugged at the bottle that sat in a bucket of ice. "Come on over here, and let's give it a try."

Belle crossed the room and sat in the matching chair on the

other side of the table. "I've never had champagne," she said as she wrung her hands.

"Neither have I." Travis popped the cork, making Belle jump.

She giggled at her surprise.

Travis chuckled and carefully filled their glasses. "To us," he said as he handed her a glass.

"Yes, to us." The bubbles tickled her nose. "It's delicious,"

Travis nodded. "But not as delicious as you."

"What?"

"Oh…umm…I'm sorry, I didn't mean to say that out loud."

Belle smiled. She went to him and sat on his lap, nestling in his warmth.

"I think you are pretty great too." She pressed her lips to his then pulled back, wanting to read his eyes, hoping her kiss pleased him.

Travis locked his lips on hers, taking her breath away. Tingles ran through Belle as sensations she had never experienced before frightened her. She bounced up off his lap and tried to breathe. The butterflies returned to her stomach. Hell, they were not butterflies; they were condors, sweeping up her nerves. She hugged her middle and tried to calm down.

"I'm sorry, honey." Travis approached her.

She didn't mean to, but she took a step back. "I'm sorry, Travis, but this is so new, so many things I'm feeling that I've never felt."

"Belle, how much do you know about what happens between a husband and wife? Did your mother or grandmother tell you anything?"

"Well, kinda, I mean basic stuff, but, Travis, I was a bounty hunter for three years. I spent a lot of time in saloons. I know what goes on."

"Belle, knowledge and experience are different, and the relations men and women have in saloons are not about love. In marriage, you have intimacy with love, and it is a beautiful, wonderful gift a couple give one another, and I'm an idiot for moving so fast."

"Hey, how come you can call yourself an idiot, but I can't?" She giggled.

"Because you know there are consequences if you do."

"That isn't fair."

"Sorry, honey."

She giggled again.

"Belle, please let me hold you. I promise, right now, I just want to hold you in my arms."

Belle slowly nodded. Once his arms were around her, she began to relax. "I'm sorry, Travis, I don't mean to be such a baby."

"Hey," Travis gently pushed her chin up to look her in the eye, "this is new to you, and I scared you." He kissed her nose. "How about I kiss you again, soft like?"

Belle nodded. His lips brushed hers as he tenderly drew her in.

"Better?"

"Yes," she whispered.

"Travis?"

"Yes."

"Umm," she blushed, "will you please kiss me like that once more."

Travis grinned. "Gladly."

After a few more kisses, he lifted her into his arms and carried her to the side of the bed. He set her on her feet. Once more, he drew her rose-pink lips to his mouth. "Belle, my darlin', may I remove this? "He touched the shoulder straps of her gown."

Belle hesitated for a moment, swallowed hard, then slowly nodded her permission.

Travis brushed the straps from her shoulders, and her gown puddled to the floor. Soft moonlight streamed from the gap in the drapes, caressing her curves, illuminating her delicate skin.

Travis sat back on the bed, in awe of the beauty of his wife's form. "Belle," his voice quaked.

"Y-yes?" Belle flushed.

"Belle, you are so beautiful. I love you."

"I love you too," she whispered.

Travis stretched his arms out to her. "Please come here."

Belle walked into his arms. His hands entwined around her slender waist. She quivered at his touch.

"Are you cold?"

"No."

"Belle, I want to touch you,"

"Yes, Travis."

Travis' hands meandered down the sides of her body, pausing when he wanted to take in the sensual beauty of his wife. They slid around the curves of her breasts, into the dips of her waist, and over the roundness of her hips. "You're so warm, so soft, so tender, lovely lady mine." He kissed the top of her shoulder, trailing up her neck and finishing at her lips.

Fire ran through Belle's body, and she thought if he touched her again, she would go up in flames. She looked at him and saw hunger for her smoldered in his eyes. "Travis, may I?" She unbuttoned the top button of his shirt.

"Yes," he said, his hot breath panting in her face as she unfastened the rest of the buttons.

He yanked off his shirt. Belle ran her hands over his smooth, hard muscles, her palms moistened by the dapple of sweat coating his broad chest. She tilted her head to look at her husband and was claimed by a passionate kiss, their hands caressing and exploring each other as the kiss deepened. She felt a shudder. Did that come from him, or her? Maybe it was both of them.

Travis pulled away from her lips long enough to swoop her up in his arms and lay her on the bed.

"Travis," Belle said.

"Yes, honey?" His eyes admired her outstretched body.

"I'm a little scared."

"I know, love, but don't worry; I'll take care of you."

"I know; you always do." Belle reached up for him, and he leaned down into her warm embrace.

BELLE COULD NOT BELIEVE that only three days on a honeymoon could have filled her with so much bliss, such a deep feeling of love that she didn't know could be experienced by anyone. She reveled in the feeling of oneness and love brought by their intimate moments.

When they returned home, they fell into a normal rhythm of married life. Travis had turned in his resignation from the rangers before they were married, but finding a replacement for him proved challenging. He promised to remain an active ranger if he was needed. Still being a ranger called him away at times, leaving Belle alone. The first time Travis was called away, Belle insisted on going with him and threw the biggest fit when he said no, resulting in her inability to sit for days. When Travis was home, he worked hard at learning to be a rancher. At first, it proved difficult, but with time, he found he possessed a natural talent for ranching.

Belle settled into being a wife and made their home cozy and inviting, not because it was expected of her, but because it was what she wanted. She was determined to bring back the love and happiness she had experienced as a child to the cabin standing where her old home had once been. She loved taking care of her home, but she also helped with the care of the horses. Her skill at animal care and training gained her a reputation, leading many people to request her expertise. Belle still possessed the bounty money from the Cutter Dan incident; she could not decide what to do with it. Travis insisted it not be spent on the ranch, but on doing some good for others. Belle agreed but found it hard to decide exactly what she would donate to.

They spent as much time with her grandmother as they could. They even asked her to move in with them, which she refused, saying, "What does a newly married couple want with an old woman living under their roof, and how will I get great-grandchildren if I'm always underfoot?" Her statement brought an immediate blush to Belle's face and a stammer to Travis' words.

Belle loved reconnecting with her childhood friends, but most of all, she enjoyed the time they spent with Hank Black Hawk and Little Dove.

She worked in the kitchen preparing dinner. Hank and Little Dove were their guests that evening. Little Dove became a second mother to her and helped her learn to cook. Belle had learned some basic cooking from her mother, but living as a bounty hunter and eating jerky and hardtack did not expand her cooking skills.

"Hurry and get cleaned up, Travis," Belle ordered as he tromped in the door.

"What, no hello husband? No kiss?"

Belle smiled as she walked over to her husband and stood on the tips of her toes. He leaned down, and she gave him a quick peck on the lips.

"What was that?" Travis asked. "I know you can do better than that." He gave her a mischievous grin and a wink.

"Yes, I can, Travis Parker," she scolded, "but if I do, I'll end up in our bed, and then who will cook dinner?"

"Well, if that were to happen, I don't care who will cook dinner."

"Travis!"

"All right, honey, I'll go, but I expect that kiss later tonight."

"I think that can be arranged," Belle said with a smile.

"Yippee!" Travis picked her up and twirled her around the room.

"Travis, put me down; dinner is going to burn."

"All right, Mrs. Parker, down you go." He placed her on her feet. "I'll go get cleaned up."

"Thank goodness," Belle muttered as he left the room.

Hank Black Hawk and Little Dove arrived just after Travis disappeared to get cleaned up.

"I'm sorry. We are running a little late, but dinner should be done soon."

"Don't worry," Little Dove said, "I told Hank we are too early."

"Nonsense," Travis said as he walked back into the room.

"You're family; you can come over whenever you want."

"Thank you, Travis, but I don't think you want my husband here all the time."

"What? Not want me over here all the time. Am I not a pleasure to be around?"

"You are to me," Little Dove smiled, "but I'm not sure everyone shares my feelings."

"Dinner will be ready soon. Why don't you two sit with Travis while I finish?"

"If it's all right with you, Belle, I'd rather help you with dinner than listen to these two talk about law enforcement days."

"Sure, I welcome the help."

"Well, Hank, I guess we better go sit and wait like good husbands do." Travis chuckled.

A PLATE SLID out of Belle's hand and crashed to the floor.

"You all right?" Travis asked.

"U-uh, yeah...I mean, everything's fine; it slipped out of my hand after I washed it."

"You need help cleaning it up?"

"Never you mind, Travis, I can get it," Little Dove said. "You and Hank can continue your tall tales." She smiled at him. "Travis, please finish the one you were talking about, the one about the whistling prisoner."

Yes, finish that one. Belle had dropped the plate at the afore mention of the whistling man. *The whistling man...I told the rangers about Red Boots...but I didn't remember the whistling man.*

"Ain't much more to say, but Rob Price was one of the strangest men I've ever delivered to Tyson prison."

"What were the tunes he whistled?" Belle tried to keep her voice from quivering and hoped no one noticed her shaking hands.

"That's the strangest thing of all. He kept whistling the same tune, and it weren't no song I'd ever heard off."

"Did he have a partner?" Belle did not think before she spoke.

"No, not that I know of. I only brought in one man. Why do you ask?"

"Oh, nothing, just the old bounty hunter in me, I suppose. I guess if he did have a partner, he probably ran him off with the whistling." She forced a laugh. "Can you remember the tune?" Belle asked.

"Why you want to know, honey?"

"Oh, no special reason, just curious," Belle lied.

"Let me think." Travis rubbed his chin.

"Well, it kinda went like this." Travis began to whistle.

Belle turned and held on to the side of the sink lest she crumple to the floor. It was his tune, one of the murderers. She tried to swallow, but her mouth dried, and if her throat continued to constrict, she believed she would suffocate.

I need to tell Travis, but I can't...I don't know why. This is something I need to take care of myself. Breathe, Belle, get a hold of yourself.

Hank's thundering laughter filled the room as Belle tried to focus on the dirty dishes, her mind totally filled with the maddening sound of that wretched whistle song. *I've got to go to that prison. I must talk to that man.*

"Belle, darlin'," Travis said as he sat at the table watching Belle clean up their breakfast dishes the next morning.

"Yes?" she answered as she continued her flurry of work.

"Stop," Travis said as he grabbed her arm and pulled her onto his lap.

"Travis, I have to finish the dishes; they're not gonna wash themselves," she snapped.

"Belle Alston Parker, don't you get snippy with me, little girl."

"I'm sorry, Travis, guess I'm not feeling myself today."

"Or yesterday or the day before, Belle, I know something is troubling you. You need to tell me what it is."

"I can't," she answered. "It's something I have to deal with on my own."

"I don't like you keeping things from me, Belle, but I know sometimes you need to sort things out. Does this have to do with your parents?"

She nodded as she fidgeted with a button on his shirt.

"Belle," Travis grasped her hand to stop her, "I need you to use words when you speak to me."

"Yes, Travis, it has to do with my parents."

"Aw, Belle, baby," he brushed a lock of hair from her face, "maybe I should stay home."

"No, no, no, you can't; you just can't!"

"Why? Are you that desperate to get rid of me?"

"Well, yes," Belle put on her best fake smile. "This is an important cattle buy, and you can't put it off. Besides, I'll enjoy the peace and quiet."

"Oh, you will, will you?" Travis danced his fingertips over her ticklish sides.

"S-stop." She cackled and squirmed to get off his lap. "Travis, please stop."

Travis kept his fingers in place as he contemplated stopping. "All right," he said as he removed his fingers from her sides and wrapped his arms around her waist. He kissed her cheek. "Seriously, Belle," his voice took on a stern tone, "I expect you to tell me what is going on with you when I get back, or there will be consequences." He patted her backside.

"I-I will Travis, I promise."

"Good. Now get up, darlin', I need to get going. Hank will be waiting on me."

Belle got on her feet as Travis reached for his saddle bag hanging over his chair. She walked him to the front door.

Travis turned and wiped a stray tear from her cheek with his thumb. "Hey, now, don't cry. I want to see a happy face when I leave."

"Sorry," Belle said with a sniffle. "I already miss you."

"And I miss you too."

She smiled at him.

Travis leaned down and placed a tender kiss on her soft pink lips. "Honey," he said as he drew back from her lips, "I wish you would stay with your grandmother or Little Dove while I'm gone."

Belle's hand flew to her hips as a bit of Fury pushed through. "Travis Parker, we have already been through this. You know I can handle myself. I shoot better than you, and besides, Little Dove will be checking in on me, and so will Grandma."

"All right, Miss Feisty Pants." He kissed her again. "But you still are not a better shot than I am."

"Am so," Belle yelled as he shut the door. She waited to hear him step off the porch before she ran to their room. She ran to the window to check. She wanted to reassure herself that Travis was gone. She chewed her thumbnail as her eyes trailed his steps to the barn, and in a few moments, she watched as he rode out. Travis' mount scaled the small hill and then disappeared.

Belle flew into action. She opened the bottom drawer of her dresser. Crouching down, she reached deep into the back of the drawer and pulled out Fury's clothes. She tossed the clothing on the bed and stood for a moment, staring at the heap that represented her other life. *A sense that I would need to live my former life once more, is that why I kept the clothes?* she asked herself. She shrugged. *No need wondering; I need them, and they are here.*

She placed her hands on her hips and took a deep breath. Thoughts raced in her head and the sound of her heartbeat pulsed in her ears. *I thought I was done with you, Fury, but you are a part of me, and deep down, I knew you would come back.*

The sleek, soft fabric of her nightgown skimmed her delicate skin as it slid down her body and puddled at her feet. Belle picked up the faded blue shirt. The fabric felt rough and worn.

I almost forgot what it was like to be Fury.

Each article of clothing Belle put on, each button she fastened, helped to bring Fury back.

Belle opened the wardrobe. Hidden and forgotten in a dark corner of the wardrobe sat an ordinary box. She retrieved the box and placed it on the bed, removing the lid, She gazed at the contents. Carefully, she lifted Fury's hat and placed it on her head. Then, without thinking twice, she grabbed the gun belt and strapped it around her small waist. She noticed the weight of the gun when she placed it in the holster. *That's it.* She turned and closed the wardrobe door, only to see her image in the mirrored door. *Fury has returned, and she will have her vengeance.*

I got no time to gawk at myself. She flung open the bedroom door and ran down the stairs. Fury grabbed one of the two rifles from the gun cabinet and headed for the door. She stopped. *Travis. I can't leave without a word.*

Fury laid the rifle on the table. She found paper and a fountain pen in the small desk they kept near the fireplace.

I'm sorry, Travis, but this is something I must do, or I will never be at peace. The man you and Hank spoke of last night, the whistling man, I am certain was one of my parents' murderers. I am going to question him and find his partner. Do not bother to search for me. By the time you read this note, I hope it will be over.

If I do not return, remember I love you.

Always, your Belle

A FEW TEARS splashed on the stationery. Fury folded the letter and placed it on the mantel where she was sure Travis would find it when he returned home in a few days. Then she scanned the room, hoping in her heart that this would not be the last time she saw her home.

Max paced in the barn as Fury saddled Swift.

"Don't you worry, boy; I know what I'm doing."

The shabby dog sat watching his master. Max whimpered and licked his nose, shifting his weight on his front paws.

"Come on, Max," Fury said, picking up on the animal's anxiety. "It will be all right. You stay here, boy, where you will be safe. Swift and I can handle this."

Fury mounted her horse and made her way out of the barn. Max produced a groaning sound and followed.

"Max, stay," Fury ordered.

Fury nudged her horse forward, and Max continued to follow.

"Max, you need to stay. Travis needs you to be here when he gets back."

The dog cocked his head.

"All right, old friend, you can come, but watch yourself, boy; things are liable to get dangerous."

CHAPTER 17

The dark grey stone walls of the Tyson Prison loomed before Fury. The walls were at least ten feet tall, with barbed wire strung across the top. On either side of the prison walls rose the watchtowers, great dark sentinels watching over the convicts. These sentinels watched the refuse of society come and go. A few walked out, but most were carried out in pine boxes. Their cold foreboding shadow made Fury's stomach clench from the sense of being under their scrutiny.

She could make out the murky silhouettes of armed guards watching from atop the towers. The figures stopped; they had spotted her. Rifles homed in on her.

"Easy, girl," Fury whispered to Swift. "Let's go slow and easy; these boys look jumpy." Raising her arms to demonstrate that she was no threat, Fury approached the prison gate flanked by two guards.

"Halt!" the older guard commanded when Fury neared the gate.

"I have come to see a prisoner, name of Rob Price."

"Wait here. Burke, keep your gun on this young fella while I check the log."

The younger guard nodded, keeping Fury in his sights.

"No one's been cleared to visit today," said the older guard as he exited the small guardhouse. "What's your name?"

"Fury."

The guard's body stiffened. He knew Fury's reputation, and the unexpected visitor standing before him fit the description, down to the painted horse and mutt.

"Well, Fury," the man's voice shook, "being that you ain't on the visit list, I will have to clear you with the warden. That is if he ain't busy. You might wait a spell."

"I don't have time to waste," Fury chided. "What's your warden's name?"

"Mr. Benjamin Sims is the warden of this prison, and ya don't get to see him just because ya wanna, even if you are Fury."

"Smiley Ben Sims." Fury chuckled.

"You know him, son?"

"Do I know him? Why, I brought in plenty of wanted men for him when he was sheriff at Appleton. Tell me, does he still tell those awful jokes?"

"He sure enough does." The guard chuckled. "Since you know him, I'm gonna tell him you're here. I will be right back, Burke."

Once more, Burke nodded his reply, keeping his gun fixed on Fury."

In a matter of moments, the old guard returned. "Come on in; warden's waitin' on you."

The ancient iron gate creaked and squeaked as the hinges groaned, swinging the gate open.

"Fury!" Smiley extended his hand as he walked over to greet her. "Good to see you, boy!" he said as he furiously shook Fury's hand.

"Good to see you too, sir," Fury answered, remembering to use her lower male voice.

"Come on, Fury, sit down and tell me what you been up to. You want something to drink?"

"No, thank you, Smiley. I don't mean to be rude, but I'm pressed for time, so let me get to the point. I need to speak to one of your prisoners by the name of Rob Price.

"Price?" The smile left the warden's face as he poured himself a drink from the decanter he kept on his desk. "Fury, I can't possibly think of a reason someone would want to speak to that lunatic."

"He may have been involved in an important double murder I'm investigating. Price and his partner are suspected of murdering a prominent judge and his wife, almost four years ago. I need to question him."

"All right, Fury," the warden answered as he scratched the top of his bald head. "I doubt you will get any information from him. He's already here for murder; he'll hang soon. Rob Price is a vicious man; he beat a man to death."

Smiley crossed his office floor and opened the door. "Guard!" he shouted.

"Yes, sir."

"Escort Fury here to Price's cell and stay with him. He has questions he wants to ask the prisoner."

"Thank you, Smiley."

"I don't know if you should thank me; you haven't met Price yet.

Fury followed her escort down the hallway. The walls and floor were stone, light streamed in from bared windows, and the echo of their boots clopping and scraping against the stone floor were the only sounds in the long corridor. Fury followed the guard to the left, and the world around her began to change. They stopped when they reached a massive, iron barred gate. The monstrosity spanned from the ceiling to the floor and stretched from one wall to the other. A lone guard stood by the gate.

"Someone to see a prisoner."

Fury's escort handed the guard a form, written by the warden, granting Fury the opportunity to see Rob Price. The guard grunted and removed a large ring of keys hanging from his belt.

The keys clanged as he opened the gate. A sick dread sank into Fury's gut when she heard the gate slam shut and the keys turning. She was locked in, and now the real prison emerged.

She had seen her share of jails but not the inside of a prison. No crisp sunlight filtered through the dirty barred windows. Fury shuddered, feeling herself encased in a dank, dreary, coldness. This place held no familiarity. It bore no resemblance to any establishment she had ever visited. *This is prison.* As they approached the cells, the smell of sweat, mildew, and despair overwhelmed her. Fury cleared her throat, hoping she would not sicken from the rancid odor.

She glanced at the inmates as she passed their cells. Some yelled obscenities as she walked by. Others stood by the bars, staring with blank empty eyes, and some were huddled on their cots.

Fury didn't know how many cells they had passed when they stopped at another gate, similar to the one they'd already passed through. Two guards stood watch.

"Why another gate?" Fury asked.

"These are the worst prisoners; this is death row."

The gate moaned open, and the guard motioned her to enter.

The atmosphere, heavy with despair and fear, caused a sense of panic to curl inside Fury. She tried to breathe, but the repulsive air stung the back of her throat. They walked by the first cell. One inmate ran to the bars, shouting his innocence.

"Get back, Morris." The guard banged his club against the bars. "There were two eyewitnesses who saw you kill the old man."

The inmate in the next cell sat crying and praying for forgiveness. The guard walked by, taking no note of the man.

They stopped at the third cell. "This here is Price," the guard said as he pounded on the cell bars with his club. "Get up, Price, you got a visitor."

Price crouched on the edge of his cot like a vulture on a limb of a tree. He whistled, the same melodious tune Fury had heard that night.

Fury swayed; she rubbed her forehead. *"Don't faint, please, don't faint."*

"Who the hell wants to see me? "Price answered in a low, raspy voice.

"How the hell should I know why anyone wants to talk to the likes of you? Get your ass off that cot and come over here."

Price did not budge. The guard slammed his club against the bars. "Now, Price!"

Price groaned and dragged himself to his feet. "All right."

Fury's pulsing heart leapt to her throat as one of the men who had killed her parents emerged from the dark shadows of his cell. He paused at the bars and glared at Fury with dark, dead eyes. Rob Price was a massive man; he would have no problem beating a man to death. Greasy black hair lay flat on his large head. Price's face was wide, his complexion mottled with pox scars. A long, solitary scar trailed down the right side of his face.

A hammer pounded an anvil in Fury's head. Her throat was a desert, and her chest rose and fell with sharp, rapid breaths. Fury feared she might lose the ability to speak. *Get a hold of yourself. Remember, you are Fury. You must put Belle and her emotions away for now, so you can talk to this lousy bastard.*

"Well, well, what do we have here?" The tone of his voice reflected the condition of his soul—each gruff word that spewed from his lips shrouded in hatred.

Fury smelled the foul scent of his stale, hot breath as he spoke to her.

"What you want, boy?"

Fury steeled herself. "I need you to answer some questions."

"Questions?" Price roared with laughter. "Why in the hell would I answer your questions?"

Price turned his back on her and began to walk back to his cot, but Fury was not going to give up. "My questions pertain to a double murder I believe you and someone else committed," Fury shouted.

Price stopped and looked over his shoulder at Fury. "I killed a lot of people, son, ya think I remember every one of them?"

"The victims were a prominent judge and his wife. After you and your partner killed the couple, you set their home on fire." Fury's throat constricted as the memory of that day became vivid in her mind.

"A judge, you say?" Price stopped and turned to face Fury; she'd sparked his attention. It seemed he delighted in talking about the murders he had committed.

"And his wife," Fury added.

Price stepped closer to Fury. "Whereabouts did this take place?" His words were lit with excitement.

"Faulkner."

Price cackled like a wild animal.

"What's so funny about the murder of two people, you sadistic prick?"

Her words propelled Price back to the bars. He wrapped his gritty hands around the cold steel. "Watch your mouth, boy, lessen you want me to beat you too," he hissed.

Fury's insides quaked, but she shoved down her fear. "How you plan on doing that, genius? Seems to me, you ain't doing anything to anyone anymore."

Fury jumped back as Rob's hand lurched at her through the bars. An idea came to her. It was a gamble, but it might pay off. "Let's go, guard. If I'd been Price's partner, I woulda done the same thing and left him here to rot."

"You son of a bitch," Price roared. "What the hell do you know about that bastard?"

"Not much." Fury shrugged. "Why don't you tell me about him? Is he the reason you got caught?"

"The hell he is." Every muscle in Price's body tensed as he paced like a caged animal. "That rotten son of a bitch, yeah, he's the reason I'm in here." Price flung at the bars once more. "He's the reason I'm going to fucking hang," Price screeched.

"Well then," Fury said, keeping an even tone. "Then I can help you."

"You, help me?" Price cackled.

"Unless you plan on breaking me out, how you gonna help me?"

"You're right. I can't get you out of here, but what I can do is make sure that your so-called partner gets what's comin' to him."

"I'm listening," Price said.

"If he is the man I'm looking for, then if you help me track him down, you'll get your revenge."

Price was quiet. Fury could see his feeble mind working. Fury knew the seductive power of revenge, how it rooted deep within a person. Revenge, the powerful motivator, made her certain he would not be able to resist her offer.

"All right," Price said as he nodded. "All right. It would serve him right. He was smarter than me. We robbed a bank a few days before, so we had money and were itching to spend it. After we put some miles between us and the posse, we decided to stop at the next town and have some fun. We were at a saloon, and he left me gambling while he went upstairs with one of the girls. I got in a fight over a card game and beat the lousy cheat. The sheriff came and took me to jail. He told me later that the man died, and I would hang for it. I didn't care. I knowed my partner would come help me. He did come to see me in the jail, said he would bust me out. He needed to know where I hid my share of the money. I was a damn fool and told him. He never came to bust me out; he just high tailed it out of there with all the money."

"And you never thought of turning him in for anything?"

"Nah, it would be my word against his."

Fury nodded. "You tell me where to find him, and I'll get him for both of us."

"All right, kid." He nodded. "It would serve him right to get caught by a scrawny kid like you." He chuckled.

"Goes by Red. Don't know where he is exactly, but he does have a saloon whore in Haven he sees pretty regular."

"Anything about him stand out? I mean, what does he look like?"

"Nothing special, dark hair, 'bout as tall as me."

"Dark hair? Why does he go by Red?" Fury held her breath, hoping she knew the answer.

"Oh, fer some reason, he likes wearing red boots. I told him once it would get him in trouble, cause folks would remember his boots, but it never did. Well, not until now."

"I have one more question." Fury tried not to quake in her boots. "Did he kill the judge and his wife?"

"Yeah, he did it, said something about the judge hanging his brother."

"So, he wanted vengeance."

"Yeah."

"I think that's all I need to know. Let's get out of here, guard."

Fury turned and left Price standing in his cell.

"Get him, kid," Fury heard Price yell.

"That's the plan," she muttered.

The wind whipped at Fury's face as she galloped away from the prison. Knowing her parents' murder had resulted from an act of revenge only served to stir her own deep-seated desire for vengeance. Her mind grew consumed with one thought—find Red and kill him.

CHAPTER 18

*T*he warmth of the day would soon fade into cool evening air when Fury arrived in Haven. She wasted no time in finding a livery for her exhausted horse.

"Anyone here?" Fury yelled.

Amongst the whinny of horses and the shuffle of hooves she heard the gruff voice. "I'm a comin'."

Fury glanced at Swift. A morsel of regret settled in her gut when she realized the condition of her poor horse, and she'd left Max somewhere on the trail. Or did he leave her? She never knew with that dog. "I can't think about that now," Fury murmured as she pushed down her emotions once more.

"Can't do what, young fella?"

"Never you mind," Fury said to the rotund, old man. "Can you board my horse?"

The old man squinted his eyes as he surveyed his stalls. "Yes, sir, I can take her."

"Good, and where can I stay for the night?"

"Nan's place, called the Bedford Inn, down Main Street past the general store. You can't miss it; it's white with big green shutters."

"Good, and one more thing before I leave."

The old man scrutinized Fury.

"How many saloons in this town?"

"Well, there is the Lucky Clover; it's across the street. And then there is Lily's; you go straight down this side of main, and you'll find it."

"Just two saloons?"

"Yep, ain't that enough?" The old man chuckled.

AN ANGEL STOOD by the bar, Stormy, a saloon-girl whore. Her long auburn hair, meant to be free flowing to her waist, sat stacked on the top of her head. Wisps of copper and mahogany strands brushed the nape of her slender neck. Thick, pancake makeup covered her milky skin, obscuring the innocent freckles dusting her nose and cheeks. Her lips, sweet as a cherub's, were painted fiery red, and a shadow of hopelessness replaced the natural glisten born to her emerald green eyes.

Stormy, the angelic whore, waited for her shift to end. She stood with one arm leaning on the bar and the other hand resting on her cocked-out hip. This was her spot where she stood when she worked.

Always the same routine. Same bar. Same men. Same worn out skimpy, red dress. That's my life. Stand by the bar, Stormy, be friendly, flirt with the customers to get them to buy you a drink. Sure. It was more like be friendly with a pack of pigs grunting and snorting around you, hoping their money would buy more than a drink. Sometimes it did. Hell, I gotta live. Could be, Stormy girl, things might be getting better, Could be, soon, you'll have one man instead of the herds of vermin who stagger in and out of this fine establishment. Could be?

Stormy glanced at the clock on the wall as the minute hand trudged along, ticking from one minute to the next. Time tortured her, refusing her a speedy release. the last few minutes always an eternity to her weary body. She usually didn't work during the day, but they were short of help. Morning chores consisted of cleaning and preparing for the flood of rowdy customers who filled the saloon at night, but she'd worked last night, and fatigue weighed down her body and ground her nerves. Her normal quitting time, seven a.m., came and went, and now it was late afternoon. Stormy did not want to deal with the growing number of men coming in to start their evening early. She was relieved her second shift would be over soon and she would be able to get off her feet. Her body began to relax at the thought of collapsing in bed, but hope vanished when she felt the tight grip of a drunk's arm envelop her slender waist.

The smell of rancid whiskey breath misted on the nape of her neck. The drunk rubbed his oily, stubbled face against her soft cheek. Stormy's body stiffened. The smell of his whiskey breath mingled with the odor of old, dried sweat. Over the years, she had grown accustomed to the stench of working in a saloon, but at this moment, Stormy wanted to wretch.

"Get your disgusting hands off me, Yancy!"

He spun her toward himself and slapped her face, leaving a blazing handprint on her cheek.

Stormy's hand rubbed her wounded cheek as she fought back the tears. Crying never helped a saloon girl. More often than not, shedding tears increased her troubles. In her line of work, she met many men. Some were kind, and others enjoyed seeing a woman cry; it gave them a sense of power and pleasure, so Stormy had learned early on to hold her tears. No one would come to the aid of a whore anyway, unless the beating got out of hand and the proprietor believed he would lose revenue. A battered girl could not work. Women like Stormy were refuse, mere objects to be used and abused.

"Come on, gal, it ain't like you've never been hit before. I'm a paying customer, and you're what I pay fer."

"Yancy, even if you *had* money, I wouldn't drink with you or anything else."

Hey, gal, you wanting another wallop to that purdy face?

"Phil, Phil," Yancy hollered at the bartender.

The bartender gave him an uninterested glance.

"This here woman, workin' fer you," Yancy jutted his meaty index finger at the girl, "won't let me buy her a drink."

"Stormy, keep the customers happy, or git another job," Phil growled.

"I didn't say you couldn't buy me a drink. I said I wouldn't drink with you, cause I don't drink with filthy, grunting animals."

"Who ya calling an animal, you whore?"

Stormy cowered, hoping to save herself from the next blow to her face.

Yancy raised his hand to strike the girl but froze when he heard a gun click.

A curious silence fell upon the patrons of the bar as they watched the altercation, anticipating some excitement.

"Hey, mister," the bartender broke the silence, "take it outside. I don't want any trouble."

"Trouble depends on this fella," the gunman said.

"This ain't none of your concern, little man."

"Ma'am," the gunman asked, "you all right? You want him to leave you alone?"

Stormy turned to see a young man aiming his gun at Yancy. Never in her life could she recollect anyone standing up for her. Never.

"I-I'm all right, mister." Stormy rubbed the sting on her face."

"Those welts coming up on your face tell me different."

"I'm all right; really, I am."

"So, what's the trouble?"

"I just wanted him to leave me alone."

"You heard the lady, mister." Fury used her gun to point at the drunk. "Shove off. The lady doesn't like your company. I can't say I blame her; I've smelled pig sties that smelled better than you."

"Lady?" Yancy bellowed out a laugh." Mister, she ain't no lady, and who the hell are you to tell me what to do? I could squash you like a bug."

"Name's Fury."

The color drained from Yancy's face faster than a lantern being blown out. "Did you say Fury? Is you Fury, the bounty hunter?"

"That would be me."

"I-I'm sorry, Mr. Fury. I'll leave her be; there's plenty more of her kind in here."

"Before you go trying to *romance* another poor girl, you need to apologize to this lady."

"Fer what? I done said I'd leave her alone."

"Apologize for hitting her and for what you called her," Fury ordered.

The drunk hesitated, shifting his weight from one foot to the other.

"My trigger finger is getting mighty tired," Fury sighed.

"All right, Mr. Fury, I apologize fer hitting her."

"Don't apologize to me, you dope, apologize to the lady."

Yancy sucked in a deep breath. "I'm sorry fer hittin' you, Stormy," he spit out the words. His face turned a deep purple when he switched his gaze back to Fury. Yancy took a step to leave.

"Hold up."

Yancy froze. "I done what ya said. I apologized."

"You apologized for hitting her, now apologize for what you called her."

"A whore? But that's what she is."

"Apologize, and do it quick. I'm getting mighty tired of holding this gun."

"All right." Yancy's jaw twitched. "I apologize fer callin' ya a whore." Yancy's face scrunched like he'd sucked a lemon.

Stormy nodded to the drunk.

Yancy glanced at Fury.

"Go on." Fury cocked her head in a sideways nod.

The drunk scampered away, and Fury returned her gun to its holster. The disappointed patrons returned to their drinking and carousing.

"Whatcha havin', mister?" the bartender asked.

"Whiskey."

The bartender placed a glass in front of Fury and poured a meager amount of liquor.

Fury raised the glass to her mouth, hoping she would not spew the contents all over the bar. It had been a while since she had drunk whiskey, and she couldn't predict how her insides would take the once familiar liquor.

"Why did you do that?"

Fury turned toward the woman still standing at the bar. "Do what?"

Fury took a swig of her drink, hoping that would be better than guzzling it down as she used to do in her former life. She recognized the familiar warmth and made a note to revisit the issue of drink with Travis when she went home—if she went home.

"Why did you help me with Yancy, and why did you make him apologize for what he called me? After all, I *am* a whore."

"And he's a loudmouth bastard."

Stormy tried to suppress a laugh.

Fury grinned.

"But really, mister," Stormy's tone flattened, "why? Why did you help the likes of me? No one in my life has ever stood up for me or even apologized to me."

Fury finished the last of her drink and placed it on the bar.

She turned and looked Stormy in the eye. "Because you are a human being, and you needed help."

"But you know what I am; people don't help the likes of me."

"May I call you Stormy?"

Stormy nodded.

"Stormy, I don't know why you do what you do. Maybe you want to, or maybe you must. I reckon most women sell themselves because they must, and I'm betting you're one of them. But anyway, no one has the right to hit someone to make themselves feel big."

"But I'm a whore."

"You're a human being, Stormy."

"I ain't got no right to ask you, mister, but will you sit and talk with me fer a spell? No one ever said things to me like you before, and I don't know, I'd like to hear more."

Great. I don't have time for this. "Well, Stormy, I suppose, but I'm on a job, and I ain't got a lot of time."

"Thank you, Mr. Fury."

"It's Fury, just plain Fury."

"All right, Fury." Stormy smiled. "Let's sit down."

Stormy led Fury to a table in the corner of the saloon. "Thank you, Fury."

"Hey, Stormy," the bartender yelled from across the room, "you only sit with paying customers."

"My shift is over, Phil."

"If you're here, you're workin'," the bartender snapped.

Stormy blushed. "Oh, I'm sorry, Fury, you don't—

Fury held up her hand. "Don't worry about it. Bartender," Fury yelled, "two glasses of—whiskey all right with you, Stormy?"

She nodded.

"Two whiskeys."

"Thank you," Stormy said, "and thank you, again, for helping me. I wish I could pay you back. Maybe I could help you with your job. You did say you were a bounty hunter. Saloon girls do hear a lot of gossip and bragging from men."

"Maybe you can."

Stormy sipped her drink. "I know who you are. I mean, I've heard about Fury, and that's you, right?"

Fury nodded.

"I heared Fury was small and mean."

"Shh, Stormy." Fury put her index finger over her lips. "I'd like to keep that quiet. I don't like to attract attention." *You don't want to attract attention, and you just pulled a gun on a man? You must be loco.*

"Tell me about who you're after."

"I will, but first I want to add something to what we were talking about earlier. About me being Fury—about what I do for a livin'. I'm a bounty hunter, not the best way to earn a living, but for the longest time it's all I thought I was, all I thought I would ever be."

"And that's changed?" Stormy leaned closer.

"Yes. Someone came into my life and showed me there's more out there in this world if I want it and I was willing to work for it. A home, for instance, instead of living in a saddle and eatin' jerky day in and day out. You can do a different kinda work—raising cattle or sewing or cooking or running a restaurant."

"Me?" Stormy pointed to herself and laughed. "Raise cattle? I couldn't do that, or those other jobs. I don't know how to do anything."

"But you can learn. Believe me, Stormy, there are good folks out there, folks who will help you."

"And not judge me?"

"Yes, and not judge you. I ain't saying it's easy, but it is possible. Who knows, Stormy, with help, you could be running your own business or married with a baby on the way—or both."

Stormy giggled. "Maybe so, but those kinda people you're

talking about don't come in here. How am I supposed to find someone to help me?"

"You got something I can write on?"

"Let me check up at the bar."

Fury took a swallow of her whiskey while she waited for Stormy to return. She hoped she wasn't making a mistake.

"Here," Stormy said as she handed Fury a small scrap of paper and a pencil."

Stormy sat as Fury scribbled on the paper.

"Take this, Stormy." Fury handed her the slip of paper. "Can you make out what it says?"

"If you're asking if I can read, I can, well, a little, but I can read this. Who is this person?"

"A friend of mine; she will help you."

Stormy smiled and tucked the scrap of paper down the front of her dress, nestling it between her breasts. "I'll think on it. Who knows, maybe I will get married someday. I kinda got a beau."

Fury hesitated. "You do?"

"Can I tell you about him?"

"Sure, Stormy, but I don't have much time. I know you ain't got any kin to advise you, so before you tell me about him, can I ask you some questions about this man?"

"A-all right, I guess that would be fine."

"Is he a good man? Does he treat you right?" Fury asked, knowing the character of the men Stormy met in her line of work to be highly questionable.

"Well, I know you got a man to find, so I'll try to be quick about it. I met him a few months back. I was standing in my usual place by the bar, you know, right where I was when you came in."

Fury nodded, fearing this quick story would not be so quick.

"He come right up to me and said, 'Ma'am, you're the purdiest thing I've ever seen.' Well, you coulda knocked me over with a feather. I blushed. Can you believe it, me of all people, blushing like an innocent schoolgirl?" Adoration shone in Stormy's eyes.

She clasped her hands together and heaved a dreamy sigh. For a moment, she did indeed resemble a love-smitten schoolgirl. "I liked him right off cause he talked sweet to me, not like all the others who talk dirty all the time. And he's tall too. I like tall men. Oh, I'm sorry, Fury, it don't mean I don't think your nice or anything. It's just—

"I understand," Fury said, holding back a smirk. "I know I ain't as tall as most men."

Stormy let a nervous giggle slip her lips. "He's around six foot, I would say, and he's got black hair and real dark eyes."

"I can see you are quite smitten with him," Fury said, hoping to end the conversation, but she felt she needed to ask one more question. "Is he ever mean to you?"

Stormy stilled. Her eyes dropped as the color faded from her cheeks. She sighed. "I gotta admit, he can get mean, and those eyes get darker and wild lookin'. Kinda scares me a bit."

"Stop right there, Stormy." Fury raised her palm.

"If he scares you, even if he's sweet at times, then you best forget him. A man who loves you should never scare you. Do you really know much about him?"

"Well, to tell the truth, no. But I don't think he's really tryin' to be mean to me. It must be me overreacting cause I deal with so many mean men. He don't live here, don't really know where he lives. I don't rightly know what he does for a living, either. But whatever he does, he takes the time to come here and see me. It ain't no set amount of time. Sometimes it's a week, sometimes a few days. I don't ever know for sure when I'll see him."

Stormy looked down at her glass. "I really don't know much about him," she muttered and took a swig of her whiskey. "Anyhow, he usually stays down at the old livery stables, the one that's just out of town. Folks are glad the old livery stable is outside of town cause they say old Melvin don't keep it cleaned up, and it causes a mighty stench on a hot day. They say old Melvin will let outlaws hide out there, for a price, but I don't know if that's true.

Most folks use Bill Stone's livery. He keeps it nice and clean—but he charges more."

"Stormy," Fury stopped the useless, nervous babble, "what's his name?"

"I don't know his real name, just what he goes by." Her head dropped. "I guess I really don't know him, do I?"

Fury nodded in agreement.

"He does have a funny nickname, though." Stormy forced a smile. "Want to hear it?"

"Sure," Fury answered, even though she was weary of this conversation.

"It's Red."

"He's got red hair?" Fury asked. "No, wait, you said his hair is black."

"It ain't fer his hair; it's his boots. His full nick is Red Boots. For some reason, he likes to wear red boots. Told me that's all he ever buys. Kinda peculiar, ain't it? Fury? You all right?

Fury could swear something had sucked the air from the room. She couldn't breathe. The noise of conversations droned in her ears, and she heard distant laughter. The room spun, and Fury felt sick. *No. I can't. I got to get control. I gotta shove Belle back and bring out more hard, cold Fury.* She closed her eyes, forced a deep breath, and fought her way back in charge of her emotions.

"You all right, Fury? You don't look so good." Stormy's hand nudged Fury's shoulder.

"I-I'm fine. Tell me more about this," panic clawed at her throat as she choked out his name, "Red Boots."

"Don't know much more."

"You said he stays at the livery?"

"Yes. The one outside town. Sometimes he stays with me." Stormy hung her head. "But mostly, if'n he comes to see me, he comes for one thing. He said he stays at the livery so he don't pay more at the hotel. Red also told me he likes staying there so he can have his horse nearby, so he can leave quick if'n he needs to.

Now I know why." Stormy's shoulders sank. "He's a hunted man, ain't he?"

"Yes." Fury tightened her grip around her glass. "He definitely is hunted."

"He's the one you're lookin' fer. Ain't he?" she mumbled.

"Stormy—"

"No. He is. I can see it now. He's no good. I wanted so much for someone to care about me. I-I didn't see the signs; guess I didn't wanna." Stormy's head drooped. "Oh, how could I be so stupid?" She buried her face in her hands.

"Stormy, don't fall apart; you gonna draw some unwanted attention."

She raised her head. "How can I help you git him?"

"First, I only want your help if you know you can stay safe. I don't want him to hurt you."

"I can take care of myself."

"Is he in town?"

"No, he ain't. He should be here soon, though; it's been a while since I last saw him."

"Hopefully, I'll have time to get ready."

"Ready for what? You ain't gonna have a shoot-out?" Stormy wrung her delicate hands.

"I hope not, Stormy." *Who am I kidding? I don't want to take him in. I want to kill him.*

"What do you want me to do?" Stormy asked.

"I'm gonna be at the hotel. I know it may be a few days, but let me know if you see him. Be careful, Stormy, I don't want him to hurt you."

"I will, and I will be careful."

"Thank you, Stormy. I gotta go. I'll be at the hotel if you need me and, Stormy, don't forget that slip of paper I gave you. I know my friend can help you."

A weak smile crossed her lips. "Thank you, Fury."

Fury left then and crossed the road to the hotel. She needed time to think. She stumbled into her room. Nightfall was still a few hours away, but she already ached from exhaustion. She staggered to the small bed and sat on the edge of the thin mattress. She threw her hat on the worn chair by the window and surveyed the paltry surroundings.

The room appeared as tired as she felt. Dingy lace curtains hung on the window, the glass in dire need of cleaning. Fury shuddered to think what vermin had inhabited the bed and rickety dresser against the wall. The small hairbrush that lay on the dresser more than likely was a haven for lice. The walls had long lost their color to the dirt, and the floor looked as if it had never met a mop. Fury smirked and rubbed her tired eyes. *Since when did Fury care about her living conditions?* But she no longer lived as Fury, the small voice in her head answered—she lived in a cozy home with Travis, the man she loved.

Her yearning for Travis filled her, allowing a delicate tear to escape from the corner of her eye. "No time for tears," she lectured herself. "If you want Travis and home, you gotta clear your mind and get the job done. But how? I've no idea when Red will be here or even if he will be here. But the livery, that's where he stays, the trick is to get to the livery before he does and wait for him, but I can't live at the livery, can I?"

Fury leaned back. Her eyelids began to droop, only to pop open at the rapid rapping on her door. Fury pulled out her gun, an old instinct that apparently had never left her.

"Fury, Fury? Please, Fury, open; it's Stormy."

"Stormy!" Fury flung the door open.

"I can't stay, Fury, please I gotta be quick. He's here, Fury, Red Boots is here." Fury could hear the high-strung panic in her voice. "I was on my way home when I saw him ride by; he headed toward the saloon. He smiled, when I looked up, and waved. I'm sure he will be hunting for me later. Probably coming to my place, after he takes his horse to the livery. I live in a shack on Main Street. It's on the poor end of town. Ain't too far from Melvin's livery, the last one on the left."

"Does he come to you at a regular time?"

"He comes at night but no regular time."

"Stormy, I'm gonna ask you to do something dangerous."

"Go ahead, Fury. You helped me, now I can pay you back."

"I don't know, the pay back ain't gonna be equal?"

Stormy cocked her head. "It's got ta do with me helping you get Red."

"Yes, Stormy, but it's your decision."

"I'll help, Fury, what you want me to do?"

"He's at the saloon, so I'm gonna hightail it to the livery and wait. That will give me the advantage. I can surprise him there." Adrenaline surged through her. She took in a deep breath. She needed control, to calm her emotions so she could think clearly and not make a mistake. "Does he ride his horse to your home?"

"No, he's got no need to. Like I said, the livery ain't too far."

"What color is his horse?"

"It's black, right hoof has a white sock. I can't remember much. I only seen him a few times when Red was riding into town."

"That's good, Stormy, thank you. You go on home usual like. I'm going to the livery."

"You plan on *killing* him?"

"I'm gonna take him in to the law. I don't plan on killing him unless I have to."

"He don't come till dark, so wait till dusk. Fury. I don't know how long you will have to wait for him; sometimes he don't go back till morning," Stormy hung her head. "I might kin tell him I'm sick, then he won't stay—I hope."

"That's fine, Stormy, but don't do anything that will make him suspicious."

Stormy nodded.

"Thank you, Stormy, you'd better go."

Fury closed the door. She sat in the dusty chair collecting her thoughts. *Gotta think this through; gotta keep calm and come up with a plan.*

～

HINTS of golden rose blended with lavender began to swirl in the western sky, signaling the death of the day as Fury made her way to the livery. She wanted to gallop, to get there quickly, but that would attract attention. She needed to be casual, someone out for a ride. She reminded herself to keep an eye out for Stormy's home, the place she knew Red Boots would visit.

The well-kept businesses and immaculate homes began to be replaced by abandoned buildings and shanties. *This is it, the poor side of town.*

Every town, every city, big or small, has one, whether the respectable people called it 'the poor side of town' or 'across the railroad tracks', everyone knew it meant the deplorable portion of the town, the part of town existing for the outcasts, the unwanted, the unclean, and the good poor, who had no choice but to live there. No self-respecting person would step foot there amongst the seedy underbelly of society, at least not in broad daylight. But when the night fell, especially on the darkest of nights, some of the *good souls* of town ventured there to the shacks of the prostitutes and the peddlers of spirits. Anything they heard preached against in the pews of their Sunday church might be found there.

What promised to be a short ride stretched out to an eternity for Fury. Finally, she came upon Stormy's shack. Stormy didn't lie, her home indeed a run-down shack, with shutters hanging by a nail, the remains of a picket fence, and a couple of boarded windows. Once, probably a lovely home, now barely a shelter for a thrown away young girl. Fury coaxed her horse on, keeping her steady pace. She needed to get to the livery.

A vise tightened around her chest. There, a few feet away, walking in her direction, she saw an outline of a figure wearing red boots. Adrenaline guzzled into Fury's body. Her stomach clenched. The thud in her chest made it hard for her to take a deep breath. Her hand brushed the top of her gun. *Shoot him! Shoot him now!*

Innocent laughter reached her ears, as a gaggle of children passed in front of her. Fury's focus changed to the people still wandering the streets. Her hand moved away from her gun. *Not now, don't want anyone hurt. Calm. You've gotta stay calm, or you are going to mess this up. Stay alert. Breathe. Don't look at his face. Go right by him. For God's sake, calm down!* Fury commanded herself to keep breathing. She painted on an indifferent face, relaxed her body, and passed him. A quiver ran down her spine as if death had passed by.

Fury agreed with the town; the livery's stench was so foul, she could find it by following the smell. Still fighting panic, she arrived at the livery. She dismounted her horse, willing her weak legs not to buckle under her.

"Sorry, Swift," Fury said as she patted the horse's velvet nose. "I promise I won't leave you in this dump."

"Hey, there."

Fury saw a man in dirty coveralls come her way. "I'm about to close down."

"I'm a paying customer. You gonna say no to money?"

"Yep, I'm done for the day, goin' home."

"What if I pay double and put my horse in a stall? You'll go home with more money in your pocket."

Melvin rubbed his grit-matted beard. "Why you want to use my stable so bad, mister?"

"I was told you didn't ask questions for the right price."

Melvin huffed. "You heard right." He held out his dirty hand to Fury.

Fury placed a wad of cash into his greasy, grasping hand.

The man grunted his approval and walked away.

"Come on, Swift, let's see if we can find you a decent stall. Damn it!" Fury caught her balance. "What the hell is that?" She lit a small lantern she found by the door. "A water trough, what a stupid place to have a trough, right where folks walk." She stepped around the trough and held the light high as she walked to the back of the barn.

Fury put Swift in the first open stall then searched for Red's horse. A dark brown horse occupied the next stall, and across from him, was a grey. Fury almost gave up finding Red's horse until she heard a whinny from the back of the barn. No natural light leaked to the back of the barn, so in the shroud of darkness, the black horse stood hidden. Fury raised the lantern and passed it over the horse. One quick glance revealed the white sock on the right hoof. "Got ya," Fury whispered.

She turned to go back to Swift's stall. Fury glanced out the front of the barn. The evening pastel pinks, purples, and oranges melted away and were replaced with the velvet blue-black night. The soft glow of moonlight streamed into the barn.

Fury blew out the lantern. She shrunk into the darkness of Swift's stall. Gripping her gun in her trembling hand, Fury waited.

CHAPTER 19

"*H*ow?" Stormy's body quivered. "How do I act *normal* with him? I gotta keep him here for a while, so Fury can make it to the livery, but I also gotta convince him not to stay all night."

She heard the familiar creak of her door. Stormy knew it was him but did not move to look. She felt the slither of his arm around her waist. The bliss that once came from his touch was now replaced by dread. Could he feel her fear? Would he know something was wrong, that something had changed?

Act normal! she ordered herself.

Stormy's face warmed from the spray of his whiskey-breath as he kissed her cheek.

"Say hi to your man," his raspy voice whispered in her ear.

Stormy forced herself to lean her body against his. Reaching over her shoulders, she cupped her hands around his grizzly face and shimmied her body over his. "Hi, Red," she answered in the husky voice she knew he expected.

"Umm, girl, you sure know how to say hi." He turned her to face him.

She gazed into his eyes and saw empty lust, her romantic

delusions shattered. Before she could prepare herself to endure his advances like she did with every man she was forced to be with, his thin lips clamped down on hers. It was not a gentle, romantic kiss given from a lover's heart. This kiss came from a cold heart that takes but does not give; it was savage, not gentle, insistent, and not romantic. Stormy felt sick from the taste of his rotten mouth. Her body recoiled in revulsion as she pushed him back.

"What the hell's wrong with you, bitch!"

"I-I'm sorry, Red. I must still be shook up from Yancy grabbing me in the saloon and hitting me."

"Why the hell should that bother you? Lots of men grab and hit whores, and you are *just* a whore."

Stormy placed her hand on her chest, fearing the reality of his words would slash her heart into tiny bits. No use to cling to the thread of hope that Fury was wrong, that Red was a good man and he truly loved her. The sting of the truth told her she was nothing more to him than his favorite toy.

She swallowed back tears and placed a false smile on her face. "Oh, well," she threw back her head and released a fake laugh, "you're so right, Red, guess I plum forgot what I am."

She saw some of the tension leave his body and a lusty smile creep across his face.

"Hey, Red," Stormy said, trying to interrupt his carnal thoughts shining in his eyes, "you want some coffee, or I could fix you something to eat?"

"Shut up," Red said as he grabbed a chunk of her auburn hair. "You know I don't come here to drink coffee and eat."

A tremble sped throughout her body, drawing out sweat beads on her upper lip.

"I know there is something worrying you, but I don't really care," Red sneered. He forced another slobbering kiss on her as he wound her hair tighter and tighter around his fist. Red was the predator and Stormy, his prey, unable to free herself from his suffocating trap. He pulled his mouth from her lips she could see the animal lust in his eyes as he ripped the top of her dress.

Fury's note drifted to the floor.

"What the hell is this? Ya got another beau leavin' ya love notes?"

He did not release his grip from her hair as he bent to retrieve the slip of paper, and the sudden jerk shot tears to her eyes.

"*Who* the hell is *Belle Alston Parker?* And why is the word *Faulkner* writ next to it?" He studied the words. "Alston? Alston… in Faulkner?"

Stormy saw recognition spread across his face, his lustful look replaced by crazed hatred. "The judge."

The burning sting of her scalp drove tears from her eyes as he yanked her hair once more. "What judge?" she yelped like a wounded animal.

"Never you mind, what judge. Who gave you the note?" Red used his grip on her hair to drag her face close to his.

Stormy smelled his stale breath reaching her face in short, hot blasts. His features became grotesque and distorted from wild rage. His brows arched, creating deep forehead furrows. Madness glowed in his dark eyes as his lips thinned and stretched. Cold horror sprang in her being as he revealed his innermost monster, his true self.

"Tell me, girl." He shook his hold on her hair. "Tell me who ya got the note from, or I'll beat it outta ya, whore!" Red released her hair and backhanded her.

A starburst of lights blinded her, followed by a burst of pain on her jaw. The rough wood of the floor slammed into her body, driving small splinters into the exposed flesh of her arm and leg. *He's gonna kill me.* Self-preservation won. "Fury gave me the note, and he's lookin' for you."

"Fury."

Red grinned as he walked to the livery. "Stormy, that

betraying bitch, I shoulda killed her. Maybe later; gotta deal with Fury first.

THE BITTER TASTE of bile rose in Fury's mouth, her heart pounded in her ears, and her breathing hitched. *What's wrong with me? Fury, the bounty hunter—nervous?* The once familiar feel of her fingers laced around the gun grip now felt foreign. If only she could stop her hand from shaking.

Steady yourself. Fury took a deep breath and tightened her grip. *This is it. The moment you've lived for. Wait. What? Is it? Is this really the moment I live for? What was that?*

A muffled footstep. Another. Finally, a moonlit figure framed in the barn door.

Self-preservation urged Fury to retreat to the dark corner of the stall, but she drew on her faltering courage and remained planted where she could see him.

The figure stepped forward. A hint of moonlight illuminated him. *Red Boots!*

Terror from the past seeped into her mind, forcing memories of that night. Although her body remained partially hidden in the stall, her mind raced to the past, to that closet, re-living her nightmare. She needed to shoot, but fear made her body a petrified stone.

"Where are ya, little gal? Miss Alston is it?" the words slithered from Red Boot's tongue.

What the hell! How does he know who I am?

"Fury?" He chuckled.

Fury heard the jingle of his spurs. She peered between the slats of wood, hoping to see his whereabouts. A slight relief rested on her as she saw his figure sitting on a hay bale. His repose granted her a few desperate moments to gather her thoughts and her courage. Did he have a gun drawn, waiting to shoot her? Damn, if she could only see.

"Well now, Fury or Miss Alston, what's your plan? Ya gonna jump out from wherever you're hidin' and shoot me between the eyes?" He tapped his red boots on the ground, pretending to wait. "Nah, I don't think so. You're trapped. Right now, I own you. I could kill you, or maybe I'll let you live if'n you're nice to me." He roared with laughter. "Funny, I kinda like this power I have. Decidin' if someone lives or dies, makes me feel like some sorta king." He dug into his pocket. "Lookie here, Fury, got me a nickel. Should I toss it? Heads, you live, tails, you die?"

He *does* own this moment, like a murderous king on a tarnished throne, ruling over the beast and the dung. How appropriate. Fury heard the scraping sound of a match being lit. The glow of the flame cast eerie shadows as he brought it up to his lips to light a stale cigar. The air began to fill with the rancid haze. Fury's throat burned as she squelched a cough. The glow of the cigar waxed and waned as he silently puffed. Minutes grew long.

He's taking his time, trying to rattle me. I know that game. Hell, I used to play it, stretch the wait out, make them sweat. It's working.

"So, the great Fury wants me. I'm honored," he said, his voice coated in sarcasm. Red Boots dragged out a puff. "Let's light this place up."

A soft glow of light floated toward the lantern hanging on a post as he lit it with his cigar. A golden flame cast light on Red Boots and part of the barn.

Fury glared at him. For the first time, she got a good look at her parents' murderer. Greasy black hair framed his square face. His protruding and angular features were exaggerated by the shadows from the light, adding a grotesque appearance to his face. Bushy, black eyebrows framed his dark eyes. Stubble grew from olive-colored skin. And in the grip of his hand, he held his gun. Fury's blood turned to ice.

"Seems we got a friend in common. Stormy. You remember Stormy, don't you, Fury? But I reckon you might not recognize her."

What the hell did that bastard do to Stormy? Oh God, it's my fault. 'Emotions, they can hurt you out there; keep 'em in check.' Hank's words rang in her ears alongside her self-recriminations. Think, Fury, think. A glint from her gun caught her eye.

Damn. Why didn't I shoot? Why don't I shoot? He's in my sights. Would it be murder? I've shot men before, but always in self-defense, never cold-blooded. Didn't think it would matter when it came to him or his partner. Do it now, Fury, or don't do it at all. Shoot, or take him prisoner.

"Hold it," she heard herself say. "Don't move unless you want to die. Toss the gun."

Red boots hesitated, then he tossed the gun to the ground.

"I wanna see your hands; raise 'em up, then stand up nice and slow like."

Red boots rose up from the hay bales, his hands slightly raised.

Fury stepped out from the shadows. "Well now. There you are." She locked her gun on him and inched forward. Sweat slid down the curve of her face.

"Come on out, so I kin get a better look at you," he said.

"Keep your damn hands up high."

He crept them up.

"Higher, you jackass, or I'll shoot you now!"

"Calm down, Fury." He laughed. "You ain't no bigger than a bug." A smirk crossed his lips. "I squash bugs."

One quick sweep of his hand, and down the lantern crashed, igniting the hay-strewn floor that lay between them. He swept up his gun and ran.

Fury shot too late, her bullet went wild.

"Join your folks!"

Fury heard him scramble from the flames.

The flames sprinted across the dry hay, widening their path. Soon, they would be licking the walls of the barn. Fury needed to move and move fast. But she couldn't. Frozen, petrified, she was unable to move, unable to think.

The shrill whinnying of horses, accompanied by their pounding hooves, filled the air with the sound of terror, snapping Fury free from her paralysis. The water trough, the one she nearly fell into when she entered the barn, she had wondered why it was placed there, but now it was a Godsend. A bucket hung over the trough. Fury dipped it into the water and began to douse the flames, bucket after bucket, but to no avail. Only a small path was free, but was it enough? It had to be enough.

The thick smoke choked her. She coughed. Fury covered her mouth with her kerchief in a feeble attempt to protect her lungs. She needed to make a run for it. Swift whinnied, terrified from the flames. *Damn, the horses.*

Fury ran to the stalls, throwing the doors open, hoping the horses would run. She opened Swift's stall. The horse's eyes were wild. "Calm down, girl. Trust me, and we will get out." Her words tried to convince herself as well as the horse.

The other horses still pounded their stalls, afraid to leave.

"Swift, you gotta get all of us out. They'll follow you; I know they will. Just trust me, Swift." Fury threw herself on Swift's bare back. She sprawled her body on the horse's back, her head resting on the horse. She kicked the horse's sides, and they were out of the stalls, but Swift bucked when they approached the fire.

"Shh, shh, girl," Fury said gently. She could see the narrow path through the flames.

"Girl, trust me. Let's play blind man. Find Max!" She covered the horse's eyes with her hands and kicked her sides. Something in Swift's memory caused her to snap to attention; she snorted then took off.

Fury heard the pounding of Swift's hooves followed by the hollow sound of other hooves behind them. The intense heat engulfed her and Fury. She feared the horse would stop, but Swift continued her gallop. Then the heat vanished, replaced by a cool, clean breeze. They were out.

A gunshot.

A scream.

A thump.

What happened?

Swift continued her gallop. "Whoa," Fury's voice squeaked. "Whoa, Swift, we're all right, whoa."

The animal's body slowed, and finally she stopped.

Fury slid off. She staggered a few feet, and the world spun. Her legs buckled. She felt herself falling but something— someone—caught her in strong arms and gently picked her up.

CHAPTER 20

A gentle breeze brushed her cheek, calling Belle back to consciousness. Her eyes flickered at the bright light. Her vision sharpened on the window. The open gingham curtains fluttered in the cool breeze, revealing a crisp blue sky.

Why am I in a bed? Where am I? She dragged herself up on her elbows and scanned her unfamiliar surroundings.

Belle found herself in a small bedroom. The brass on the bed looked worn, as did the faded quilt. Her body caught up with her consciousness, and pain began to awaken before she could determine the color of the wall. Belle's head spun, and she slid back down into the mattress. Tightness in her chest made breathing difficult. Her throat burned, and her skin felt sunburned. Belle rubbed her forehead and tried to breathe.

Indiscernible voices drifted in from the adjacent room and distracted her from her ailments.

"Travis?"

"Doc, why hasn't she woken up? How is she? I-I mean, is she gonna be all right? Why doesn't she wake up?" Travis' voice wavered as he tried to maintain control.

"Ranger, the burns are not significant. It's amazing she didn't get worse ones. As for her lungs, we will have to wait. I have no idea how much smoke she breathed, and I can't—

"What the hell!" Travis jumped at the sound of a crash. He flung open the bedroom door, to find Belle on the floor. He swooped his wife into his arms. "Belle, honey, you all right?"

Belle touched her throat with her hand, as if to protect it from the pain of speaking. "Yes," she answered in a raspy voice. "I tried to get up, and everything went black. Travis, put me down. I want to get dressed and out of here."

Travis' face flashed from concern to stern. "Not likely," he growled at his little wife. "You are staying in bed until Doc says otherwise." Travis laid her in bed and covered her with the quilt, making sure he tucked it around her to keep her warm.

"Really, Travis," Belle rubbed her throat, "I'm fine."

"Let me be the judge of that," Doc answered before Travis could speak. "I got to get my bag from the other room, be back in a minute." The old man plodded along, closing the door behind him.

Belle avoided Travis' eyes, but it didn't help. She could still feel his disapproving gaze burning through her.

"I know what you are doing, young lady," he said, his voice deep. "Look at me."

Belle slowly raised her gaze to meet her husband's eyes. There he stood, the man she loved, arms crossed, his dark gaze locked on her, his clenched jaw twitching with anger. *This must be what a volcano looks like before it blows.*

Butterflies soared in her stomach. She managed a painful hard swallow. "I'm in big trouble," her voice whimpered.

"Big, big trouble." Travis nodded. "Do you remember what happened?"

Belle slowly nodded. "Yes." She swallowed hard. "I tracked down Red Boots. I found his girl, Stormy—oh my God, Stormy! Travis, you gotta find her. He hurt her. Please, Travis."

"Don't worry, honey, I found her. She told me where to look for you."

"Is she all right."

Travis hesitated.

Belle read the tension in his face. "She's not, is she? He hurt her, and it's my fault."

"Shh, Belle. Yes, he beat her, but that ain't your fault. Red hurt her, not you."

"But, Travis, she helped me. That's why he hurt her. Where is she?"

"Here, in the next room. Doc's taking care of her."

"Is she gonna be all right?" Belle's voice pleaded.

"Doc thinks she will be."

"I gotta go to her, Travis, I gotta take care of her." Belle sat up and pushed her blankets down.

"Oh, no, you don't." Travis guided her back down on the bed. He tucked the blankets around her. "You can't help no one if you ain't well. Don't worry; she's in very good hands. I'm sure the doc will let you see her once you both are strong enough."

"Travis, how did you know I was here?"

"The morning I left with Hank, I knew something was wrong with you." He gave a weak laugh. "Guess I was right. I fretted so much, Hank told me to go back home and he would go on to buy the cattle. Imagine my surprise, to come home and find a note instead of my wife. I went to Tyson Prison. Price wouldn't talk, but lucky for me, the guard overheard your conversation, and I headed to Haven. By the way, on the way here, I picked up a straggler on the road."

"Max? Where is he?"

"Don't you worry about him; he's with Swift. The bartender at the Lucky Clover said you were there, talking to Stormy. It was gettin' dark, but I made it to Stormy. Her neighbor heard me call for help. I left Stormy with her neighbor and went outside in time to see the livery in flames."

"You're the one who caught me when I got off Swift?"

Travis nodded. He removed his hat and tunneled his fingers through his hair. "Belle, why? Why did you go after him alone? You shoulda told me."

"I know. I wanted to be the one who brought him in. I wanted to do it for Mama and Papa."

"No, Belle, sweetheart, you know this isn't what your parents wanted; this is what *you* wanted."

Belle quivered as his words sank in. He was right; she wanted revenge, and she wanted it for herself.

"I'm sorry, Travis." Tears ran down her face.

Travis sat by her and wiped her tears. "You're forgiven, Belle," he said as he kissed her forehead.

"So, you're not mad anymore? Does that mean you're not gonna—

"Spank you? Oh, no, little darlin', you have earned yourself one hell of a spanking, but not until you are well."

"Sorry." Belle sunk into the bed, wishing she could hide.

"You need to get some sleep."

"Travis, please don't go."

"I ain't going anywhere. I'm gonna sit in that chair and watch you like a hawk."

"T-Travis?" Belle spoke in an anguished whisper.

"You all right, honey?" He sat next to her on the bed and grabbed her hand.

"I'm all right, Travis. W-will you tell me what happened to Red Boots?"

She felt his grip on her hand tighten. "Belle, he died."

Horror filled her eyes. "Did I kill him?"

"No, no, no, baby." He drew her hand up to his lips and kissed it. Travis brushed back her hair. "You didn't kill him; it was the horses."

"The horses?"

"Yes, Sheriff said it looked like he was standing in front of the barn when they came running out. He shot his gun, but it was too late to save himself."

"Then I must've killed him. Swift and I were the first out of the barn. I felt a thump. We trampled him; I know we did!" Belle felt sick.

"Belle, remember who you are talking about. This man killed your parents and attempted to kill you."

"I know, I know, but for a moment in the barn, I thought of shooting him in cold blood."

"But you didn't. You're no murderer, Belle." Travis scooted Belle over and lay in the bed next to her. He drew her to his side and laid her head on his shoulder. He stroked her hair. "Go to sleep, Belle. I'm right here. I'll take care of you."

Belle drifted to sleep in his arms.

BELLE CHEWED HER THUMBNAIL.

"Belle, what's wrong, honey?" Travis asked as he rescued her thumb.

"You know what's wrong, Travis," she huffed, "I've been here for days. Today had better be the day Doc says I can go home, or I'll leave on my own."

"Belle, you will do what the doctor tells you or else." Travis raised an eyebrow.

"Where is he anyhow?" Belle huffed.

"He said he needed to find his bag."

"He always needs to find his bag."

The door crept open, and the doctor came in the room. "Sorry, folks, couldn't find my bag. Well, little lady, let's see how you are doing."

"Doc, I'm fine. I promise, really, I am."

"Belle Parker! You be still and let the doctor look you over."

"Oh, all right," Belle pouted.

"Well, little lady," Doc put his instrument away, "much better. Son." Belle hated when the doctor turned his attention to Travis and forgot she was there.

"She can travel now, but easy going; make sure you stop to rest."

"Oh, she'll rest," Travis said as he shifted his gaze to Belle.

"I didn't say I wouldn't, Travis. Honestly, Doctor, why do you insist on talking to Travis instead of me?"

"Because he knows I'll make sure you obey his orders," Travis answered.

"I didn't ask you." Belle glared at him.

"You two, work it out." The old doctor chuckled.

"Wait, Doc," Belle called out. "What about Stormy? Will she be able to leave soon?"

"Not yet; she needs to stay a while longer."

"Oh." Belle's voice sank.

"Don't worry, Mrs. Parker, she will be all right."

"Thank you, Doctor."

The doctor nodded and left the room.

"Travis, you think I could visit Stormy before we leave?"

"I don't see why not. I'll check with the doc, but you, little girl, need to take a nap. I want you well rested before we leave for home tomorrow."

"Travis," Belle whined, "all you want me to do is eat and sleep. Can't we go for a walk or sit on Doc's porch or even," she arched her eyebrows and gave him a wink, "something we both would find pleasurable?"

"Why Mrs. Parker, are you trying to bribe me?"

"That depends. Is it working?"

"Oh, Belle, there ain't nothing I want to do more, but not here, so you'll have to settle for sitting on the porch but not until after your nap."

Belle huffed and dropped her bottom lip.

"No pouting." Travis chuckled and tapped the tip of her nose. "Sleep, my love." He kissed her.

"*H*urry up, Belle," Travis said.

"I'll be right down; I want to say goodbye to Stormy."

"All right, don't keep me waiting, honey."

Belle rapped on the door.

"Come on in."

"Stormy," Belle looked at her friend, "I didn't want to leave without saying goodbye." Belle stood at Stormy's bedside. The bruises were still visible but were fading. "Stormy, I'm so sorry this happened to you. It's my fault. I shouldn't have gotten you involved."

"It ain't your fault, Belle, I wanted to help you…um…Fury…I don't know what I mean."

"I know." Belle laughed. "Sometimes I don't even know who I am."

"You are so brave, Belle. I could never be brave."

"Are you joking? You are one of the bravest persons I've ever known."

"Thank you, Belle. I'll never forget you."

"I hope not. We can write each other, and when you feel strong enough, you can visit with me in Faulkner."

"Me? Visit you? Now, who's joking? You don't want a saloon whore to visit your home."

"Stormy," Belle's hands flew to her hips, " I want my friend to visit, and don't talk bad about yourself."

"But it's true. I'm a whore; it's all I'll ever be."

"No, you're not, and you can be whatever you want to be."

"I doubt that. Besides, it takes money to live or learn something new. I ain't got money, and I only know one way to get it."

Belle's eyes lit up. "Oh, Stormy, I've got the most amazing idea."

"What?"

Belle pulled a wad of money from her reticule. Good thing she had given it to Travis to take to the cattle auction, in case he needed more cash. She picked up Stormy's hand and placed the cash in the palm of her hand, then she closed the girl's hands around the money. "This is yours, and before you argue with me, it's a gift and you can't turn down a gift from a friend."

Stormy's eyes widened as she realized the large amount of money in her possession. "B-but, but, Belle, I can't—

"Stormy, I told you it's a gift." She sat next to Stormy's bed and clasped her hands. "Please, Stormy, let me help you. With this, you can be what you want; you can change your life."

Tears burst from Stormy's eyes. "Thank you, Belle." She pulled Belle into a tight hug.

"No need to thank me." Belle pulled back. "Just get better and keep in touch."

"I will."

"Belle!" a thundering voice rose to the window.

"That would be my beloved husband calling. I gotta go." Belle hugged her friend one last time and left to join her husband.

The trip home seemed to take ages, with Travis insisting she stop and rest.

When they finally arrived, Hank, little Dove, and Belle's grandmother stood on the porch, ready to greet them.

"Belle Alston," her grandmother, scolded.

"It's Parker, Belle Alston Parker," Travis corrected.

"Yes, whatever. I should take a switch to you."

"That's my job," Travis corrected again.

"Belle, I'm so angry with you but so relieved you are home." The woman hugged her. "Little Dove cooked us a fine dinner; let's go in and celebrate."

"Please go ahead, everyone; there is something I must do before I join you."

No one asked any questions. They did as Belle wished and went in the house, all except for Travis.

Belle bent over the flowerbed and picked a bouquet of daisies. "They were my mother's favorites," Belle murmured.

"They're very pretty," Travis said, and he wrapped his arms around her waist.

"Travis, will you walk with me to my parents' graves?"

"Of course, sweetheart." He wrapped her tiny hand in his.

They knelt by the graves. Belle wiped a tear with the back of her hand and lay the flowers on their graves. "Papa." Her voice quivered.

Travis squeezed her hand.

"Papa, Mama, I miss you so much." The tears trickled, dropping to the sacred ground. "I love you, and I want you to know it took a while, and some persuading." She smiled at Travis, and he wiped a tear from her eye with his thumb. "But I found what you wanted for me. I'm gonna live like you said, Papa. I'm gonna remember my happy times growing up here, and I'm gonna tell your grandchildren all about you. I found something to live for, and he's sitting here with me."

Travis pulled her close and kissed her tender lips. "I love you, Belle."

"I love you too."

Travis stood and brushed the dirt from his pants. "Let's go in, before your grandmother comes after us."

Belle laughed. She held up her hand, and he helped her to her feet.

"Travis," Belle asked as they walked to the house.

"Do you think we could work on those grandchildren I promised my parents, later tonight?"

"I would love to." Travis winked. "But it may have to wait."

"Why?" Belle stopped.

Travis placed his hands on her waist and lowered his gaze until they were eye to eye. "Because, Belle, you know there's no pleasure after punishment."

Belle frowned. "Oh, I forgot."

"Don't worry, Belle. I might change my mind."

"About the spanking?"

"Oh, no, you're getting your cute little butt roasted, but the way I feel right now, I don't think I can put off the pleasure."

The End

TESS MATTHEWS

After raising her children and retiring from a career in education, Tess Matthews is following her passion – writing romance. Her stories are full of adventure, intrigue and above all romance, but not your ordinary vanilla romance, Tess writes about strong men who love their feisty women and take them in hand when needed. Although she enjoys all types of romance stories, her favorites take place in the old west – after all, who can resist those cowboys!

Tess lives on the foothills of the Appalachian Mountains in northern Alabama with her husband and a variety of dogs, cats and chickens.

Don't miss these exciting titles by Tess Matthews and Blushing Books!

Fury's Love
The Sheriff Takes A Bride
Cassidy's Gentleman
Under The Mistletoe

BLUSHING BOOKS

Blushing Books is one of the oldest eBook publishers on the web. We've been running websites that publish spanking and BDSM related romance and erotica since 1999, and we have been selling eBooks since 2003. We hope you'll check out our hundreds of offerings at http://www.blushingbooks.com.

BLUSHING BOOKS NEWSLETTER

Please join the Blushing Books newsletter
to receive updates & special promotional offers.
You can also join by using your mobile phone:
Just text BLUSHING to 22828.